And the Hills Opened Up

Also by David Oppegaard

The Suicide Collectors
Wormwood, Nevada
The Ragged Mountains

And the Hills Opened Up

David Oppegaard

Burnt Bridge || New Orleans || San Francisco

And the Hills Opened Up is a work of fiction. Names, characters, places, and incidents are the products of the author's imagination or are used fictitiously. Any resemblance to actual events, locales, or persons, living or dead, is entirely coincedental.

www.burntbridge.net

Cover and book design by Mark Rapacz

LIBRARY OF CONGRESS CATALOGING-IN-PUBLICATION DATA

ISBN-13: 978-0-9886727-1-0
ISBN-10: 0988672715

For Alan Oppegaard and Tom Norman,
two of the good guys

PART ONE

Red Earth, Wyoming
1890

1

Covered in sweat and half-delirious, Hank Chambers poked his head into the main adit and shouted for his men to clear the goddamn mine. After a lengthy, ponderous moment, two lollygaggers popped out of the darkness, rushed past the foreman, and sprinted down the hillside, hurdling clumps of sagebrush as they loped along.

The foreman scowled and shook his head at such boyish behavior. A lean, sinewy man of forty-three, Chambers had been running a fever for two days, his skin hot to the touch and his mind prone to strange wanderings. He took it slow as he descended the rocky hillside toward the crowd of miners gathered below, digging in his heels to keep his weight back. He saw no need to break his neck before God and man.

"What do you think, Mr. Chambers?"

"I need to make a fresh count, Andrew."

"Yes, sir. You just give the word."

Chambers considered his crew. Filthy in appearance, the entire water-sodden lot was squinting beneath the hot July sun like a bunch of moles that'd never seen the sky before. His first headcount reckoned seventy-eight, his second count eighty. They had seventy-nine men on the books and he was certain the whole crop was here today. The men loved a good blasting, to hear the dynamite shake the hills. They liked to whoop and holler and forget there wasn't much else to do in Red Earth except drink strong spirits and copulate with the same dozen whores.

The foreman counted a third time and came up with seventy-nine. He should have been in bed, sweating the fever out and awaiting lucidity, but he wasn't getting paid by the Dennison Mining Company to lie abed. He was getting paid to extract as much copper ore from this stubborn old mountain as fast as he could do it. Every hour in a mining operation was precious, every second was money spent, and Chambers had a bottom line that Mr. Dennison expected him to meet.

The crowd of men below shifted on their feet and coughed into their hands—they wondered what he was waiting for. Chambers considered asking Andrew to make a headcount himself, to see if their numbers matched up, but when the foreman looked at his shift boss, a thin young man with a somber, expectant look, he decided to sit with the third figure. Sometimes you just had to play the part, even if you weren't feeling it.

"All right, Andrew. Tell them to light it up."

The shift boss smiled and called into the mine, where a miner named Tol Gregerson was waiting for the signal to light the fuse. Gregerson hollered back from inside the mine and Chambers started down the hillside, taking it slow, while Andrew skipped ahead of him like a pup. The miners quieted as the foreman neared, watching him sweat, but he ignored their prying and turned to face the mine's opening.

Somebody coughed and spat on the ground.

A crow flew across the sky and settled on a tree.

Old Tol Gregerson emerged from the mine's entrance, moving fast and kicking up dust. He lost his footing halfway down and skidded the rest on his backside. The hillside shuddered, sending dirt and rocks tumbling down. A great puff of black smoke rolled out of the mine's entrance and drifted into the sky, causing the men to whoop in approbation. Chambers peered into the dark cloud as it continued to climb—the smoke seemed darker and more abundant than you'd expect, reminding him of an oilfield fire he'd seen once near Carbon City.

Andrew slapped his hat against his thigh. Chambers wiped the sweat out of his eyes, recalling himself.

"That was a good one, boss. Felt the whole damn valley shift."

Chambers rubbed his warm cheek. "Gregerson used the normal amount of sticks, didn't he?"

Andrew frowned and looked back at Gregerson. The old man was shaking hands with the other miners like he'd done something special. Somebody brought out a flask and passed it around.

"I think so, boss. I could ask him and make certain."

Chambers waved the idea away with his hand. "Don't bother. Gregerson knows his business."

"Sure does," Andrew said. "I swear I felt the earth itself shake out."

Chambers nodded, his exhaustion returning as the cloud of smoke broke apart and the sky returned to blue. Nothing man did lingered too long around here—the mountains had a way of outlasting everything without seeming to make an effort. Man was just an ant in Wyoming, scrambling to bring his heavy crumbs back to the hill.

Andrew set his hat on his head and plucked at the brim. "How long do you think we should wait?"

"Give her twenty minutes to let the dust clear and the hill stay put," Chambers said, pulling out his pocket watch. "Then go in and make sure everything's stable before you send the men back down. Clearing the rubble should keep 'em busy rest of the day."

"Yes, sir."

Chamber put his watch away and squinted at the hillside. "I'm headed back for the afternoon. Send for me if there are difficulties."

The shift boss nodded, solemn as a judge as he contemplated the duties lying ahead of him. "I think that's a good idea, Mr. Chambers. Some rest will do you a world of good."

"I didn't ask you what you thought, Andrew."

"No, sir. You did not."

Chambers turned away from the shift boss and began walking down the hillside. He felt a heaviness resting on his shoulders, like the hills themselves were pushing down on him. He did not like being sick with a summer fever and he did not like the memory of that black smoke, billowing out of the mine while the men applauded.

The foreman covered the half-mile into camp, moving slow but sure in his feverish ambulation. Red Earth, founded two years prior in 1888, was only big enough to support the operations and will of the Dennison Mining Company. Connected to civilization by a weekly stagecoach and one treacherous mountain road, the company town lay seventy miles southeast of Rawlins and was surrounded by mountains on all sides. Winter came early and left late, sometimes bogging the camp down in ten feet of snow and nearly killing off anything with a pulse. The locals, who numbered roughly one hundred and sixty souls, joked that you didn't so much live in Red Earth as survive the bastard, and some days it didn't feel like much of a joke at all.

Comprised mostly of shacks and cabins, the largest buildings in town were the Runoff Saloon, the Copper Hotel, and the Cooke House. They also had a small church, a general store, a livery, and two bunkhouses for the bachelor miners, with most of the residential shacks and cabins clumped together on the north side of town. Chambers touched his cap several times as he entered the outskirts of town, acknowledging the usual assortment of gentlemen loafers who hung about smoking cigars and passing the time of day. Most were old miners, ushered into retirement either by injury, drink, or general decrepitude. He didn't know how they got by but come summertime they always hung around town, swapping lies and speculating where their next fortune lay.

As Chambers passed the general store Milo Atkins rushed out and joined him in the street. The sheriff didn't have his own office, just a desk at the front of the general store where he could sit and watch traffic go by. If he needed to lock up a drunk for the night, Atkins chained him to an iron ring set into the store's wooden floor, an uncomfortable indignity that kept most men from visiting a second time.

"Howdy, Sheriff," Chambers said, touching his hat. "You're moving mighty fast for such a hot day."

"I didn't want to miss you, Mr. Chambers."

Chambers nodded, waiting for the sheriff to explain himself. The sheriff was a young man of twenty-five who'd gotten the job of town sheriff because he was handy with a gun and willing to work cheap. The Dennison Mining Company paid his salary and never once had Atkins complained about how small it was. He probably thought the experience would help when he moved on to a bigger town, such as Saratoga or Rock Springs. Atkins had a lanky frame, dark hair, brown eyes, and bushy eyebrows. Chambers supposed he had Italian blood, or some Cherokee to him.

"I heard the explosion down at the mine," Atkins said, looking over Chambers' shoulder. "You blasting today?"

"Yup," Chambers said, "that was us. Thought it was time to bust open that Brink Lode some more."

Atkins frowned, shoving his eyebrows together.

"I wish you'd let me know in advance."

"Oh?"

"I like to know what's happening in my town. Maybe I could help you clear the area beforehand."

Chambers blinked, sweat trickling down from his hat band and into his eyes. Was it the fever or had the sheriff called Red Earth his town? As if Mr. Dennison, on a rich man's whim, couldn't have the whole place torn down in a week's time? Hell, even that weasel Cooke, living in that stone mansion of his, outranked them both.

"Thank you, Sherriff, but you don't have to worry on that score. My men and I have been blasting for over two years and we haven't lost a soul yet."

"Sure, but I was thinking—"

"If we need a drunk hogtied, Atkins, we'll be sure to call you," Chambers said, starting down the street again. "I'm sure you have a fine touch with a rope."

The sheriff offered no reply, but Chambers could feel his unhappy stare following him as he walked away. He didn't care. He just wanted to be home now, stripped naked and beneath a blanket. His legs felt weak and light at the same time, his mouth dry. He passed the two boarding houses for the company miners, a scattering of roughhewn shacks that had gone up in a week, and came to his own cabin.

His wife came out into the yard as he approached, shading her eyes against the sun. Younger than himself by seven years, Bonnie Chambers was pleasant enough on the eyes, even with her dark hair drawn back in a school teacher's bun. She had French blood, though she didn't like to admit it. When she blushed, her cheeks turned a pretty thistle pink.

"You look like you're about to swoon, Hank Chambers."

"Yes, ma'am, swooning might be a possibility."

Bonnie shook her head.

"I knew I shouldn't have let you get out of bed this morning. I'm sure the boys could have lit that fuse without you."

Chambers shrugged and kissed his wife on the cheek, too weary to argue. Bonnie frowned and felt his forehead with the back of her hand.

"Good lord, Hank. You're burning worse than ever."

"That so?"

Bonnie grabbed his elbow and led him inside their cabin, as if he were an old timer with bad legs.

"Get those clothes off and hop into bed right now, Mr. Chambers. I'm not about to become a widow because you're too stubborn to rest. I'll bring you water and heat some soup."

"Fine by me, darling."

Chambers shook off his wife's grasp and passed through the cabin. It was cooler inside, out of the sun's glare, and the cabin smelled like pine sap. Bonnie had strung up a white sheet to separate their bed from the rest of the cabin, though Chambers didn't know how much good it did—it was hard to pretend you were alone when you could hear everything going on past the sheet. Chambers stood in this half-room, staring at nothing while he took off his clothes. The ground seemed to rise and fall, bending beneath his feet. Bonnie drew back the sheet and handed him a tin cup.

"There's your first. Plenty more to come."

Chambers took the cup and drank, naked except for his socks. Bonnie watched him down the water, her lips pressed with worry.

"Don't look so put out," he said, handing her the emptied cup. "It's only a summer fever."

"I know that. You think I don't know that?"

Bonnie drummed her nails on the tin cup. Chambers parted the covers and slid into the bed. The sheets felt cool on his bare skin.

"I slept poorly last night," Bonnie said. "I dreamt it snowed in the middle of summer. It snowed and snowed until the whole town was buried in white. We couldn't dig our way out, it was that bad. Nobody could move and it seemed like there wasn't a town here at all."

Chambers licked his lips, ready for more water.

"Then what? The snow melt and wash everything out?"

"Nothing. We just stayed snowed in and quiet. Then I woke up and it was morning."

Chambers turned onto his side, deciding to forget about the water.

"Hank, how much longer do you think we'll stay here?"

"I don't know. Till the copper runs out, I suppose."

"And how long do you think that'll be?"

Chambers yawned, picturing the mine with its web of tunnels, all sloping down. They'd dug deep already, but there was still a fair amount of good ore left in that hill.

"Might yield five more years or so, I reckon."

Bonnie sighed and he knew what she was thinking—five more years away from civilization. Away from fancy restaurants, dramatic plays, and respectable dress shops.

"We're making good money here," Chambers said. "Five years of this kind of money and we'll be doing fair."

"Fair enough that we can move to Cheyenne and you can ease back?"

"Sure," Chambers said, drifting toward sleep. His wife left the partitioned room quietly, staring at the empty cup in her hands. She pictured a deep well, the kind you couldn't climb out of once you'd fallen in.

2

Father Lynch sat in the narrow front room of his empty church, smoking his pipe and wondering if it was too early yet for the day's first sip. Like Bonnie Chambers, his sleep had been troubled, though his nightmares had been more of a muddled sort, various scenes that blurred together into one long, hellish roll of imagery he could vaguely remember. Something involving a scuttling, many-limbed creature, perhaps, and the unpleasant smell of sulfur.

A gaunt man of sixty-two years, Father Lynch cut his hair with a straight razor and shaved every morning. He kept the wooly, silver hairs upon his head cropped short, hoping to set an example of comeliness for the camp's miners—filthy, work-trodden beasts that they were. Lynch preached that cleanliness was next to godliness, yet still they came to service each week with bits of soil hanging from their unkempt beards and peppering their greasy hair, their breath reeking of whiskey and beer while they wiped their oily palms upon their mud-stained trousers.

Well, at least they came, and were generous enough when the offertory basket was passed, providing funds to keep the church running and his belly full. Lynch had been forced to leave Cheyenne the year before due to a lack of interest and support, his small Catholic church overwhelmed by the various religious tendrils already in place. That and his failure to lure enough cattle barons to his services—they did not like his bare bones view of the Bible and its teachings. They wanted to believe that a rich man could easily get into heaven, the greedy sods, and wanted none of the unpleasantness a true spiritual scouring brought upon the seeking believer. Indulgence, they cried. Let us atone for our sins through coin—we have not the time for good deeds and a quiet hour of prayer now and again. We're men of business and must tend to that, Father, lest our earthly kingdoms fall apart.

Good Lord, the shit ran deep in Cheyenne, and the waste their beloved bovines excreted was the least of it.

Father Lynch stood up and stretched, looking at the bottle of gin corked beside his bed. The sun was high enough—it must have been two o'clock by now, and two was closing in on four, and four was nearly dinnertime....

A knocking brought Lynch out of his reverie. Someone was at the church's back door, pounding away. "Yes, yes, I'm coming," the priest called out, setting aside his pipe. He ran a hand across his hair and glanced around his bedroom, which contained a small writing desk, a chair, a cot, a potbellied stove, and two shelves stocked with food. A small space, indeed, yet it contained everything Father Lynch needed to live as he administered to the camp's souls.

The priest opened his bedroom door and entered the church proper. The entire building had been built with volunteer help the summer before, from chopping down the pine trees in the surrounding hills to shaving them into planks to plugging it all together. Dozens of miners, many of whom hadn't crossed the church's threshold since, had shown up on their Sunday off to aid in the church's construction, working with a quiet ferocity Father Lynch had found surprising. They might not have all believed in God, but the men of Red Earth definitely believed in having a church in town. Perhaps they thought having a church would make the town appear softer to women-folk, more welcoming, or maybe they'd donated their time and sweat in hope of banking the universe's goodwill. Lord knew they could use it—they hadn't had a major accident in the mine yet, but when you spent your days with so much rock above you, even sturdy copper-ore, it got you to thinking about what may come next.

Father Lynch made his way down the sanctuary's center aisle. A dozen wooden benches made up the sanctuary's seating, each one as roughly crafted as the church itself, and on Easter and Christmas there was plenty of standing room behind them. Four windows, two on the east side and two on the west, let in enough light to see by.

Lynch opened the back door, which was heavy and wide. Four women stood outside on the back porch clad in lacy, tight-fitting dresses the pushed the swell of their breasts forward, as if their bosoms had been placed upon a shelf. Lynch averted his eyes from the swelling, trying to keep his gaze above their chins. The afternoon sunlight was dazzling after the dim interior of the church and made the exposed, pale skin of each woman seem to glow doubly.

"Good afternoon, ladies. Is it Saturday already?"

"Afternoon, Father," the oldest, Madam Petrov, replied. A stout, fifty-year-old Russian with broad shoulders, she was as devoutly Russian Orthodox as she was adept at minding her girls. She never missed a Sunday service, despite the difference between her faith and his.

"Yes, here is Saturday again."

Father Lynch smiled and rubbed his hands.

"Excellent. Who would like to go first?"

The younger women looked to each other, then the madam.

Madam Petrov sighed and clucked her tongue.

"Can you not even decide something as small as this by yourselves?"

"We could start with you, Madam—"

"No, I go last. It feels good to be away from the saloon and stand here in the sunshine. Did you hear the blasting, Father?"

"Yes, I heard some rumblings. Are they opening a new section today?"

"Who cares? What they are going to do is blow us all to pieces. It is not enough for them to hack underground like madmen, sniffing and hunting for their precious copper. They must destroy the mountains as well."

Father Lynch smiled and folded his hands at his waist. "I'm sure it's not as bad as all that, Mrs. Petrov. Mr. Chambers wouldn't do anything foolish to endanger his men or the town."

Mrs. Petrov snorted. "You must make joke, Father. Miners will do anything for extra coin in their pocket. Even intelligent man like Mr. Chambers has itch for coin—it's as strong as his men itching for my little sparrows here. He will blast and blast if he thinks it will bring company more money."

Father Lynch shook his head.

"You do have a way with words, Madam."

"Thank you. I study—"

"I'll go," one of the young women said, stepping forward. "I'll go first."

Madam Petrov paused, then closed her mouth.

"Fine, now you speak up, Ingrid. Right when we are talking of superior matters."

"My apologies, Madam—"

"Go on. Do not keep the good Father waiting any longer."

Ingrid frowned, as if this invitation was a trap she must skirt. Father Lynch stepped back into the church, inviting her inside with a theatrical sweep of his arm.

"Please, Ingrid. Come in."

The young woman stepped inside. Father Lynch nodded to Madam Petrov and the other two girls and shut the door.

"Please, have a seat."

The prostitute sat on the nearest bench, facing the front of the church. Father Lynch sat down as well, keeping a foot of space between them. Ingrid was in her late twenties, with curls of blond hair spilling out from beneath her hat and a full figure that drew your attention from her pinched face, which looked perpetually tired, the eyebrows drawn in dazed perplexity above her blue eyes. She was originally from Minnesota, Lynch recalled. She'd run off with a young man at fifteen who'd brought her as far as the Black Hills before dying from cholera, leaving her without an income or trade, in permanent exile from her own family and home.

Ingrid's story was more or less similar to the tales he'd heard during Saturday confession over the past year, when he opened the church's doors to Madam Petrov's girls so they wouldn't disturb his male parishioners with their presence. The church had no confessional, so Father Lynch preferred to sit like this instead, side by side, facing the large wooden cross nailed above the altar. He felt no need for the penitent to kneel during these conversations—he'd leave such grand gestures to the priests in bigger cities, to those who craved power over their flock any way they could get it. In a scrabbling town like Red Earth, he was glad to have any penitents at all.

Ingrid bowed her head and clasped her hands. She'd taken out a rosary from the pocket of her dress and held it clenched between her hands. She crossed herself, and took a deep breath.

"Forgive me, Father, for I sinned..."

Father Lynch tucked his chin against his chest, half-listening as Ingrid got into it. These Saturday confessions seemed nearly identical to each other, the usual listing of petty sins and grievances that occur in a brothel—the ivory combs stolen, the men cheated out of their pay, the strange sexual perversions yielded to for money or the lust for perversion itself. The sudden tears that emerged when speaking of an aborted child or a child given up in the distant past. And, within these stories, ample evidence of the bad luck and bad decisions that had brought these women to Red Earth in the first place.

He could sample the favors of any of these women, Lynch knew. It would only take a few coins to convince them to follow him to the back room and his little cot. He'd known the favors of women before joining the church—he could still remember the softness of their touch, the pliable flesh of their breasts and the rich smell between their legs. These women—these bodies—from thirty years ago still haunted Lynch in the night, hovering above his thoughts like lewd, enticing angels. He'd told no one of these encounters when he'd entered the priesthood, fearing they'd cast him out before he could formally enter, and he'd carried them in his heart ever since, not as a burden, exactly, but as memories both cherished and disquieting.

Ingrid paused, taking a deep breath. He'd said the necessary words, when she'd needed to hear them, and the stream of her confession was flowing toward its end. Father Lynch avoided looking at the young woman while she spoke, keeping his eyes fixed on the cross ahead. He could see her pale bosom in the corner of his eye, rising and falling as she spoke. She smelled sweetly of that perfume they all wore, the cheap rosewater from the general store. It covered the musked smell of her natural body odor, though not completely. He could imagine the feel of his body, pressing so gently down upon hers....

The church was silent. Ingrid had finished her confession and was waiting for his reply. Father Lynch frowned, as if deep in thought, and charged her with a penance of fifty Hail

Mary's before giving her absolution.

"Amen," Ingrid said, nodding.

"Your sins are truly forgiven. Go in peace, child."

"Thanks be to God."

Ingrid rose and started for the back door, her scent lingering in the pew. Father Lynch remained seated, his eyes fixed on the cross. He already felt worn and tired, the July heat filling the church with humidity similar to the hot, panting breath of a dog. He heard the door open behind him and sunlight swept into the church. Floorboards creaked as the next penitent entered, seeking absolution of her own.

3

Sherriff Milo Atkins circled the town's perimeter slowly, not wanting to go round too fast. Twenty minutes was all it took to walk Red Earth and he didn't want to eat up the ground before he'd cooled off some.

It was that damn Hank Chambers who'd gotten his blood boiling. Mr. Fancy Words Mining Foreman, Mr. The Dennison Mining Company is All-Powerful and Rules Above Us All. Sure, old man Dennison paid the bills around here, including Atkins' own salary, but that didn't mean you could blast away without giving the town some kind of warning, even five minutes notice, so you weren't snoozing at your desk when it happened, a loud enough bang that you woke up and tipped back in your chair, much to the goddamned amusement of anybody who happened to be in the general store. Haw-haw-haw.

It was probably Atkins' age that made Chambers forget about him like that, like a town sheriff was nothing but an itty bitty old fly fit for the swatting. Atkins' pa, who'd been a lawman for thirty years himself, in Wichita, Kansas, had warned it would be like this for the first few years—in half-wild towns like Red Earth grown men didn't cotton to twenty-five-year-old sheriffs, all bright-eyed and damp behind the ears. Didn't matter how good you were at the job, or how well you handled a gun. Men who'd lived long enough with the wilderness at their heels weren't keen on much authority at all, much less a man wearing tin long before he'd turned thirty.

But you had to start somewhere. Atkins had brought his wife and boy out here promising the next town would be located somewhere properly civilized, with an actual railroad running through it. If putting up with some ignorant jawing would keep them all warm and fed, and give him some experience to boot, he'd just have to do it, no matter how it galled.

Atkins was walking behind the two boarding houses when some rocks broke loose and rolled down from the hills beyond, kicking up dust as they tumbled down to the valley floor, harming nothing. Atkins followed the trail of dust up the hillside with his eye and found an old mountain goat looking right back at him, horns and all.

"What you doing up there? You bent on disturbing the peace?"

The goat chewed whatever the hell he was chewing. Atkins unbuttoned his holster and pulled out his revolver, lining its sight up with the goat's face. The goat made no move to flee—he just stared back at Atkins, mute and as dumb as the rocks he'd kicked. It'd be a tricky shot, but Atkins reckoned he could hit it right between the eyes if he'd wanted, since he'd been practicing with a revolver for as long as he could hold onto one. He'd wanted to be a cowboy as a youngster, like Billy the Kid, or Wild Bill Hickok, not knowing that the Wild West was already long over and that it hadn't really been such a grand shootout to begin with. Even Wyoming was getting settled now as the ranchers put up their fences and the oil and coal outfits hawked in, everybody looking to get rich.

Atkins sighed and lowered the gun.

"Go on. Git!"

The mountain goat lowered its horned head and sniffed the ground. It nibbled something green.

"On your own schedule, is that it?"

The goat ignored him and kept nibbling. Atkins took aim and fired a shot about a foot's distance from the beast's nose. The shot echoed loudly off the hills and kicked up a puff of dust, causing the goat to buck and scramble upward, fast and nimble. Atkins holstered his revolver as its fluffy white backside grew smaller and smaller, finally disappearing into a clump of pines.

"That's more like it," Atkins said, hitching up his belt. "That's how you show some goddamn respect."

Atkins circled around the boarding houses and started back up Main Street, which was nothing but cracked earth beneath the July sun, so dried out it was painful to look at, with Revis Cooke's house the only proper building lining it in either direction. Set on the east side of the street, south of the church and the Copper Hotel, the Cooke House was two stories tall, with limestone walls built to hold up against anything from a winter's storm to an angry mob. The front door, which had been shipped out from San Francisco, was made out of solid iron and had a narrow viewing slot for security purposes. And, for every narrow window of the place, you could pull a cord from inside and a steel shutter would drop over it, like scales covering a dragon's hide.

Cooke paid the miners once a month, throwing open the door to his little fortress and dolling out the Dennison payroll from his desk on the first floor, scribbling names and figures into his notebook while the miners stood waiting in line, dirty hats in hand. The payroll line ran out the front door and far down the street, the men outside loud and jovial, reckoning aloud how they'd spend their pay, while the men inside kept as quiet as church mice, their eyes focused on the stack of coins piled at Cooke's elbow.

Part of Atkins' job was to watch over payday, which meant he needed to stand behind Cooke the whole time, arms crossed and gun strapped to his hip. Occasionally, one of the men would get a wild hair up his arse to make a run for that pile of coins, or to try and threaten Mr. Cooke when his payout didn't meet his expectations or need—Atkins escorted these gentlemen outside the house with a firm hand and, according to how riled up they'd gotten, either sent them on their way, whooped them with the butt of his pistol, or escorted them to the edge of town and told them to get the hell out while they still could. So far, in a year and a half's service, he'd had to whoop three unrulies and banished two violent, wild-eyed drunks.

Ah, the life of a small town lawman. Almost as fancy as being the President of the United States, or the King of England.

Atkins passed a prospector on the street and touched the brim of his hat in greeting. The prospector, who smelled like whiskey through every pore, grunted and nodded back, a pickaxe resting easily on his shoulder, as if he'd forgotten it there. The prospectors had only come to town in the past year, trickling in one by one, and they kept mostly to themselves, bunking in the Copper Hotel during the summer and heading home when winter came on, wherever home was. They were all looking for a new copper seam they could turn and sell to the Dennison Mining Company, not guessing or believing Dennison had already sounded out this hunk of the Sierra Madres.

One of the men squatting in front of the general store, an old man named Butch Hastings, waved to Atkins from across the street. The sheriff gritted his teeth and pretended not to see the flagging, keeping his eyes fixed straight ahead. He'd already spun enough bull with the loafers for one day—talking with bored souls was one of the hazards of Atkin's job, since his desk was just inside the store and prone to all manner of disruption from their kind. They'd talk to anyone, about anything, until their listener's ears fell off, and even that might not serve to halt their yammering.

Atkins decided to keep on walking and check in at home. He'd taken his lunch there only three hours pervious but you never knew what fires might need putting out. Last spring their boy, Billy, had brought in a jar of red ants and set them loose to see what would happen (what happened was they bit the hell out of everybody, especially the dog, until Atkins had killed them all with a mixture of honey and arsenic, including the dog, who'd stupidly followed the ants' lead). Every day was something new with that boy, some fresh trial he liked to set upon his poor mother, and more often than not Atkins was reminded of his own father years ago, shouting himself hoarse.

Their cabin was on the far north of town with nothing but mountains behind it. Last in a row of cabins, you had to walk past everything else in town to get there. Atkins preferred some distance from the center of town, where he often had to break something up, or talk somebody down. Miners in general didn't often carry guns but they did carry knives, one and all, and they liked to use them on each other when they got riled. Atkins had seen men lose ears, fingers, and entire chunks of cheek before he could so much as draw his gun—why would any sane man with a family want to live next door to that?

Their door was propped open with a rock. Atkins went inside and removed his hat, hanging it on a nail peg beside the doorway. Violet was sitting in the rocking chair by the fireplace, her knitting on her lap. She smiled dreamily at him and tilted her head.

"You look like an angel, Milo, standing there with the sunlight behind you."

"I do?"

"Sure do. You stop by to take me up to Heaven?"

"I hope not," Atkins said, leaning down and kissing his wife on the cheek. "I'd hate to get there and find out I'm not allowed."

Violet laughed softly, rocking in her chair. She had hazel eyes and fine brown hair that hung to the middle of her back, which she braided on Christmas, Easter, and his birthday.

Atkins glanced around the room.

"He in the bedroom or behind the cabin?"

"Behind."

"Playing with those dolls of his, I reckon."

Violet closed her eyes and sighed. "They're not dolls, Milo. I told you. They're his stickmen. He has wars and all kinds of things like that with them."

"Fine. I'll go visit the general and let you get back to it."

Atkins kissed his wife on the forehead and started back toward the door.

"Milo?"

Atkins turned, looping a thumb into his gun belt.

"Yes, ma'am?"

"Was there any special reason you stopped by like this, mid-day?"

"No, nothing special."

"Those old men at the general aren't getting under your collar, are they? Teasing and the like?"

"Oh, only the usual. Nothing too bad."

"Still, I don't see why Mr. Cooke makes you keep your office at the general. Seems like he'd have plenty of room for you in his house."

Atkins shrugged.

"I don't know if that'd be much better, Vi. You know how Cooke is. So particular and the like. You can't sneeze without him scowling at you and grumbling beneath his breath."

"I suppose. I don't know him like you do."

"No," Atkins said, grabbing his hat as he headed out the door. "You sure don't."

As foretold, young William Atkins was playing behind the cabin, his back turned to the world. He was hunched over several piles of sticks, each bundled together with a strip of old burlap. Violet and Billy had made the stickmen together, right before Christmas, and ever since they'd been Billy's inseparable companions, getting dragged along wherever the seven-year-old went, from the public outhouse to church on Sundays to his bed.

The sheriff leaned against his cabin, watching his son play. He counted seven stickmen, all of them a-smashing into each other while his son made crashing noises with his mouth. Either the game or the sun had brought out the blood in the boy's soft, downy cheeks, giving him a flushed look that reminded Atkins of what his wife had said about him looking like an angel.

"Hey there, Billy."

"Hi, Pa."

His son continued playing without turning to look back. Atkins stepped forward and squatted beside him, pinching a blade of grass between his fingers and setting it in his mouth.

"What game you playing there?"

"One against all," Billy said, glancing up. "It's when one stickman fights everybody else."

Atkins chewed the grass and squinted up into the hills.

"That doesn't sound too fair. One against six."

"No, it's fair," Billy said, solemnly nodding. "The one stickman is really strong, stronger than all the others. He's winning."

Atkins rose from his heels and straightened up.

"That sounds all right, then. You keep on playing that."

"Yes, sir. I will."

Atkins spat out the blade of grass. Billy looked up from his stickmen, frowning with a thought.

"Pa, it's not dinnertime already?"

Atkins tousled the boy's hair, which was dark and fine, like his mother's.

"No, sonny. It's not."

Billy grinned, so wide and happy Atkins had to look away. The stickmen resumed their crashing and you could hear the old straw in them, so dry and cracking you expected a brushfire any moment, rising all around.

4

Ingrid Blomvik made the short walk from the church back to the Runoff Saloon alone, not waiting for Madam Petrov or the other girls. Two men, sitting out on the Copper Hotel's front porch, whistled their appreciation as she passed by. Ingrid ignored them and crossed the empty street, slowing as she approached the Runoff Saloon's porch. Five girls stood propped up on its banister, doing their best to look attractive while they sweated through their cheap dresses. Nobody was used to this kind of heat, not this high in the mountains, and when it did come to visit for a few days, usually in July or August, it felt hotter than the salt flats of Utah.

The porch girls murmured hello as Ingrid mounted the steps and swept past them. Madam Petrov made the regular girls display themselves like goods at a mercantile. She said it attracted more customers, which was doubtful, since nearly every man in town spent his days below the earth, breaking rocks and hauling the mess out (every man who could afford a whore, that was). She let the girls work the porch in shifts during the daytime, four hours on then four hours off, with everybody on the porch starting at five, no matter what. About one hour into a porch shift you ran out of talk, if you'd had any in the first place, and from there the conversation dragged along like a lame mule, nearly as bad as the time you spent with your legs parted beneath some sweaty, unwashed man.

Not that Ingrid dealt much with sweaty men these days—the sole use of her services were reserved by Revis Cooke, who paid a high sum for such special treatment, and Revis Cooke kept himself clean with a particular vehemence that bordered on insanity, his skin so buffed and soft it reminded her of a baby's bum.

The saloon's interior was dark and cool, a large, open space with plenty of tables and chairs and a fireplace to one side. A few customers sat at the island bar in the middle of the room, drinking without talking. Caleb sat on a stool behind the bar, whittling a block of wood. The young man looked up as she came inside and nodded.

"What's it going to be this time, Caleb?"

"Beaver."

Ingrid laughed and started up the saloon's stairway, running her hand along the smooth banister.

"A beaver? With a fat tail and all?"

"Figured we could set it above the fireplace, right next to the cow skull."

"That skull could use some company," Ingrid said, stepping onto the second floor landing. "Being dead must get awful lonely."

Caleb made no reply, already forgetting her as he returned to his work, shaving off another layer of curls from the block. Ingrid turned right, passing three bedrooms until she came to her own, which overlooked the street below. The girls used their own bedrooms for business, seven upstairs and seven down, with the extra rooms for Madam Petrov's bedroom, office, and the bartender's room. Ingrid's room was as small as any, just big enough for a bed and a chest of drawers. It wasn't too glamorous, entertaining a distasteful man in the same room you slept in, but it beat the hell out of a being a girl of the line in some noisy city like Butte, set up in a row of hot wooden shacks like you was nothing but a pumping doll.

Ingrid opened the top drawer of the bureau, rifled through her collection of undergarments, and pulled out a small leather bound book. She sat down on the edge of her bed, kicked off her shoes, and opened the slim volume on her lap, enjoying the way its binding creaked as it spread. It was a book of poetry her deceased husband Erik had given her when they'd been courting back in Minnesota—"In Memoriam", by Lord Alfred Tennyson. The poems were about his dead friend Arthur, about how sad and heartbroken he'd felt at Arthur's sudden death. The book had seemed like a strange thing to give a girl you were courting, especially since they'd both been so young back then, only thirty-two years between them, but it made perfect sense now, with Erik buried in the Black Hills for six long years.

A photograph slid out of the book as Ingrid turned the pages. They'd had the picture taken right after they'd gotten married in Rapid City, spending money on it they couldn't really afford, but she'd rather have it now than a hundred cash dollars. She'd worn a dress her mother had made, a blue and white checkered she'd outgrown since and given away to another girl, and Erik looked so handsome in his good suit, his eyes brimming over with life and jubilation. They'd both been children still, really, not knowing that nothing but cholera and heartbreak was waiting for them around the bend.

Somebody knocked on her door. Ingrid wiped the damp from her eyes, slipped the photograph back inside, and returned the book to its hiding spot at the back of her bureau drawer. "Come in," she called out, sitting back. The door opened and a young woman stepped inside. She was on the short side, with curly dark hair and chestnut brown skin. She was a favorite with the men, all plump curves and wide, beautiful brown eyes.

"Howdy, Anita."

"Hey, Ingrid. Sorry to bother, but Mr. Cooke is here."

Ingrid sighed and tucked a strand of hair behind her ear. They'd lain together the night before and she'd hoped to have an evening's reprieve.

"Send him up, Anita."

"You sure?"

"I am."

The young whore made to leave, then poked her head back inside. "Your eyes, Ingrid. They look red."

"Don't worry about that. Just send the bastard up and mind the slime."

Revis Cooke knocked once on her door and opened it himself, not standing on manners. He was a tall man given to wearing costly suits fitted with small pockets. He always carried a gold fob watch and checked it every five minutes, like he had some place important to be. He claimed to be forty but Ingrid thought he looked older than that, like a grouchy old man in training. He had dark, unsmiling eyes, a hawkish nose, and a pinched mouth that looked prissy if you couldn't sense the sharp teeth hiding behind it. He kept his hair slicked down with the old fashioned pomade fur trappers had used a hundred years before, the kind made with bear fat instead of petroleum.

"I regret to intrude on your leisure hours, Miss Ingrid, but matters would not permit me to visit you later this evening, nor the next day."

Ingrid smiled and rose from the side of her bed. She did not like to sit while her visitor stood beside her bed—it brought her to eye-level with his crotch and the inevitable rising therein.

"I'm delighted to see you, Mr. Cooke. The Runoff Saloon

always appreciates your patronage."

"And do you, Miss Ingrid? Appreciate my patronage?"

Ingrid widened her eyes, willing their blue to sparkle.

"Why sure, Mr. Cooke. Aren't I the one you show the most favor to? And wouldn't it be most natural for me to return it?"

Mr. Cooke stepped forward and set his hands upon her waist, his eyes gleaming as he absorbed her cleavage. "That's what I like most about you, Ingrid. You know a real man when you see one. Not like the rest of this goddamned town, populated as it is with dirt encrusted miners and the usual camp vultures."

"You find it so bad, Mr. Cooke?"

"Bad? Red Earth isn't enough for such a word. This town is a banality and a banality is a worse sin to me by far."

Ingrid didn't know what Mr. Cooke was talking about, but she rarely did. He'd gone to university back East, the only man in town who'd done as much, and liked to hear the wind of his own words. She knew it got him agitated, talking like this, using fine language and big words, and knew you just had to wait out the talking and try not to laugh. Men hated it when you laughed at something you weren't supposed to laugh at.

"You look delectable, Miss Ingrid. You make me feel like the Big Bad Wolf, about to sup."

Ingrid giggled stupidly as the accountant leaned in and nibbled on her neck. The room's heat, combined with the smell of Cooke's pomade, was making her feel faint. How could he stand his own smell? He worked inside a building, as she did. He was no cowboy riding along the open plains, no mountain man Jim Bridger.

Cooke's hands cupped her breasts and began to fumble with her bodice, threatening to bust a few buttons or more—he talked fine, but acted the slop when it came to undressing a woman. Ingrid pushed his hands away and undid the corsage herself, not wanting it harmed, and let it fall to the floor. It took only a few seconds more before she stood naked in the hot room, a bead of sweat slipping between her breasts.

"Ah, yes. Indeed."

The accountant stepped back, fumbling with his own belt in his eagerness to be rid of it. A small pink bit of tongue slipped out between his teeth as he dropped his pants and drawers and kicked the mess of clothes away. His prick was hard and at the ready, wobbling as he came forward and pushed her onto the bed. Cooke had kept his suit coat on, as he always did, and its fine fabric felt over-slick as he climbed onto her and nudged her legs apart with his knees. Ingrid fought against the urge to close her thighs and scream, still there after all these years of whoring, and allowed her eyes to drift away as the accountant entered her and began his thrusting. She tried her best to remember her young husband, the feel of Erik Blomvik's body as they once preformed this same act on a woolen blanket, hidden away in his father's hayloft on a sunny afternoon much like this one. The strength in Erik's shoulders and back as she clutched him to her, so happy as he kissed her neck, her cheeks, her lips. She drew on the memory as if it were a spell of protection, keeping her slightly distant from the slippery, pomaded man on top of her, no matter how deeply he tried to enter.

Some men fell asleep, afterwards, into a deep and untroubled slumber she allowed for a few minutes as she washed between her legs and dried off. Not Revis Cooke, however. Revis Cooke liked to talk.

"This whole town is nothing but a single operation, you know. If Mr. Dennison felt an urge, he could have the whole setup collapsed and put away in a week's time, like taking down a circus."

"Is that so?"

Ingrid wished Cooke would get dressed, or at least put his drawers back on. She didn't need to look at his prick, now soft and gleaming with the juice of his seed, any more than she already had. She'd tell him as much, too, if he wasn't already paying so dearly for their time.

"Yes, it is. But that won't happen for several years more. Not until the mine runs dry and more profit can be found somewhere else. Until then, you ladies will have livelihood enough in these hills."

Mr. Cooke ran his hand along her thigh and set it upon her knee. "Do you recall that matter I mentioned, when I first entered your room?"

"I sure do. You said it would keep you from calling tonight."

Mr. Cooke smiled. No, not a smile, exactly—a hooking of the lip that made Ingrid shiver, though the room was as hot and baking as ever. Out of all the rough and strange men she'd known in five years of whoring, he had to be the most worrisome of all. Maybe it was the fine words and business man's clothes, maybe it was something else.

"The coach is coming in this evening, Miss Ingrid."

"The coach? But it's not Wednesday."

"The coach from San Francisco. The bank coach."

Ingrid drew the sheet up to her waist, though she wasn't cold. She could still see his hand beneath the sheet, lumped like a coiled snake in the grass. Hopefully he had nothing more on his mind for today.

"It comes only once a month, you know," Mr. Cooke said, glancing at her from the corner of his eye. "The coach travels with five guards in addition to the driver himself. Shotguns, they call them. In two years, they haven't missed a delivery yet. They are men you can set your clock by."

Ingrid smiled and set her head on Mr. Cooke's shoulder, though that brought her closer to his slick scalp.

"Like you, Mr. Cooke. I could set a clock by you as well."

"Perhaps you could," he said, drawing his hand back and shifting onto his side, so he could face her. "Being a payroll accountant is a vital job, Miss Ingrid. Each month, I need to count the delivery and dole it out to the appropriate recipients. You'd marvel to see it, all that money laid out on my desk in high stacks. More money than you've ever seen in your life."

Ingrid closed her eyes, imagining that money stacked on her own dresser. Enough money to buy a person free of this town, free of all these mountains and the winters that seemed to begin as soon as they'd ended. With a pile of money like that you could take the train back East. You could go back to Minnesota and show everybody how you'd become something after all.

"I know I'm no whiskey guzzling hard-rocker," Cooke said, squeezing her left breast as if feeling a tomato for soft spots. "But if anybody tried me around here, they'd find enough trouble to last them."

Ingrid nodded. They all talked big like that, afterward.

5

The four outlaws heard the heavy-laden coach descending. They left the winding mountain road, dismounting from their horses and leading them into a short ravine. The horses pawed at the ground as they entered a dense grove of pines, uncertain of the footing and why they were being led into a valley with no visible exit. The outlaws murmured reassuringly to the horses as they brought them round, so that the entire group, now hidden, faced the road. The gang was led by a slim, brown-eyed man named Elwood Hayes. They'd come up from Colorado the day before.

They listened as the coach rumbled closer, its noisy passage echoing off the surrounding hillside, knocking scree loose and moving faster than sanity would seem to allow on such a twisting path.

"Goddamn, they're making a racket."

"Hush, Roach."

"What for? They won't hear nothing above all that. Might as well be riding through a thunderstorm."

Roach Clayton was right—they did not seem to care about how much noise they made or who heard it. That meant a heavy guard, Elwood decided. An escort of either cocky young roosters, too certain their guns made them safe, or grizzled veterans, too hardened by time and experience to care much what happened to them now. Either way, they'd put up one hell of a fight if fallen upon.

All right, then. They'd do this Owen's way, even if it meant him getting a swelled and prideful head.

You could hear the clopping of hooves separate from the rattling wheels. Clem Stubbs lifted his rifle and pointed toward the road with it. Clem was stout and broad-shouldered, with an enormous red beard not unlike the burning bush once revealed to Moses. What few teeth Clem still had in his jaw were yellow and worn, the last stubborn survivors of his mighty love of sweets.

"What you think, El? Should we give 'em lead and set on them from behind?"

Hayes shook his head.

"No. We'll wait till they make the delivery and wander off to the saloon. They won't be as eager to come running to the aid of the Dennison man after spending a few hours drinking and whoring."

Roach Clayton dropped to one knee as if to pray. He was a short, wiry man with round spectacles that gleamed at odd moments, catching you off guard. He looked more fit to minding a hardware store than trail living, but he could outride any man and was startlingly handy with a camp knife.

"You think we can break the Dennison man? He'll be guarding that money chest with his life. Those company men are like that."

"I'll break him," Johnny Miller said. "Just get me in that room with him."

Elwood glanced at the young man. Miller had joined up with them in Denver the month before, a rat-faced youngster who said he wanted to make some easy money and hurt somebody, and not necessarily in that order.

Roach said something else Elwood couldn't hear. The stagecoach was visible now, accompanied by two guards on horseback in front and two in back. A lookout rode beside the driver, his rifle laid out across his lap. The lookout's eyes swept from one side of the road to the other, never quite resting on one spot as the coach jostled along. He looked grizzled enough and so did the other guards, none of whom appeared younger than thirty.

Hayes rubbed his jaw, wondering how exactly they'd finagle all this. You had to take all the specifics into account when you were robbing a man or things could turn on you in a hurry.

The stagecoach and its escort disappeared around a bend in the mountain road, leaving a cloud of dust to slowly settle back on the stony ground. They brought the horses out of the ravine and remounted. Elwood brushed the dirt and pine needles from his pants, mindful of the need for respectable appearance as they approached town. Even in a tiny spider hole like this you didn't want to alarm anyone unduly, not before the silver was in your pocket and the wind at your back.

Clem Stubbs rode up beside Hayes—the road was too narrow for more than two riders to get along comfortably. It was a miracle a stagecoach could fit on such a poor stretch, regardless of its speed.

"You satisfied with your handsomeness, Elwood?"

"I am."

"A man should be tidy, if he's going to rob a tidy sum."

Hayes smiled, letting his horse pick his way down the slanting road. "I like that, Clem. You figure that yourself?"

"Yes, sir. Right now, in my very own Christian mind."

"Mercy," Elwood said, shaking his head. "What wonders hath God wrought in His creation."

The road leveled out some. Elwood kicked his horse to a trot and the other men trailing him followed suit. Down below, you could make out a cloud of dust rising above the trees as the stagecoach rushed onward, heading toward a small town laid out on the valley floor. The town, naught but a few dozen buildings, seemed to be hunched away from the mountains surrounding it, like a nervous wagon train making camp for the night.

Red Earth, his brother had called it. Red Earth, Wyoming.

And such a beauty of a day.

Elwood slowed his horse as they rode down the last steep length of mountain road and reached the valley floor. Felt good to be on flat ground again, to ride without worrying about pitching forward, but Elwood Hayes resisted the urge to let his horse out. They weren't going to act the cowboy, whooping and raising hell as they pounded into town. No, that sort of tomfoolery got a group of men noticed.

They passed the copper mine, which was nothing much to see besides a few buildings and a dark hole in the hillside. Elwood noted the unsettling fact that there seemed to be only one torturous road in and out of camp. If a group of like-minded men, angry and well-armed, managed to cut them off before they'd started upward...well, that could lead to a bloody encounter for all involved.

About a half-mile past the mine's entrance, they came to the first buildings on the outskirts of town. They stabled their horses at the livery barn and left the stable two at a time, with Roach and Johnny going first, headed straight for the saloon downtown, while Hayes and Clem held back a minute before crossing the street.

"That's sharp, splitting us up like that," Clem said, scratching his beard. "Four men stick out more than two."

"That's why I'm in charge, Stubbs. You let me do the hard figuring."

A few old timers were sitting on the porch outside the

town's general store. Elwood touched the brim of his hat and one nodded back.

"You reckon your brother's working in the mine these days, Elwood?"

"No, it don't seem likely. He's worried by dark and crowded places. That's why he only prospects, and does poorly at that. He thinks silver and gold can still be found around these hills, popping out of the ground like prairie dogs."

They crossed the street and came to a handful of shacks that smelled about the same as the livery stables. A man sat cross-legged in a doorway, cradling a jug in his lap. His blond beard was gnarled and unkempt and his hair looked like it might not have seen a barber's shears in a year or more. Elwood kicked the man's leg and he jerked awake, his eyes red and bleary.

"Hey, hoss. No call for kicking."

Stubbs and Elwood laughed.

"Lord Almighty," Elwood said. "Don't you look poorly, you little skunk."

The drunk shaded his eyes.

"El, is that you?"

"Sure is, you drunken fool."

"Well, I'll be."

Owen Hayes set aside the jug and stood up, leaning against the boarding house's doorway for support. He smiled, showing his tobacco-stained teeth, and staggered forward to embrace his older brother. Elwood tolerated the contact a moment before pushing his brother away.

"I can hardly believe it. You came, Ellie. You got my letter and you came."

"I did. It wasn't a pile of nonsense, was it, Owen? I've got three men with me and none of us is going to be too happy with you if you was spinning tales."

"I wasn't spinning tales," Owen said, looking at Stubbs.

"I might be a drunk, El, and a poor excuse for a prospector, but I'm no liar. Payday is tomorrow. That Dennison man will be sitting on that cashbox tonight like a goose in a fairy tale, waiting for its fat gold egg to hatch."

Hayes glanced at Stubbs.

"We saw the stagecoach on the way in. Had a sizable escort."

"That's it, all right. That's the National Bank coach. Comes once a month to Mr. Cooke's house."

"What's Cooke like?" Stubbs asked. "You met him before?"

"No, not myself," Owen said, wiping the sweat off his brow. "But I seen him plenty around town and heard folks talk. Thinks he's smarter than everybody and tougher, too. About what you'd think a big company man to be like in a place like this, I suppose."

Elwood scratched beneath his hat. He'd sweated through the brim and his throat felt dry enough to close up permanently.

"Let's get ourselves a drink. I'm thinking Roach and Johnny have already started without us."

Owen's face broke into another one of those tobacco juice grins.

"I could use a sip myself, brother."

"Kid," Stubbs said, roping him against his chest with one broad arm, "I think you better stick to coffee from here on out."

Owen's vexed eyes went to Elwood, who kept his expression flat.

"Robbing the Dennison Mining Company is no drinking game." Elwood reached into his coat and pulled out a .38 revolver. "You remember how to shoot?"

Owen took the revolver and pointed it across the street, looking down its sight with one eye closed.

"Been awhile, but I can recall."

"That's good. Now tuck it away until you need it."

"This a Remington, ain't it?"

"Don't matter what it is. Shoots bullets well enough. Just don't shoot yourself or any of us."

"Thank you, brother. I will strive to remember that."

Elwood Hayes, like the other men in his gang, wore his pistol in a holster strapped to the small of his back. He believed it did no good to show your gun to the world, reckoned that it only made you a bigger target, both to the law and to hot-tempered drunkards. Also, he liked the look bank tellers and rich folk got in their eyes when you pulled your gun on them like a magic trick. Folks always underestimated a man with empty hands and that alone could give you an opening, if you knew where to look for it. The other men had taken awhile to see the wisdom of this, but Elwood had made it a rule if they wanted to ride with him, a known man in Colorado with three successful holdups already under his belt. Folks said you lost time reaching back for your revolver, which was true, but if you got used to drawing that way it was only a moment and you could overcome that and more through surprise.

Elwood allowed his younger brother to take the lead and show them to the Runoff Saloon, figuring the town without acting too obvious about it. He picked out the accountant's house straight off, seeing as it was the only building in Red Earth that looked permanent, two-stories tall with stone walls, a proper chimney, and small, narrow windows only a cat could pass through.

"I can feel them," Stubbs grumbled beside Hayes. "I can feel their eyes at this very moment, feeling me out."

Elwood opened his mouth, about to ask who exactly Stubbs thought was watching them, but then he saw the girls gathered on the front porch of the saloon, fanning themselves as they sat in the shade, their bare arms glowing. Elwood closed his mouth and swallowed, abruptly aware of the sweat rising along the brim of his hat and the smell of horse upon his skin.

Stubbs crossed himself.

"May the Good Lord preserve me from temptation and deliver me…"

Clem Stubbs was married, somehow, and always started up like this when they ran into women. The prayers must not have been as feverish or pure as the Good Lord wanted, however, since Stubbs usually gave into temptation around his third drink.

Owen glanced back at them and grinned.

"Don't worry about the doves, gentlemen. They do like to flutter around this particular area."

Elwood nodded to the ladies as they climbed the porch steps and passed through, his hand on Stubbs' shoulder to help him along. The ladies flicked their fans like peacock tails, giggling (as he knew they would) while their perfume lifted sweetly off their powdered skin and into the summer air. Elwood and Clem Stubbs stopped just inside the saloon as Owen continued on, allowing their eyes to adjust to the dimness. On Elwood's left were several round tables, all of them empty except one near the saloon's front windows, where three of the stagecoach guards sat playing cards. On Elwood's right was a stairway to the saloon's second floor and behind that a hallway that led to several rooms. The saloon smelled like spilt beer, stale cigar smoke, and the burning kerosene lamps that hung about on pegs.

Roach Clayton and Johnny Miller were sitting by themselves at a rectangular bar in the middle of the room. Elwood headed in their direction, looking sideways at the other tables. The bartender, a young man with a tangle of dark hair over his eyes, came up as Elwood sat down on a stool beside Roach and set his feet on the brass foot rail.

"What'll you have?"

"Beer."

"Caleb here is my good pal," Owen said, sitting on Elwood's

right side, with Clem a third stool down. "Good old Caleb, the greatest bartender Wyoming's ever known."

Elwood grimaced—his brother's breath was as foul as if he'd been chewing on a dead buzzard for the past hour.

"Don't know about greatest," Caleb said, setting a cup of coffee in front of Owen. "About the fanciest concoction I can make is pink gin."

Owen frowned, looking at his coffee. Caleb filled a mug of beer from a keg under the bar and set it in front of Hayes, who tipped it toward the bartender in salute before drinking. Stubbs ordered a beer and a whiskey and Elwood turned to Roach Clayton while the bartender was occupied.

"You see anything strange about them guards?"

Roach shook his head and stared into the bar's varnished top. "Two went upstairs with a girl each, the rest is playing poker. They've been drinking beer and whiskey steady but don't seem bent on getting wild."

"They laugh like goddamn donkeys," Johnny said, leaning across Roach and only bothering to half-whisper. "Bunch of asses, is what they are."

Elwood stared into Johnny's eyes a moment, pondering the glassy rage he saw inside them. Miller wasn't built for the thieving life—he should have been out fighting in a war somewhere, riding on the front lines, charging up hills and such. The only stealth and cunning he had to him was the shrewdness of a cornered animal, already wounded and ready to die fighting.

"You said only two went with the girls, Roach?"

"I did."

"But I counted six on the road. Four riders, one driver, one lookout."

"Lookout's not here," Roach said, and sipped at his beer. "I'm thinking he's over at the Dennison man's place, having dinner or whatnot while they count the money delivered."

Elwood thought about this, imagining the two men talking quietly over fat beef steaks. Their shirtsleeves would be rolled. The house would be cool and padded with fine oriental carpets. Heavy furniture.

"The Cooke House looks like a tough nut to crack. Thick stone walls with hardly a weak point to it."

Roach nodded and belched. Hayes turned to his brother, who was still frowning at his coffee cup.

"You didn't say nothing about a stone fort, Owen."

"I don't want coffee, Elwood. I want a beer, like you got."

"How'd you reckon we'd get at that cashbox if it's surrounded like that?"

"Figured you'd have your ways," Owen said, smiling as he looked up at the high ceiling. "What's a few stones to a famous bandit like Elwood Hayes?"

Hayes took a breath and finished his beer. He felt like cuffing his younger brother on the ears, but it would draw too much attention. He'd have to wait and cuff him later, when they were counting all their money.

Owen sniffed and picked up his coffee, smelling it like an animal expecting poison. "No, El, I suppose I never really thought that far, to be honest," he admitted. "I didn't think you'd actually show up as such, ready for business. How long's it been since we seen each other?"

"Since Gran died, I reckon."

"Four years, that'd be. Four years, Elwood."

Elwood's gaze fell on the bartender, who was whittling on a block of wood. The shavings curled from his knife and drifted to the floor like snowflakes.

"Four years is a long time to be without kin, ain't it?"

"Yup," Elwood said. "But we're here together now, ain't we?"

"Sure. Sure we are."

Elwood set his empty mug on the bar, hoping this would be the last of family talk. Caleb came over and poured him another beer, which tasted almost as good as the first. Behind them, at the tables, the stagecoach guards laughed and cussed at each other, their voices growing louder. A chair scraped on the floor as one of the guards got to his feet. Leaning back on his stool, Elwood watched the man approach the bar from the corner of his eye and saddle up beside Johnny Miller. The guard had two empty mugs in one fist and one in the other. He pounded all three against the bar.

"More beer, tender! More beer!"

Caleb set his whittling aside and filled the mugs without comment. The guard reached into his pocket and smacked a palm full of coins onto the counter, causing both the bartender and Johnny to flinch. On Elwood's right, Owen laughed and raised his coffee cup in salute.

"The man knows what he wants, doesn't he?"

"Damn right, I do," the guard said, looking down the bar. "You fellers prospecting around here?"

"Something like that," Roach said. Elwood glanced back at the tables, where the other guards were making a show of not watching.

"Don't look much like rock moles," the guard said. "Usually y'all are covered with so much grime you can barely make out your eyes."

The guard smiled, but nobody laughed. He collected the filled mugs and lifted them off the bar. His heavier right hand wavered for a moment, tipping one of the mugs and spilling beer on Johnny Miller's knee. The young man sprang up from his stool and pulled out his pistol, leveling it directly at the guard's chest. Miller moved so swiftly Elwood only had time to open his mouth and inhale a burst of gunpowder before the stagecoach guard dropped to the floor, beer and all.

6

Old Tol Gregerson, who had a touch of firebug in him, had used more dynamite than he ought've and blown the newest section of the Dennison mine all to hell, leaving the third level's north corner a mess of heaped rock and pooled water.

But Tol was nowhere to be seen now, of course, Hans Berg noticed as he shoveled stone into an ore car, one of six strung behind a patient mule and his drowsing skinner. The old man always seemed to be absent when the time came to put rock in the box—Tol Gregerson liked to make the hills go boom but wasn't as eager to pick up his mess after.

Two other swampers, Jake Keller and Bear Tollackson, worked alongside Berg at the foot of the freshly opened chamber, filling the cars with sediment and raw ore as they slowly opened the room. Their shared excitement from earlier in the day, when they'd gotten to break and watch the big thump from outside the mine, had worn off four or five ore trains back. Conversation, which had started loud and rowdy as they started in on the freshly loosened rock, had fallen off to the occasional observation as the hours passed and the rubble showed no signs of letting up. It always made you feel low when you realized how much mountain you had left, no matter how much you'd dug out already or how badly your back ached.

"We'll have work for a month or more at this end," Jake Keller announced, dumping another shovelful into the cars. "No need to worry about getting paid."

"It's not pay that worries me," Bear Tollackson said. "Did you boys see how Chambers sweated before the blasting? Reminded me of the yellow fever."

Hans Berg dumped out a shovelful and paused.

"You've seen the Yellow Jack, Bear?"

"Aye. I worked a silver mine in Argentina, some ten years back. A hellish place, that was. Men dropping on both sides of you while shifts went day and night, sometimes running sixteen, eighteen hours a man."

Hans Berg imagined a mine buried deep beneath layers of teeming jungle and snakes. The only mine he'd known beside the Red Earth had been back in Michigan's Upper Peninsula. He'd worked the Quincy Mine in Copper Country for five long years before getting soaked one night and showing up for work too drunk and accidently crushing another miner's knee with a misplaced strike.

And now here he was, a year later and fourteen hundred miles distant, still trying to forget the man's screams.

"Mr. Chambers is a hard one," Jake Keller said. "Fever won't keep a stubborn fella like that down for long."

The other men grunted in agreement. The foreman could be ornery at times but he was easily the finest man any of them had ever worked for. Hank Chambers begrudged no man his lunch break, his drink, or his pay, long as he worked hard and steady and caused no foolish accident. With him there were no unnecessary words, no skull knocking, no blustering to show how rough he could make it for the rest of them. He expected you to work as hard as he did and even the orneriest miners couldn't bellyache about that.

They topped off the line of ore cars and woke the skinner, a kindly old coot who must have been seventy if he was a day. The skinner cracked his whip over his mule's head, passing on the message, and soon the entire train was rolling into the tunnel and out of sight. Hans imagined the ore train rolling out of their tunnel and switching onto the main track, which would lead to the third level's adit entrance, where the ore would be sifted out from the dirt and rock and dumped into a haul wagon. When the wagon was filled, it'd be sent on its way up the mountain road toward Rawlins, where it'd be processed into proper copper at a smelting plant, a foul inferno also owned and operated by Mr. Dennison.

"Must be near six," Bear Tollackson said, leaning his ample frame against his shovel's handle. They all rested upon their shovels now, breathing heavily as they sweated in the cool air. By the waxy yellow glow of candlelight, they looked like dirty ghosts exhausted by their ghostly labors.

"I hope so," Jake said, wiping his brow with a piece of burlap. "I could use a few pints at the Runoff, sooner rather than later. And some beef stew over at the Copper, as well. Three bowls, I'll handle."

A light appeared down the tunnel running from the room, appearing in the same spot where the mule-drawn ore train had disappeared. The light hovered in the darkness like a moth, swinging slowly back and fourth and illuminating the tunnel's azurite-spotted walls as it approached.

A face appeared beside the light—Andrew Klieg, shift boss and second-in-command. He stepped out of the tunnel's mouth and entered the high-ceilinged chamber.

"Bear, I need your crew up on Level One to help carry out a heavy fragment. You can leave this heap till tomorrow."

"Sure enough, Mr. Klieg. We'll head up."

The shift boss nodded and turned back down the track.

They gathered their tools and followed the shift boss at a distance, letting Klieg gain on them. Halfway down the tunnel, Hans noticed he'd left his candle behind in the new room.

"Forgot my light," Hans called out, causing the other men to chuckle and glance back at him. "I'll catch up."

Bear waved him down the tunnel, his eyes twinkling. He liked to call Hans "Forgetful Freddy" and this would only add fuel to the fire.

But heck.

You needed light to see.

The rooms of the Red Earth Mine felt cold and unfriendly if you happened to find yourself alone in one, your flickering candle raised before you. The walls of the Quincy Mine, back in Michigan, had seemed only quiet and worn, like an old man wanting nothing more than to be left to his dreamless sleep. Those extensive, productive shaft mines had been worked for nearly forty years before Hans Berg had arrived to add his shoulder to the load—here, the Red Earth Mine was only two years old, still a fresh burrow inside the heart of Flannery Peak. The mountain had not yet had time to fully understand that it had been invaded, that men had appeared in this remote part of the world bent on plundering its core, yet Hans could tell it was unhappy nonetheless, like a lion with a thorn in its paw.

So, when the newly blasted chamber's ceiling split apart ten feet ahead of him, Hans Berg fully expected the entire mountain to collapse upon his trespasser's head and crush him where he stood, exacting a swift and furious revenge. Instead, it merely dumped a fresh pile of rock along the tracks, scaring the water out of him. "Jaspers," Hans whispered, lifting his candle to better view the pile of rock and scree. A cloud rose above the fallen rock, thick with dirt, and the familiar smell of smoke filled the air.

Hans blinked from the dust and examined the hole in the

tunnel's roof. The light of his candle only reached so far—he could make out nothing except a patch of black overhead, though he might have felt a faint gust of air, coming from somewhere. He turned his attention back to the pile of newly fallen rock, which looked about the same as all the other turquoise-spotted rubble they'd extracted from the room so far.

Except....

Something was buried under this rubble.

Something big.

"Sweet Mary," Hans whispered, setting down his candle to free his hands. He dug off the loose rock and flung the larger stones behind him. The rocks fell away and gave up the shape below—it was a man with skin so badly charred it encased him like a mummy's wrap, as if he'd been dipped in a volcano and left out to cool. But it was a man, all right—some poor son-of-a-bitch who might have been buried inside the mountain for the past thousand years.

A burnt man, who still smelled like smoke and had curled, claw-like fingers. Hans Berg wiped his brow, his eyes wide from the sight before him. The smell of roasted flesh filled the chamber, thickening. Hans laughed aloud, imagining the reception he'd get back in town—the many drinks the other men would buy him, the fawning attention of the Runoff's whores—and leaned over to get a closer look at his prize.

The burnt man's eyelids parted, showing eyes with no light to them. Then, quick as that, the burnt man was sitting up and reaching out with his spindly arms, his clawed fingers squeezing Hans' windpipe with a grip so crushing and fierce it felt like an ache. The miner's vision filled with floating spots as he thrashed about, trying to free himself.

The spots spread into dark and widening pools, then into darkness all around.

Hans barely had time to wonder about any of it.

PART TWO

Death Above, Death Below

7

When Elwood Hayes envisioned robbing the Dennison Mining Company, he'd figured something might go wrong, some unexpected devilry that might cost them a bullet or two. Hayes had been on the wrong side of law for three years, ever since he'd struck a man too square in an alley fight and sent the dumb bastard to an early grave. He'd learned to expect nasty surprises when you tried to part a man from his money—some chicken-headed local who appeared out of nowhere to gape and blink, a farmer's kid who favored himself a hero and yearned to see his picture in the paper. Any time you tried to conduct yourself in some profitable yet illegal business, trouble was bound to show its ugly, bucktoothed head.

But Lord, this was a new one, even to him.

"Hell, Johnny."

"You saw him, Mr. Hayes. You saw him provocate me."

"He spilt some beer."

"Right on my knee, he spilt it. Right after that smart mouth talk about us being rock moles."

The whores on the saloon's front porch had stuck their heads inside to watch the action. The stagecoach guard was lying on the floor, kicking his feet as he bled out on the barroom floor, surrounded by a large pool of spilled beer and broken glass. His friends had gotten to their feet to remove their hats and watch him die. They hadn't drawn their pistols yet but Hayes knew it was only a matter of time until they forgot their shock and turned against Johnny. The question of the moment was whether the Hayes Gang should stand with the fool or hand him over. Johnny had killed the man straight out, with no eye to robbery or common sense. They should have left the kid back in Denver, with the other thin-skinned young men who dwelt there, and it was Elwood's own fault Johnny had traveled with them this far. He'd shown the boy too much kindness in the face of too many obvious faults and now a time of reckoning had come.

"What you thinking, El?"

Elwood turned to see his own reflection in Roach Clayton's spectacles. He looked pale and out of sorts. Almost like one of his men had done something so goddamn stupid it defied the mind's powers.

"We go down a man, it's just going to make it harder to bust into that fortress down the street."

Johnny, perhaps stunned himself, had joined the coach guards as they stood above their dying friend. One of the guards was pressing at the wound with a rag from the bar, but the blood kept seeping through. The bartender, Caleb, had stepped outside to see if he could scare up the town sheriff.

"We've got your brother now," Roach whispered back, his breath smelling like whiskey. "We can make do with four."

Elwood looked past Roach and saw that Clem and Owen had spread out down the bar and dropped their hands to their sides. They expected a shootout, but they didn't see the two guards who'd left their whores to stand along the upstairs balcony and watch the commotion below. They were standing in their dirty skivvies, each holding a rifle as they watched everything play out with a clear and steady gaze. After a hard ride, they hadn't had time enough to get properly drunk and they'd been interrupted in their attentions—they might as well have been two sleeping rattlesnakes Johnny Miller had poked with a stick for the hell of it.

"Jesus!" the dying man shouted, then kicked up his feet in one last mighty convulsion before falling still. Johnny Miller laughed and looked back at the bar, his eyes gleaming in an uncanny way.

"How you like that, fellas? A banker's errand boy calling out to the Good Lord in his last moment, like he'd never heard of those moneylenders getting driven out of the temple."

The stagecoach guards turned in unison to regard young Johnny Miller and a new stillness fell upon the barroom. Hayes felt a tickling on the nape of his neck that signaled the proximity of Death. He paused in uncertainty no longer, striding across the barroom floor and dropping Miller with one punch across the right temple. The surprised young man collapsed to the floor with a thud and Hayes stepped back to shake the heat out of his fist.

"There, fellas. He's all yours."

After some discussion, two guards went off and fetched one of the cheap pine coffins Leg Jameson kept stocked in his general store. Then the guards lifted the dead man into the coffin and hammered the lid on right there. When the box was sealed, the four living guards sat down around it and began drinking again, using the coffin for a table. When the unconscious Johnny Miller showed signs of stirring, they trussed him up with a rope, also fetched from the store, and gagged him with a handkerchief. They debated the young man's fate between them, loudly proclaiming they didn't know if it were best to hang Miller outright or turn him over to the law in Rawlins, where the killing could be done properly in front of a large crowd.

Elwood Hayes didn't like any of this, but he made himself stay in the bar and bear witness to what he saw as a breakdown of discretion and leadership. The Hayes Gang had moved to a table on the opposite side of the bar, about as far as they could possibly get from the coach guards within the confines of the building, but they could still hear enough to put them off their drink.

"I'd like to shut them all up for good."

Elwood turned to his younger brother, now sitting at his elbow.

"That right?"

"Yeah. Sure, they lost one of theirs, but they don't have to act so sore about it. They probably didn't even like the fella."

Elwood took a drink of whiskey and rolled it along his tongue. "They're blowing off steam," Clem Stubbs said, picking at the table with his pocket knife, his bushy red beard sweeping across the tabletop as he worked. "By the end of the night, they're likely to open that box up and dance their man across the bar, just to make the whores laugh."

Roach Clayton crossed his arms.

"Who cares? We'll be gone by then, with their money in our pockets."

The saloon door creaked open and Hayes looked up, hoping it was the head guard, the one who'd stayed back with the Dennison accountant after the payroll delivery. Instead, two other men entered the bar, a gray-haired priest and a smooth cheeked lawman who couldn't have been older than twenty-five. They glanced around the room, nodded to the bartender, and went directly toward the stagecoach guards, who got to their feet as a group. The sheriff asked them something and they all looked at Johnny Miller, tied and gagged on the floor.

The preacher circled round the men and stopped at the foot of the coffin. He lowered his head and clasped his hands, praying over the body. The sheriff and the other men fell silent for a moment and looked at the coffin, too, as if they could all see through its cheap pine lid.

"Maybe they'll bury them side to side," Owen said. "The killer and the killed."

"Now, isn't that a sweet notion," Stubbs said, digging a deep new furrow into the table and filling the air with the scent of wood shavings.

Hayes shifted in his seat, the weight of his revolver pressing against the small of his back.

"Whatever the hell they do, I wish they'd take the whole circus outside."

The sheriff looked over at their table, frowning. One of the shotguns jawed in the lawman's ear. Finally, after he'd been jawed at enough, the sheriff broke away and ordered the others to take the coffin outside along with Johnny Miller. The guards did as they were told, three of them lifting the coffin between them while the fourth grabbed Miller by his ropes and dragged him to his feet. Johnny shouted through his gag, his words unintelligible and distressed. One of the guards punched Johnny in the stomach, knocking the wind from him, and a moment later Miller was dragged quietly from the saloon, his feet as heavy as if they'd been filled with wet clay. The preacher followed behind the prisoner, head bowed and hands clasped. The sheriff walked toward their table with a pained looked upon his boyish face.

"Evening, gentlemen."

Hayes nodded and removed his hat.

"Evening, Sheriff."

"That was your friend who shot the National man?"

"Yes, sir. His name is Johnny Miller."

The sheriff took a notepad from his pocket and a pencil and scribbled something down. Stubbs and Roach glanced at Elwood, who kept his face blank.

"They wanted to hang Mr. Miller straight off, but I convinced them to hold up and send him to Rawlins for a proper trial." The sheriff glanced up from his notepad. "This isn't the lawless Old West anymore, even out here. Mr. Dennison expects Red Earth to run smoothly and he pays my salary to make sure that happens."

Elwood nodded, keeping his eyes focused on the sheriff's. He expected the kid to flinch and look away, but he looked right back. He'd be one to deal with later.

"So what brings you gentlemen to Red Earth? You prospecting?"

Elwood smiled and glanced at Roach. "Prospecting for work is more like it. We were hoping Dennison was hiring still."

The sheriff scribbled some more and stuffed the notebook back into his pocket. "You'll have to talk to Hank Chambers about that. He's the foreman. The company shift ends at six. You'll find him at home sometime after."

"Thank you, Sheriff," Owen said. "We surely appreciate that information."

The sheriff glanced at the younger Hayes.

"Say, I know you, don't I?"

"Yes, sir, I'm Owen Hayes, and I've been doing some independent prospecting in the area. You probably seen me around town."

"Find anything worth working?"

"Not yet."

"I'd be surprised if you did. Dennison's men have surveyed this whole valley and they can sniff out good ore like they planted it there themselves."

Owen grinned and looked around the bar stupidly. Elwood willed his younger brother to shut his mouth and leave it at that but, of course, he could not do so.

"Damn it all," Owen said, slapping the table. "Why didn't

anyone tell me that in the first place? I might as well pack up my kit tonight."

The young sheriff looked toward the saloon's front door, unsmiling. A few of the whores had come out of their rooms up on the second floor and were leaning over the railing in a suggestive manner.

"Well, gentlemen," the sheriff said, "sometimes moving on doesn't hurt none, either."

8

Hank Chambers emerged from his feverish afternoon nap to find a man looming above his bed. The foreman raised his head, his tongue stuck to the roof of his mouth and a terrible thirst stuffed in his throat. The visitor tilted his chin, watching Chambers with undisguised curiosity. The visitor's face was deeply lined, wrinkled around the eyes and scorched acorn brown from a lifetime of working beneath the sun. He wore a broken old straw hat with a tattered brim.

"Pa."

The visitor nodded. He removed his hat and fanned himself with it, as if he could actually feel the cabin's trapped heat and had not been in the ground for over twenty long years. Chambers swung his leg over the bed's edge, making to stand. His body trembled from the effort.

"Goodness, Pa. I've missed you so much. Everybody has—"

Noise from another part of the cabin. His wife, asking if he needed something. Chambers turned his head, as if he could see through the partition sheet and make out whatever lay beyond it.

When he turned back, his visitor was gone.

The foreman sighed and lay back in bed. His wife came into the room with a cup of water, frowning. "I thought you might have been calling for water," she said, her eyebrows folding in on each other. "Was that it?"

"I saw him, Bonnie."

"Who?"

"Pa. I thought I saw my pa standing right here, clear as day. He was even wearing that beat-up straw hat he favored."

His wife leaned over the bed and felt Chambers' forehead with the back of her hand. It felt cool and nice and he found himself reaching up from beneath the cotton sheet to cup one of her heavy breasts. It felt as good as ever in his palm, possessing a calming weight that returned him to the world of the living.

Bonnie leaned into his groping, kissed his hot forehead, and pulled back to adjust her hair.

"Mr. Chambers, please. You need your rest."

"Yes, ma'am."

She handed him the cup of water, which made him sit up again and lean against the headboard.

"Drink all of that."

Chambers did so, gladly.

"I'll fetch you another so you can drink that, too. And a fresh cloth for your forehead. You could cook eggs on it."

Chambers smiled and watched his wife go back through the partition's doorway. That was a good woman, there. He'd done well for himself by marrying Bonnie and she seemed to feel the same about him. Any way you looked at it, it wasn't every woman who'd pick up house every few years and haul out to another goddamn mining camp, where she was sure to deal with more dust and disorderly behavior.

The foreman closed his eyes and had started to drift back to sleep when somebody hammered on the cabin's door. He heard the front door creak as Bonnie answered and the sound of her voice, trying to hush the visitor. The visitor replied in a low but excited tone and whatever he said must have had a strong effect, because suddenly Bonnie was beside the bed, wringing her hands.

"Randy Bale's here, Hank. He says there's been some kind of accident in the mine."

Chambers was on his feet and moving before he knew exactly what he was about. He found his clothes piled on the floor, still damp with his earlier sweat. He pulled on his shirt and drawers and trousers while Bonnie tisked.

"Please, Hank. You're too poorly. Can't Andrew handle this? Isn't this what a shift-boss is for?"

"I'm the foreman. This is what I'm for."

Bonnie wrapped her arms around him, ready to throw him back down in bed herself. Chambers took a deep breath, trying to clear his thoughts, and felt his wife's bosom press against his own.

"I'll be home before you know it," Chambers whispered, squeezing his wife with both arms. "I'll guzzle all the water you see fit."

Randy Bale was standing outside the cabin, his gaze fixed south of town. He was only sixteen or so, the kind of fleet-footed kid they'd have sent if something had gone wrong. Normally, Randy would be mucking the stables and tending to the mules not on shift.

Chambers clapped the kid on the shoulder, making him jump.

"Easy, boy. Easy."

They started walking toward the mine, speaking as they went. Chambers ignored the sun's fierce heat and the fresh dizziness that threatened to overtake him. He focused on the hills in the distance and the small, vulnerable group of buildings at their base.

"What happened?"

"Three men dead, sir."

"Cave in?"

"No. I mean, yes, sir, some rock fell in, but that wasn't what killed them."

"Then what was it?"

The boy glanced up at the foreman. "Something... something got at their throats."

Chambers pulled up. Sweat poured down in his brow in a mighty cascade of miserable salt water.

"Their throats?"

"Ripped'em clean out, sir. Blood all over."

Chambers set his hands on his hips. He felt like keeling over right there in the scrub grass.

"Run back to my cabin, Randy, and tell Bonnie to give you my rifle. Go now and catch up with me."

The boy took off like a scared antelope, moving as if glad to vent his energy. The foreman watched him run for a moment, wondering if he should have sent the boy for the sheriff and more men instead. What kind of animal might find itself lost inside a mountain and decide to start killing? Bear? Mountain lion?

Or did they have a murderer on their hands?

Chambers was swaying on his feet by the time he approached the mine's entrance, Randy Bale right on his heels. He stopped as the boy caught up and handed over his Winchester. Chambers levered the rifle open and checked the cartridge while Randy panted beside him.

"Who was it killed?"

"Hans Berg, Jake Keller, and Bear Tollackson."

The foreman clenched his teeth. All three good workers, good men, and whatever had taken down a giant like Tollackson must have been pretty formidable itself.

"Nobody saw nothing, either. They was just down in the Brink Lode, swamping out the new rock. When Mr. Klieg went to check on them, he found their candle still burning but the men lying there, dead. He thought they were pulling his leg before he saw all the blood."

Chambers nodded and looked in on the dry house, which sat about ten yards outside the mine's entrance. With its roughhewn benches and cubby holes, the dry house served as a changing room for the miners, who usually came up soaked to the bone after each shift—the temperature in the mine was pleasant enough, cool in the summer and warm in winter, but water would seep through the earth to drip upon your head and fill the gaps you'd just chiseled out.

Chambers heard Randy Bale breathing hard behind him.

"None of the men have come up?"

"No, sir. Don't look like it."

Chambers checked his pocket watch. Six-fifteen on a Saturday. The dry house should have been packed with men coming off the week's last shift.

"They must reckon it takes an army to sort out three dead men. You wait here, Randy."

"Sir?"

"Mind the entrance and tell any men coming out to wait for me in the dry house before they go into town. I want to talk to everybody before they take to drinking and whoring."

"Yes, sir."

Chambers walked into the mine's entrance. The temperature dropped mercifully as he left the daylight behind and headed down the tunnel, moving slowly to let his eyes adjust before stepping into the Main Room, which was really just a big, hollowed out room, scraped clean of any copper ore it might have once had. They kept a long supply bench in the Main Room where you could come back for dynamite, fuses, hammers, chisels, candles, and whatever else was lying around.

An old man named Lionel usually minded the bench, keeping a lamp burning and logging who took what, but he wasn't sitting in his usual chair this evening, complaining about his lame right leg to anybody who'd listen.

"Lionel? You around here?"

Chambers voice carried through the air and died out against the damp rock. He dug through the supplies piled on the bench, pulled out an oil wick lamp, and lit it on the main lamp. The amount of light in the Main Room doubled, revealing the white shine of condensation on the rocks overhead. A bat flitted across the room, dipped toward Chamber's face, and rose again as he snapped his fingers, a movement as automatic to him as scratching his ass.

The Dennison Mine was still young and growing, but it was already sizeable. Three tunnels were connected to the Main Room—left took you to the Emerald Lode, right took you to the White Lode, and straight ahead took you deep into the hillside toward the Brink Lode, which ran two levels below the main.

Hank Chambers started down the gleaming metal rails of the Brink tunnel, wondering at the quiet and wishing he weren't alone.

9

The stagecoach guards all smelled like beer and whiskey and they stumbled clumsily into the street, unsure of where to take their dead friend. Father Lynch followed the group at a distance, his thin lips pursed in distaste, and said a silent prayer that the men would not drop the coffin between them, the impact of which would surely split the cheap pine contraption Leg Jameson had the nerve to call a coffin. The killer had already been led away to the general store, where he'd be kept until the next morning. Soon enough, Johnny Miller would be rolling back through the hills toward a noose of his own and it would all mean nothing, absolutely nothing, and the Devil would be laughing mightily at the never ending stupidity of man.

"We should ask Hollis where to keep him."

"We should just load him back into the wagon. Ain't no money box inside it anymore."

"May draw flies, though."

"Chester always was a ripe one."

The men laughed and Father Lynch winced—what sort of name was Chester, anyhow? That sounded like the type of name that laid out of the path to damnation for a child before it could take its first step. Chester. The name of a born sinner.

"All right," one of the guards said. "Let's go ask."

The four men staggered toward the Cooke House with their shared load. Father Lynch sighed and rubbed his temple—if there was a more unpleasant man in the world than Revis Cooke, who harbored the duel sins of greed and arrogance in staggering abundance, Father Lynch did not want to meet him. Mr. Cooke was enough unpleasantness for anyone to encounter in the skin of one man.

The stagecoach guards dropped the coffin and conferred with each other in the way of nervous, half-intoxicated men. Finally, after some heated debate, one of their number was made to go up to the house and knock on the front door. The metal door was so stout the man's fist barely made a noise against it, only a soft *thud-thud-thud* Father Lynch had to tilt his head to hear. Nothing happened for a moment, but as the man made to knock again the door's peek-a-boo slot was thrown back and a pair of oil-black eyes appeared.

"Yes?"

"Sorry to bother you, sir, but is Hollis Wells in there with you?"

The black eyes narrowed.

"Yes, he is. We are tallying accounts. What do you want?"

The guard, now much closer to sober, took off his hat and wrung it in his hands.

"Well, sir, there's been a difficulty. We were at the saloon across the road there and one of our men was shot and killed."

"I see. We wondered at the gunfire."

The guard nodded.

"The killer was unprovoked and we're going to take him to Rawlins in the morning for trial."

"That sounds in order. What do you need Mr. Wells for, at this very minute?"

"Well, sir, we was wondering what to do with the body. With Chester's body."

Cooke blinked again from behind his metal door. Father Lynch wondered what could make a man so given toward the indoors, so fearful of God's bright firmament. Was it a love for money alone that could wreak such havoc upon a man? Or was there a greater twisting inside Cooke which required four walls to keep it at bay?

"Go ahead and stow the remains in the wagon," Cooke said. "I suppose he'll keep well enough on wheels." "No," Father Lynch called out, stepping toward the house. "Bring the coffin to the church. Chester's first night departed should be spent in the house of God. I'll watch over the body."

The stagecoach guards startled at the priest's voice, having forgotten his presence. Cooke snorted through the door.

"That's fine with me, Father. Now leave us alone."

The peek-a-boo bar slammed home. The guards looked in directionless befuddlement at the priest, a look he'd grown to know all too well. He raised his hand and lo, they followed.

Father Lynch had them set the coffin down at the rear of the church, in the standing room behind the pews. The men stepped back from the coffin, hats in hand, and stared balefully at the floor. The spirits on their breath had turned hot and sour and their clothes still smelled of the road, like horses and juniper and sweat. Inside the church, they did not seem like good or bad men. Just four mortal souls, making their path through the world as best they could.

"Thank you, gentleman. You can go back to the saloon. Your friend should be fine here for the night."

The dejected guards mumbled their thanks and went out the door. Father Lynch made a sign of the cross over the coffin and said the Lord's Prayer, as much to comfort himself as the dead man. He'd presided over hundreds of funerals during his career and spent countless nights sitting up with the dead, both with family members and alone. Many folks were made uneasy by the dead, frightened by the mirror held up to their own eventual future, but Lynch was not. He'd watched a great many men, women, and children die over the past forty years. He'd seen the light fade from their eyes and how their chests rose slowly, fell slowly, then ceased to move altogether. He'd bathed the dead and dressed them in their Sunday finest. Combed their hair. Rolled their eyes shut. He'd felt them stiffen beneath his touch, their bodies seized by the clenched fist of rigor mortis. And, as they were lowered into their final resting place, Lynch had done his best to speak a few words of comfort above their mortal bodies as their souls traveled toward the Lord, who alone could sit in judgment upon them.

Truly, Father Lynch didn't mind the company of the dead in his little church, which was always so empty during the long nights. He retrieved the bottle of gin from the back room, took a pull, and brought a chair back out with him to the sanctuary, where he sat with the coffin before him.

Outside, the descending sun broke through the clouds and brightened the room. Father Lynch imagined he was sitting among the clouds, bathed in the sun's white light as he drifted above the world. How beautiful it would be to look down upon creation from such a height. The death of this one man would seem even less than it did now, nearly insignificant in comparison to the world's mountains, lakes, deserts, forests, and frothing oceans.

And the wind blowing across it all, like God's very breath.

At six o'clock Father Lynch finished his drink, put on his hat, and headed out the door. Lynch didn't feel like cooking and Chester didn't seem to mind if he stepped out.

Across the way, the girls had come back outside the Runoff

Saloon, waiting for the Saturday night rush. Tonight the miners would drink and carouse and lay with whores. Tomorrow, twenty or so would filter into his church, bleary-eyed and penitent, fully expecting the approaching week to be exactly the same as the previous. The pattern of a mining camp was simple enough, based as it was on a great amount of work followed by a brief, stormy period of revelry, the entire town exhaling with the beginning of each shift and inhaling once again as the miners returned, eager to spend their salaries and hold women so much softer than the rock they spent their days hacking loose.

Father Lynch squinted as he walked slowly down the street, hoping to find Ingrid Blomvik among the girls placed along the Runoff Saloon's front porch. She'd seemed so sad at her confession earlier that afternoon, so full of mourning for her dead husband. He'd wanted to console and bed her at the same time, to combine his heat with her own and pray for God's forgiveness after. But the sad girl from Minnesota was not out among the other doves, which did seem to coo to each other as they fiddled with their elaborate garments.

The priest stopped in front of the Copper Hotel, went up the porch steps, and stepped inside. He found it cooler here than in the church, with the comforting murmur of men speaking to each other in a variety of tongues. The hotel's dining room, which also served as its lobby, was large enough to accommodate forty souls, with a rectangular second floor balcony rising above it from which the tenants could watch the action below. Father Lynch bought a plate and sat down at a small table in a corner of the room, content to let the numerous conversations wash over him as he prayed and began to eat.

He was well into his overcooked steak when a young man with green eyes and a shock of red hair ran into the hotel, breathing hard and waving his arms. "Three men," the boy shouted, looking wildly about the room with an oddly triumphant shine to his eyes. "Three men dead at the Dennison Mine!"

Chairs scraped on the wood floor as the diners got to their feet and began shouting questions. The boy smiled at the attention and began babbling away about three miners with their throats ripped out and blood everywhere. Pushing his unfinished steak away, Father Lynch felt a coldness settle upon his shoulders and perch there like a pink-eyed vulture, flapping its broad wings as it prepared to fly.

10

The top level of the mine was empty, the miners having abandoned their stations to run off and seek a sight of greater interest. The foreman could easily picture how the news of three men killed would have spread swiftly throughout the mine, drawing the men like ants to honey and suspending operations in every dark corner of the hillside. The sort of delay Hank Chambers would not have allowed had he been on hand and not lying abed with fever like a wilting pansy.

But done was done and they had a new situation on their hands. Chambers hooked the strap of his rifle across his shoulder and started climbing down a vertical access shaft, one hand free to grasp the metal ladder sunk into the rock wall and the other minding the oil wick lamp. At the second level, he stepped off the ladder and looked around, calling out to anyone within shouting distance. No sound of metal ringing against rock, or the grind of ore carts rolling along the tunnels. Levels Two and Three each had adits cut into the south side of the mountain, with their own set of haul wagons waiting outside to remove the ore. The tunnels to each of these exits ran a quarter of a mile long and kept the mules busy rolling out full carts and returning them empty.

Chambers returned to the vertical shaft and paused, listening to the feathery rustle of bats overhead. A wall of loose rock, blasted small enough it could be removed by hand, lay at a slant against the room's far wall. Chambers studied the stope and wondered if there was something he was missing here. A miner who knew what he was doing could walk up that angled pile of rock easily enough and pick through the rubble for a piece that suited him—but if you made a wrong step and shifted the pile too much, the whole mess could break loose and roll out under you, burying you quick and deep.

"Stop thinking, Hank," the foreman said aloud. "You're letting the fever spook you." The soles of Chambers' boots, wet from groundwater, slipped against the ladder's rungs as he climbed downward, sending the oil sloshing inside his lantern and placing an even greater strain on his clinging right arm. None of this was a new sensation—he'd been climbing up and down slick ladders half his life—but the fever had weakened Chambers considerably, dampening his palms and dripping sweat into his eyes.

The ground came up sooner than he'd expected. Chambers leaned his weight back, ignoring the rubbery nature of his arm, and lowered the lantern to get a better look at what he'd touched foot upon.

Four men looked back at him. All claw fingered, all staring upward with glassy eyes. Packed together like fish in a barrel and dead as it got.

Chambers swore beneath his breath, his voice strange to his own ears. He hooked the lantern to a rung above his head and gripped the ladder with both hands, wanting to fall less than ever. He recognized all four miners, though not by name. They'd all come recent to Red Earth, arriving after the spring thaw and looking for work.

And they'd died trying to escape it, so panicked they made

migrating lemmings seem downright rational.

"Hey there," Chambers shouted in the direction of the dead men, hoping his voice would carry through into the third level. "Anybody hear me?"

The dead men gaped back at him, silent. Chambers looked closer, searching for the mark of a bullet or a knife. He wondered if they'd suffocated somehow, but the air smelled clean enough to him.

"Sorry, fellas, but I need to get through."

The foreman brought his boot down on the chest of the nearest miner, pushing on him with nearly all his weight. A rib snapped but the body hardly budged.

"Goddamn. Y'all got wedged in there."

Chambers recalculated his aim and brought his boot down on the forehead of the man farthest back. This time, something gave way and the body slid backward. He kicked the miner again and kept his full weight on the body until it fell away. The other bodies held their spots in the shaft for a moment, waiting for gravity to catch up, then they dropped as well, landing with a thud not six feet down.

Chambers unhooked the lamp and continued downward, the rifle banging uncomfortably against his shoulder. He felt a powerful urge to change direction—to climb right the hell back up to the surface, have Bonnie pack her things, and head straight to Rawlins, where they could catch any train heading east or west. He owed the Dennison Mining Company his living, not his death.

He resisted the urge and dropped to the ground. The four men he'd kicked loose had landed facedown, exposing their backs to the yellow light of his lantern. One had a nasty wound beneath his shoulder blades, as if he'd been punctured by something sharp as he climbed. The others had no such wound, yet their necks were broken. Either the short fall down the shaft ladder had done that or something with an awfully strong grip. Chambers peered up the exit shaft once again, considering the ladder rungs. He heard his wife in his mind, telling him to git. But he also heard his father's tobacco coarsened voice, telling him it'd be a worse hell yet if he didn't see to the fate of his men, whatever that may be.

The old man won out one more time. Chambers turned right and started down the tunnel, heading toward the new room where Bear Tollackson would have been working with his crew. He saw a candle burning in the distance, still far off, and it distracted him from the next body till he nearly tripped over it, chasing the breath from his lungs and placing another curse upon his tongue.

In 1863, Hank Chambers' father, Robert Chambers, returned home from the War Between the States with one less arm, wild eyes, and a love of gruesome tales. In the evenings he'd drink rotgut whiskey as he sat before the fire, waiting for Mother to go to bed, and when she did he'd call Hank over and start talking, speaking more freely than he ever had before the war, and out would pour story after story of severed limbs, festering wounds, and men cut down by cannon fire. So many men killed they heaped upon each other in great waves, a sea of dead covering entire fields and littering the earth like grains of sand upon a beach. Men screaming for their wives, mothers, cornfield loves. Men laughing crazily as surgeons removed their limbs right before their eyes. Men crawling over each other, begging to die in the mud while frightened horses ran in every direction, trampling the fallen beneath their panicked hooves. Men dying in a deep silence worse than any scream.

What the foreman encountered on the lowest level of the Dennison Mine resembled his father's war stories, only compacted and pressed into one long tunnel with a few open rooms along the way. Dead men strewn about like forgotten toys: their eyes wide with horror, their blood pooling on the ground, and the chilled air reeking of a slaughter house's coppery tang. Some had tried to run, some had tried to fight. Many had their throats torn, as if they'd been gotten at by a bear or a wolf. Their eyes bulged, frog-like, and he could not help but wonder what ugly thing they'd seen in their final earthly moments.

Chambers tied his handkerchief over his mouth and picked his way through the crowded tunnel. He entered the first open room and found more of the same—several men had climbed the stope here, risking burial by rock in their terror. The foreman ticked off names as he identified the fallen, counting the dead into the high thirties before losing heart and giving up the reckoning. The oil lamp burned richly in his hand, hissing softly, and he wondered briefly if all this was another dream, a terrible, lucid fever dream, but the sweat dripping down his brow said otherwise, how it stung his eyes and caused him to squint as if he were looking into the sun.

The next tunnel was the worst yet, as if the tunnel had caved in except the rubble was the bodies of dead men, not rock. There were so many bodies their collective bulk would have stuffed the tunnel shut except something powerfully strong had torn through them, boring through their mass like a drill bit cutting through limestone. The resulting mess caused Chambers to pull up outside the tunnel and turn his head away—he would have retched had he'd eaten anything in the last two days.

"Jesus," he whispered, a shudder sweeping through him. "Jesus Almighty."

He could hear the tunnel's ceiling drip.

Drip, drip, drip.

The opened gore, falling from up to down. The split intestines and ruptured veins. The human body spilling forth with all its stored wonders.

Chambers set his lantern at his feet and adjusted his rifle

by its strap. His shoulder, unused to the strain, ached from wearing the gun. He focused on the minor pain, closing his eyes and hissing through his teeth. He would not be going through that tunnel. That was too much to ask any man. This would be as far he got—let the sheriff come down here and finish the investigation. Let him sort—

A scream pierced the silence, as sudden and electrifying as a bolt of lightning landing at his feet. A man's scream.

A living man.

Chambers' chin dropped against his chest. He'd heard a scream like that only once before, when a coal tunnel had partially collapsed and buried a man up to his waist in several tons of rock, pulverizing everything below his belt.

The screamer repeated himself and Chambers turned back to the dripping tunnel. He picked his lamp off the floor and climbed inside, setting his knees on a man's shoulders and scrambling forward. He'd gotten about three yards into the tunnel when he felt the wetness dripping onto his back and the bodies shifting beneath him. He tried not to imagine what fragile strings held the dead above him in place, what it would feel like if they came loose and buried him among them.

11

Six o'clock came and went without the town's miners filling the saloon as Owen had said they would. Elwood Hayes was about to ask his younger brother about this when an orange-haired boy ran into the bar, hollered three men dead in the mine, with their throats torn, and then bolted out the front door again, leaving the saloon's customers to gape at each other in surprise.

"What in hell's name?" Roach Clayton grumbled, the first at their table to speak. "Next the whole town's going to sink into the earth."

"Yes, sir," Clem Stubbs said. "And those fools will laugh the whole while."

The stagecoach guards, whom Stubbs was referring to, had returned to their table at the front of the saloon, none of them talking much as they resumed their drinking, the whores leaving them be after a few harsh words. Every so often, one of the four guards would grow a little braver and glare toward the Hayes Gang. They wanted more blood than Johnny Miller's but didn't know how to go about stepping first. Hayes supposed that after riding for the bank so long, the guards were too used to living on the defensive and protecting the treasures of men greater and richer than themselves.

But give them a poke and they'd stir like hornets.

"Wonder what killed those men," Owen said, holding his tumbler up to the light. "Mountain lion? Could a mountain lion get into a mine like that?"

"A knife," Stubbs said. "A knife could get into a mine like that. Probably some drunk Chough who owed too much money from gambling."

Elwood took in the room, watching for anything strange. The girls had all gone out to sit on porch and wait for the miners, leaving the barroom quiet. The bartender, Caleb, was running a rag up and down the bar and chatting with a stout, older woman who must have been the saloon's madam. Two old men, both caked with dirt, sat at the far end of the bar, gesturing with their hands as they swapped tales.

A pretty blond emerged from a room on the second floor and leaned over the railing, looking down into the bar. She seemed sad and sunk into herself, even for a whore.

Stubbs followed Elwood's gaze and whistled. "My, would you look at that. A blooming mountain flower."

The girl turned her head toward the table full of stagecoach guards, her nose crinkling. Suddenly Elwood could smell rank beer, pine sap, smoke, unwashed men, and the faint smell of horses, all at once.

"Not too long bloomed, either," Roach added, reseating the looping wire of his spectacles upon his ears. "A man could do worse around here than that."

Beside him, Owen laughed in the dumb, awkward way he had when he was nervous.

"That's Ingrid, fellas. You going to steal from Revis Cooke, you might as well steal her along with his gold. She sees nobody else but him. Up in her chambers, I mean. Ugly bastard must have gold pouring out his pecker."

"Ingrid," Elwood said, trying out the name. "Finnish?"

"Norwegian. The other girls say she's from Minnesota."

The longer she stood at the second floor railing, the more you could feel the eyes of the other men in the room lift in her direction and remain there.

Ingrid.

Ingrid from Minnesota.

Elwood Hayes pushed back his chair and got to his feet. He wavered a bit on his heels, drunker than expected. He ran a hand through his hair, frowned at the hopeless snarls he found there, and cleared his throat.

"Boys, I'm gonna jaw with Miss Ingrid for a minute."

"You think that's a good idea?" Stubbs asked, smiling behind his fiery beard. "Talking with a woman like that is bound to draw attention."

"I know," Elwood said, smiling back.

She pretended not to watch him climb the stairs and Elwood pretended he was fully sober while the whole bar followed his progress to the second floor. He made to remove his hat, but recalled he'd already left it on the table below so as not to be encumbered by it. So, instead of holding, he could only keep his hands at his sides, fully aware of them in a way that usually happened only when he was firing a gun.

The whore had ponderous blue eyes and hair like corn silk. When she glanced at Elwood, finally acknowledging his presence beside her, his legs weakened more than the whiskey he'd drunk would allow.

"Evening, Miss."

"Evening."

Elwood turned his gaze down to the saloon below and saw a dozen folks watching, like he and Ingrid were about to give them all a song and dance. He felt an urge to wave to the room and say something smart but he let it pass. Letting stupid urges pass you by was what separated a smart man from a fool like Johnny Miller.

"I'm spoken for, if that's what you were about to ask."

Elwood turned back to the young woman.

"Ma'am, my name is Elwood Hayes."

He waited for a response, but Ingrid's face remained blank. Maybe news didn't travel across the Colorado border anymore.

"I've been told that you're in a partnership with Mr. Revis Cooke, accountant for the Dennison Mining Company?"

"That's right. Can't say I enjoy it much, but I am."

Elwood nodded and hooked his thumbs into his pants.

"Well, how would you like to leave his employ, permanently?"

The young woman looked him up and down.

"You don't have that kind of money, Mr. Hayes."

Elwood laughed and unhooked his thumbs. "You're right about that, Miss. But, you see, my friends and I are about to change that. We're about to have a lot of money, in fact."

Ingrid smoothed the pleats in her skirt. She wore white lace gloves, like any fine lady in San Francisco.

"We're robbing Cooke. Those men down there have recently delivered a full month's payroll to his address that we intend to acquire."

"The miners need that money. They don't save a nickel around here."

"That money's insured by the bank. Next month a new delivery, twice as big, will roll into town. The miners will just have to live on credit until then, like most do anyway."

Ingrid's chest was starting to rise and fall with enhanced grandeur—she was excited by the idea, despite herself. The way her nostrils flared.

"That house is more like a bank than you think, Mr. Hayes, and Cooke is as shrewd as an old mother hen."

"Yes, Miss Blomvik, I agree with you there," Elwood said, nodding again. "That is why I am speaking to you now. If you can help us get inside that little fort, you'll get a full share of whatever we collect."

Ingrid laughed, a harsh, barking sound that surprised him.

"A full share," she said, turning to look Elwood square in the eye. "And how can I trust a road agent's word? How do I know you won't toss me aside as soon as you get your money?"

Elwood glanced up at the ceiling, wishing he'd brought his hat with him after all. It would have helped him look more like a beggar if he were holding it now, wringing it with nervousness. Worse, he could not think of single reason for this woman to trust him, nor any man in Wyoming—everybody was always after a beautiful woman for something or other.

"I can't say I do know why you should trust me, Miss Blomvik. I suppose that'll be a gamble to consider on top of the larger. But I do reckon nobody ever got out of a position like yours, or a town like this, without taking a considerable chance."

The young woman tucked a strand of blond hair behind her ear and stared at him for another moment before turning back to the railing. The older woman, the sizeable madam, was scowling up at them from her perch at the bar.

"I hate this damn town," Ingrid said in a low voice. "I'd just as well see it burned to the ground as put out a fallen candle."

Elwood held his tongue, letting her figure it for herself. Downstairs, one of the guards slammed his glass against the table, sending a loud crack through the room. The other guards laughed at whatever had been said and a whore looked in through the front doorway, peaking hopefully at the men.

"All right, Mr. Hayes. I'll throw in with your gang."

Elwood felt a world better as he descended the saloon stairs, his mind clearing from the fog of spirits and the gloom brought on by Johnny Miller's foolish actions. The holdup had looked plenty doubtful a half-hour before, but with Revis Cooke's girl in their corner they still had a chance at leaving Red Earth as wealthy men. Perhaps their luck, which had been running ragged enough for the past few months, was about to change for the better.

Two of the stagecoach guards greeted Elwood at the bottom of the stairs, hands upon their hips, near enough to their holsters. One had an overgrown mustache, like he thought he was Doc Holliday, and the other was ugly as sin, with a bald and lumpy head. The other two guards were still back at their poker table, watching the scene with interest.

"What did you want with that whore upstairs?"

Hayes grinned and coughed into his hand.

"What do you think I wanted?"

"She's spoken for."

Hayes glanced back over his shoulder, but Miss Blomvik had retired to her room. He turned back to the men, still grinning. The backs of his hands had begun to tingle.

"You know, she told me the same thing, now that you mention it."

"So why'd you hang around her then, buzzing at her like a fat old horsefly?"

"I felt like buzzing, I suppose."

The ugly bald man lunged forward and grabbed Hayes by the lapels of his jacket, lifting him an inch off the floor.

"We've been talking, and we think it's time for you to leave town. You and those other three. After what your man did to Chester, you're lucky we don't lay you all in the earth right here."

"You smell like horseshit," Hayes said. "You been rolling around the alley with the other curs?"

The bald man made to strike him with an open hand, half-releasing him, and Hayes took the opportunity to reach behind his back and pull his pistol. Before the guard could land his strike, Hayes had already cocked the pistol, brought it round, and shot him in the kneecap. The guard screamed, dropped onto the blown knee, and screamed some more. Hayes struck the guard across his bald head with the butt of his gun and dropped him to the floor.

"Yes, sir. That should settle you a while."

You could hear a deep intake of air as everyone registered the dropped man—then things started moving fast. The guard with the mustache stepped backward and fumbled for his gun. Chairs scraped as men reached for their own guns, if they had any. The bartender slowly sat down behind the bar, holding his hands above his head. The saloon's madam came around the bar and ducked under it, too, her movements swift and certain. A few porch whores poked their heads in through the front door, saw the guns being drawn, and retreated hastily.

Hayes widened his stance and aimed for the mustachioed man's gun, hoping to shoot it out of his hand, but the guard's movements were so wild he ended up shooting him in the forearm, which had the same effect, anyhow, disarming the guard as he howled in pain. Hayes ducked low and scooped the mustachioed man's pistol off the ground as the two other stagecoach guards began firing from across the room, filling the air with lead.

Chunks of stairway detonated as the guards lit into it, sending up a cloud of splinters. Elwood ran at a crouch toward the back of the room, where Roach, Clem, and Owen had taken up firing positions. He made it behind an empty table and threw his shoulder into it, lifting the table off its base and sending it crashing sideways. He checked the stolen pistol to make sure it was loaded and cocked and was about to come up firing when a man flew over the table, thumping into Elwood's chest like a sledgehammer, knocking him to the ground and causing him to drop both guns.

It was the mustachioed man, back for another round, and this time he'd drawn a knife. Elwood brought his foot up and kicked him in the chest, trying to pry some distance between them. The guard snarled and swiped the blade at him, moving fast despite the gunshot wound to his forearm. "Come on, now," Elwood shouted above the racket of gunfire, "there's no need for cutting." The guard ignored him and lunged, swiping the knife across Elwood's chest. Elwood scrambled back against the overturned tabletop, kicking furiously, and found his gun on the floor. The guard lunged again and Elwood shot him between the eyes. The guard's head snapped back and he fell to the ground. Elwood sighed and shook his pistol in the air, which was almost too hot to hold.

"I warned you off, Doc. You can't say otherwise."

12

When his ma called him to stop playing with his straw dolls and come inside, seven-year-old Billy Atkins expected to see his pa sitting at the table and the smell of cooking to fill their cabin. Instead, his pa was not home and his ma was still working at the stove, wiping the sweat from her forehead and watching over the potatoes as they boiled. They ate a lot of potatoes, all year long. Billy liked his with salt.

"Billy, I need you to go hunt up your pa. He hasn't come home for dinner yet and I have to mind the stove. It isn't like him to dawdle."

Billy smiled and stretched his arms above his head. He wasn't allowed to go downtown by himself too often.

"You think you can find your daddy's office?"

"Yes, ma'am."

"Don't talk to any miners. And don't take any money or candy from them, especially if they're acting funny."

"I won't."

"Go on then, little rabbit."

Billy Atkins didn't need to be told twice. He darted out of the cabin and sprinted down the road, passing the dozen other cabins sprinkled on the north side of Red Earth. He ran as fast as his legs would carry him, enjoying how everything blurred to the side of his vision and it felt a little like he was flying. He hoped Emma Parson was looking out her cabin window across the road. He wanted her to see how fast he could run and feel jealous about how he got to go downtown by himself. Emma was nine-years-old and thought she knew everything in the whole world just because she'd been born in Cincinnati, Ohio, which she said was a proper city.

But Billy's pa was sheriff. His pa was sheriff and he carried a gun on his belt, a big pearl handled revolver, and he could draw it so fast the gun went blurry. Men and women called his pa Sheriff Atkins and nodded politely when he passed. Why Emma Parson thought being born in Cincinnati was better than your pa being a lawman Billy Atkins had no idea, except she was a girl, and girls seemed to have all manner of queer ideas. Like how sometimes they'd be wrestling in the grass and Emma's eyes would suddenly go all soft and cloudy, like a storm was passing through them, and she'd plant a big fat kiss on his cheek and giggle and say they were married now forever and ever and Billy would say that was the worst thing he'd ever heard in his whole life.

Near downtown, Billy slowed his running to a walk. He didn't want to get to the general store too soon—he had too much to look at, like all the pretty ladies sitting on the Runoff Saloon's big front porch. The ladies always waved when he passed by, smiling real friendly-like, and he waved back as long as his ma wasn't watching. She didn't like the ladies, she said, because they were steeped in sin and wickedness—which they might have been, if wickedness included powder, perfume, and curly hair.

Tonight, though, the ladies weren't the most interesting thing. A group of men were standing outside the hotel, excited and talking loud. Billy expected to see his father but he wasn't among the hotel men, who kept looking down the street and pointing at hills in the distance. Billy couldn't see anything worth the fuss—just the same old mountains. He considered stopping to ask what they were all pointing at but then remembered his mother, standing red-faced over the stove and telling him not to talk to the miners. He couldn't tell if these men were miners or not, but if they were, it'd get back to Pa sooner or later and Ma would tan his hide for sure.

So Billy kept walking straight past, keeping his eyes on the dirt road and his hands in his pockets. Nobody called out to waylay him and soon he was climbing the steps to the general store, picking up speed again as he opened the screen door and let it bang behind him, loud as a gunshot.

"Pa!"

Billy squinted his eyes and looked around. The shop was dim, even though it was still light outside. Henry wasn't sitting in his chair behind the shop counter, where he always sat, and there weren't any customers, either. Just a stranger sitting at the sheriff's desk in the front corner of the room, all hunched over with his eyes closed.

"Who are you?"

Metal rattled as the stranger looked up. He had dark circles around his eyes and his lower lip was cracked and bleeding.

"I'm a dead man. Who are you?"

Billy took a step back and looked at the door.

"You looking for your pa?"

Billy nodded, looking from the door to the stranger and back again.

"He the sheriff?"

Billy nodded again. "Sherriff Atkins," he said, finding his tongue. "He's late for dinner and Ma sent me to fetch him."

The stranger closed his eyes.

"I could use some dinner myself, though I don't suppose

I'll see any tonight."

Billy stepped forward, wondering why the stranger was sitting so funny. When he came around the desk, he saw chains attached to the man's wrists and ankles. The chains had been looped through a giant iron ring in the floor. Billy had always wondered what the ring was for, popping out of the wood like that.

The stranger leaned forward and opened his eyes.

"Your pa ain't here, son."

"Where is he?"

"You let me out of these string beans and I'll tell you."

Billy crossed his arms.

"No, sir. I cannot do that. You're a criminal. You're wearing those chains because you did something bad."

The stranger laughed and started coughing.

"Hell, son. If everybody who did something bad in this world wore chains, nobody would be walking free at all."

Billy bit his lip and squinted, trying to figure what the stranger was getting at. His gray eyes reminded Billy of a wolf he'd seen the winter before, sniffing around their cabin in daylight, pacing back and forth. You could see the wolf's ribs poking through where fat should have been and Ma hadn't allowed Billy outside until Pa got home that evening.

"If you won't tell me, I'll just go find Mr. Leg and ask him."

"The old man left, too. He was mighty interested in seeing things for himself."

"Seeing what things?"

The stranger smiled, showing a row of crooked teeth.

"The other dead men."

The coins and bills were adding up properly but Revis Cooke took his time about it, feeling no urge to rush the accounting. Also, Cooke was enjoying the National Bank man's growing discomfort as the evening passed and his men whooped it up across the street. A man who couldn't deprive himself without squirming like a child in church was not much of a man at all.

"Seems like it's all here, Mr. Cooke."

"Perhaps, Mr. Wells. We'll see how it tallies up in the end."

The silver dollar certificates felt crisp and solid beneath Cooke's fingertips, each one adding to the payroll total as he stacked them on the large desk before him. Cooke's visitor, a man named Hollis Wells, was sitting in a stiff wooden chair across from him, his arms crossed over the front of his faded gray cavalry coat. He wore a black derby cap, which he wore tipped slightly forward, and a well-trimmed blond beard that was not uncomely. Wells appeared to be a good soldier, a trustworthy soul. Canny enough to deal with bankers, yet steely enough to command ruffians.

"Would you mind if I went across the street a moment to check on my men? They've already gotten in enough trouble for one night and I'd like to head off any more before it happens."

Cooke grinned and licked his thumb.

"Hired guns can cause more trouble than they're worth. A mercenary army is a powder keg waiting to blow."

"I don't know about mercenaries. They're good men, just a little short tempered after a long ride. That mountain trail from Rawlins is no easy thing, even in summer."

Cooke nodded.

"I remember it well—"

Gunshots erupted outside, a series of dry pops that could be heard through the house's thick limestone walls. Hollis Wells leapt to his feet like he'd been stung.

"Goddamn it, I told them."

Wells went to the front door and tried the door. The knob didn't even turn.

"It's locked."

"Of course it is. We have over a thousand dollars on the table, Mr. Wells. The company's valuables must be secured."

Wells threw back the door's view slot and looked outside. More gunshots, of various calibers, rang out from across the street. Cooke wrote down his latest tabulation and pushed his chair back, frowning. Between the miners and the transients, Red Earth was growing more unpleasant by the day.

The National Bank man turned round, his forehead pinched.

"Please unlock the door, Mr. Cooke. I need to go over there."

Cooke sighed and rolled up his shirtsleeves.

"I'm afraid I cannot fulfill your request, Mr. Wells. Company policy states that in the event of gunfire, or any disturbance of note, that I am not allow passage through this building. Passage in or out, I'm afraid."

Wells licked his lips. More gunfire cracked outside.

"Are you joking, sir? I can see clearly that nobody is within fifty feet of this building."

"No, Mr. Wells, I do not make jests about company policy. We'll have to wait out the gunfire indoors and hope your men emerge in due time. They can handle themselves, can they not?"

Mr. Wells drew himself up to his full height, which nearly matched Cooke's. His jaw shifted imperceptibly, the teeth grinding within. Cooke stared calmly back into his fidgeting eyes, wondering if the lookout was going to rush him, like a mad bull.

"Are you going to assault me, Mr. Wells? Do you cognate as poorly as your trigger-happy men?"

Wells pushed back the brim of his cap.

"I just need to get through that door, sir."

"I understand that. But the only thing that's capable of

getting through that door, as long as I'm alive and have a say in the matter, is a spirit. Are you a spirit, Mr. Wells?"

Wells looked back at the door. More gunfire erupted.

"No, sir. I am not."

Cooke smiled and returned to his seat at the table, rubbing his hands as he looked over the stacked bills and coins. "Wonderful. Let's settle our accounts while the drunkards across the street settle theirs. Neither should take too much longer."

Wells remained standing, unhappy and indecisive. Cooke did not mind, as long as the lookout did not interrupt him further. The Dennison company payroll was not going to sort itself.

On the far north end of town Bonnie Chambers also heard the gunfire, but she took it for practice shooting. She was distracted by the prolonged absence of her husband and the three dead miners he was attending to. Her mind, long adjusted to the slow pace of frontier towns, did not automatically provide room for two major calamities at once, especially when one involved her husband, who was still feverish and should have been lying in bed at that moment.

Yes, many things seemed to be happening nearly at once:

First, Randy Bale had shown up with the news and Hank had run off to the mine. Then the boy had returned asking for Hank's rifle and she'd scrambled to load it before he'd run off a second time.

Second, she'd waited for perhaps twenty minutes, agitated and bursting with the news, before she'd given in and gone next door to gossip with Susan Logan, her one and best friend in town. Susan's redheaded boy, who'd been lying in the corner feigning sleep, had popped up all of a sudden and run off toward downtown, shouting about the three dead miners to anybody with ears to listen.

Third, about five minutes after that, Sherriff Atkins had ridden out of town with a handful of men at his heels, themselves headed toward the mine. She spotted Leg and Henry Jameson among the riders and wondered who was minding the general store, if anyone, and if she would have done better to keep the news to herself until Hank came back with a full report. Sheriff Atkins was a young man, still wet behind the ears, and he was liable to fall off his horse in his rush to be a hero and break his neck.

It was all rolling downhill now. If Hank was angry with her for her loose tongue, she'd hurry to dab his forehead and tell him not to tax himself, not with his fever, and get him back in bed before he could work up much steam. They'd been together a long time, through good and bad, and she could handle him in about any kind of humor he cared to feel. They'd married at a small brick church in Springfield, Missouri, with both families in attendance. That had been in 1872, when she was still eighteen and Hank recently turned twenty-six, a tan and dashing young man edging into the prime of life. He'd already done well out West as a prospector, with some money to his name and more work waiting for him in Colorado, and their families had been on friendly terms for years and years. He said he could remember seeing Bonnie once as a little girl, running loose with other children at some festivity or other, but she did not recall seeing him at all, not until he came to call one afternoon at the bidding of her father, his tan and calloused hands gently holding yellow honeysuckle flowers like a man in a fancy magazine. He'd asked if she'd like to take a walk and, after careful reflection, Bonnie had said yes, as long as she didn't have to carry those flowers all over town.

The years had flown from there, leading them both from one town to another, from one mining operation to the next. They'd loved each other well enough, once the initial strangeness of marriage was swept away. They'd also conceived three children and buried them all, none lasting longer than a year. Bonnie still had small, hard spots in her heart she'd reserved for loving each child, little hard spots that felt like old scar tissue in her mind whenever she slowed down long enough to recall what it'd felt like to hold the poor babes in her arms. Their deaths had been hard to take, certainly, but Hank had stayed at her side at each burial, solid as the rocks he worked with, and the more desperate and lonely she'd felt as the years went by the more she'd loved him, warts and all, until she could not imagine living in a world where they did not wake side by side.

So let the foreman come home, damp with fever sweat and ornery as a wounded badger. Bonnie would hold him even as he shook his fist in the air, hot spittle flying from his mouth. Yes, just as long as it was him, with his rock smell and strong hands that had so often held her with a surprising gentleness, as if she too were a bouquet of honeysuckle held up in offering.

13

It defied physics and good sense, but the tunnel packed with the bodies of the dead and maimed did not collapse as Hank Chambers climbed across its sloppy floor, which was actually less a surface and more a constantly shifting mass of knees, elbows, and anguished faces he did not want to look upon. The bodies were freshly dead, too, which made them unpleasantly warm and given to passing noxious fluids and gases with each pressing of his weight. He did not know if it was the smell, the wetness, or his fever, but he felt his mind loosening as he slipped forward, its grinding cogs reverting to some ancient form of thought, his body an eel among eels.

His only focus was the light in his hand, which must not go out, which must not go out, which must not go out no matter what else might happen. Chambers had spent much of his life edging darkness and he would not submit to it now, even if this was his final hour. He bore the oil lamp before him with both hands, as if it were a newborn infant, or a touchy stick of dynamite, and as he scrambled on his knees and elbows more screaming came from the end of the tunnel.

Light appeared, revealing the tunnel's dripping exit.

Chambers crawled forward and poked his head above a jutted knee, looking into the section they'd opened that afternoon.

The new section was lit by at least a dozen candles. Bodies were heaped upon the ground and strewn among the piled rock. Some of the men were still quivering, like fish thrown onto dry land, and some were missing their heads entire. Among the dead and dying strode a skeletal figure clothed only in a skin of black char, as if he'd been roasted all the way through. He had long, dangling arms and enormous hands that ended in claw-like fingers. He walked like a specter made flesh, his movements swift and abrupt, a flurry of odd gestures unlike any Chambers had seen before.

The few patches of skin visible among the Charred Man's body were a pale, clammy white. Chambers noted a patch of white on the Charred Man's hip, a second on his throat, a third on his cheek, and a fourth on his knee. The spots had a mesmerizing effect, blurring together as the Charred Man circled the room, and it took Chambers a moment to recall the great danger he was in.

That was no mortal human being out there, gloating over the seventy-plus men he'd dispatched in less than an hour. This was something truly wicked, like a creature from the old German stories his grandmother had told him as a boy. This was a devil, a demon, a killer of men.

One of the wounded screamed near the tunnel's opening. Chambers sank further into the bodies piled beneath him, shielding his lamp with his hand. He heard a scuttling, a loud tear, and the man shrieked one final time before falling silent. Then came a smacking sound, somehow dry and wet at the same time.

Christ almighty.

The Charred Man was taking his own time with these final victims, like a child torturing a wounded bird, or a man savoring a fine whiskey. He was taking his time but soon enough he'd run out of food to play with and grow bored. He'd start making his way through the rest of the mine, tunnel after tunnel, until he reached an exit, emerged into the evening air, and came down from the hills.

Chambers heard more scuttling beyond the tunnel and took a deep breath. The rifle on his shoulder poked into his back, as uncomfortable as the many knees and elbows beneath him. He lifted his body enough to unsling the gun and set it beside him. It looked so small and futile now, more like a stick of wood, a twig. He reckoned a shot at the Charred Man would be neigh on impossible from this angle and would do little more than reveal his position. He'd likely get off one shot, maybe two, before the speedy devil fell upon him with those long arms and clawed fingers.

No. He needed to figure a way to stop this wickedness before it got any further. The mine's operations had somehow unleashed this creature upon the world and it was his responsibility to see it stopped before any worse could be done. He couldn't do anything more for his men, even the one's still breathing, but he could still save the town up above.

And Bonnie.

He could make sure she never met the Charred Man.

It wasn't easy to turn around in the cramped tunnel but somehow Chambers managed to do it without losing the light of his lamp or disrupting the ceiling of dead above him (even if it did appear that gravity was beginning to have its way, after all, pulling down the occasional loose arm or leg so suddenly it dropped in front of Chambers as if waving howdy). He abandoned his rifle, preferring to move with less hindrance and drag, and crawled as fast as he could back down the tunnel. He moved faster than before, less timid with the cooling bodies beneath him, rudely placing his knees and elbows wherever he damn well pleased. It was funny how a man could get used to about anything if he had to, even the close proximity of the maimed.

Still, when Chambers came out of the tunnel and stepped onto the firm rock floor, it was a relief so great his knees buckled and he was forced to lean against the wall a moment. Among all the horrors of the tunnel, he'd forgotten the smell of good clean air.

"God-damn," Chambers whispered. "God-damn."

Chambers pushed off from the wall and raised his lantern. The bodies lying on the ground in this room now seemed scarce compared to those cramming the last tunnel and the room beyond it. He made his way across the room easily enough, stepping over and around the dead, and entered the tunnel beyond, where he stepped over four more bodies and started climbing up the access shaft. He thought he heard something scuttling behind him but pushed the thought away, deciding there would be no advantage to knowing his death was approaching. Climbing was the thing to do now, so long as he could climb, so long as nothing caught him by the foot and dragged him back down.

The foreman passed the opening to the second level and kept going. Sweat ran down his forehead in rivulets—he could not tell if it was from the exertion or the fever. A feeling of buoyancy had come over him, a lightness in his bones that made climbing easier. He kept his gaze upward, ever seeking. When he reached the top of the access shaft he set his lamp above the final rung of the ladder and swung his legs over onto solid rock. It was only then, after gathering himself and getting to his feet, that the foreman allowed himself to look back down the shaft.

Nothing there.

No Charred Man, no dead men returned to life. Just an empty ladder, descending into the dark.

He understood what he'd found below was not a feverish nightmare, however. Blood, urine, and other bodily fluids covered his clothes, his skin. The bats could smell him and they kept their distance, flitting as far above him as they could get.

"You don't like that, do you? Don't like my stench much."

Chambers laughed and coughed into his sticky, foul smelling hand. In all his years working beneath the earth he'd never felt as filthy as he did now. He wasn't just one man; he was one man covered with the excretions of dozens more. If Bonnie could see him now, she'd holler murder and send him straight to the nearest creek with a bar of soap and orders to not return until every inch of his body was scrubbed pink and his clothes burned to cinders.

The foreman started down the next tunnel, reminded of the precious nature of his time. His legs were stiffening beneath him, a fiery pain arcing through his right hip, but he forced himself to maintain a steady pace. This tunnel, more than any of the others behind him, seemed to take longest of all, an exercise in sweat and torture, but Chambers at last found himself in the mine's large front room, the shelves loaded with supplies like the table of the Last Supper loaded with food.

He went straight to the dynamite.

They had four crates on hand. Chambers hauled two out of the mine, squinting at the evening light (weak as it was), and opened the other two just inside the entrance. He stuck blast caps into about two dozen sticks, ran their fuse lines outside, and set the individual sticks into as many lode bearing nooks and crannies as he could find, using a spare ladder and a hand pick to wedge more sticks into the sloping roof above the mine's entrance. He didn't have time to cap the hundred extra sticks of dynamite but he scattered them all around the chamber anyhow, hoping they'd be set off by the initial explosion. Hell, the nitroglycerine made them unstable enough already, liable to go off from a loud sneeze or good shaking.

It took Chambers about ten quick minutes to finish the whole setup. His men would have laughed to see what a slipshod job their foreman had done, how none of the sticks had been stuck inside a properly drilled hole, but it looked like it would get the job done regardless. Chambers picked up his lantern and backed through the mine's entrance until he stood ten feet on the other side, the strands of fuse wire lying tangled at his feet beside the crates of extra explosives.

Chambers wiped the sweat from his brow as he peered into the entrance. He felt called upon to speak.

"I'm sorry to leave you all like this, without a proper Christian burial and all, but I think you'd understand. What happened to you down there was a horror, a terrible, terrible horror, and you gave your lives for the Dennison Mining Company, whether you wanted to or not. Mostly not, I assume."

Chambers blinked and felt close to swooning. His fever was roaring now, like a wild and angry beast inside his mind. He'd be bedridden for a week after this, if he ever rose up again at all.

"I'll do my best to see to it that Mr. Dennison gives satisfaction to your families, but I can't make any promises. I'm sure you've all heard how tightfisted that old son-of-a-bitch can be."

Chambers chuckled and wiped away more sweat from his brow. The salty water came on and on, like he was a wet cloth being squeezed.

"May the Lord watch over you all now, far better than I did."

The wind picked up and blew into the cave. Chambers leaned over the tangle of fuses, ready to light them all with the lantern in his hand. But, as he did so, he felt something hard jab him in the back.

"You light those fuses, Mr. Chambers, and I'll have to shoot you dead."

That was the end of a pistol, he realized.

"You hear me?"

"Yes," Chambers said, still deciding as he peered into the lantern's flame.

"Why don't you step back, sir? Just step back and we can talk this over."

Chambers sighed. He felt so tired. So tired and he just wanted to be back in his bed, being fussed over.

"You know I don't want to make Bonnie a widow, Mr. Chambers."

A click as the pistol was cocked. Chambers straightened, slowly, and turned to look at who had the gun on him.

Atkins. Young Sheriff Atkins, looking as stiff and scared as a rabbit chased to the edge of a cliff, with a shiny silver star on his chest and handful of men behind him. A fresh rivulet of sweat ran into Chambers' eyes, but he let it stay there, not wanting to risk the sudden movement. A gust of foul smelling air blew out of the mine's entrance, as if the hills themselves were exhaling.

Chamber's licked his lips, wondering how best to explain himself before one more guest showed up to the party.

14

She'd known he wasn't a miner by the way he'd come up those stairs—his stride smooth and easy, with no stoop in his back. His eyes bright and ready. No miner in Red Earth carried himself in such a way, like a cat ready to spring.

Ingrid Blomvik liked that. She liked how the stranger walked.

He offered his hand and introduced himself as Elwood Hayes, pausing for a second like his name meant something. He was a good-looking man, in a hardscrabble way, and that was novelty enough in Red Earth. She almost hoped he'd ask to see her bedroom, her arrangement with Revis Cooke notwithstanding. She wouldn't have minded lying down with a comely man for once, somebody you didn't mind watching work above you.

But Mr. Elwood Hayes had not wanted any of that. His proposition was even more interesting, mad as it was. A real heist, like you'd read about in the papers. And he looked like he meant it, too, as if he were a man used to setting his will against something and seeing it through. He'd reminded her of Erik that way, except Hayes had less innocence to his eyes, less joyfulness. When he asked her to join them, to actually rob that bastard Revis Cooke blind, she'd felt her heart leap in her chest, a new wind blowing through town so clean and pure she could almost smell the Pacific Ocean on it. Even if he was planning to double cross her later, or his plan was doomed to fail, Elwood Hayes had given her a solid reason to pick up and leave town, breaking the spell of indecision that had hung over her for so long, sucking the very life out of her. She'd had enough of this perdition—Revis Cooke could play with his own pecker from here on out, if he could stand touching himself.

Ingrid had felt pure giddiness, hustling back to her room to pack her few things into a suitcase and make her getaway. A little bird of happiness fluttered inside her heart, a bird she hadn't felt in years, and it flitted around and around as she folded her clothes and packed them away with the book of Tennyson.

Then she heard a gunshot, and the bird went still.

Ingrid dropped the shawl in her hands and darted back down the hall. She ran up to the railing, heedless of the danger, and looked down into the mess below.

And it was a mess, indeed. The stagecoach guards and Elwood's gang were firing at each other from across the saloon like this was a battlefield in the Civil War. Madam Petrov had dropped behind the bar with Caleb and a bald man was lying near the foot of the stairs, knocked out cold. She could just make out Elwood Hayes through the fog of gun smoke, fighting off another guard from a sitting position. Ingrid caught a flash of metal in the guard's hand, took it for a knife, and prepared to watch her new business partner die before her eyes, stuck and bleeding onto the saloon's floor.

But then a loud crack, rising above the others, and the guard's head flew backward as if he'd been punched.

And a pistol in the hand of Elwood Hayes, where none

had been a moment before.

Ingrid's mouth formed a small, silent O as heat rose in her cheeks. Hayes scuttled back behind an overturned table while the other men continued to fire, both sides dug in behind tables of their own. The room filled with so much gunpowder smoke the air turned murky.

Emerging from behind his overturned table, Hayes began to crawl across the floor toward the two remaining guards. Ingrid's eyes watered from the smoke and she drew a handkerchief from her pocket to cover her mouth. She could see Hayes was exposed but nobody else paid him mind at all. He kept crawling, elbow after elbow, while his gang fired and the stagecoach guards fired back and nobody hit much of anything excepting table and rafter.

Their own powder was blinding them.

Ingrid bit her lip as Elwood Hayes approached the two coach guards, coming at them from an angle. When he got about five feet from their overturned table he sprung up, planted his feet, and fired a shot into each man at a range so close he could have kicked them instead.

The shooting ceased. Nothing felled Hayes. The resulting silence was both awful and grand and Ingrid heard a faint ringing in her ears.

She'd found her man.

Elwood enjoyed the scene as the smoke cleared. The saloon filled with whores, who gawked at the dead men and the blood pooling around them. The Madam cursed loudly in her home tongue as she came out from behind the counter and directed the whores to tend to the last stagecoach guard still living. They wrapped the bald man's shot knee while he came round and started to scream in great earnestness.

The bartender left the saloon to find the sheriff and arrange the delivery of three more coffins. None of the Hayes crew had kicked: Clem Stubbs was plugged in the shoulder, a bullet had grazed Owen's thigh, and Roach Clayton had cracked a spectacle lens. Elwood told himself that he'd done well, done about as good as could be expected under such circumstances, but he still wondered if three men had needed to die so he could go upstairs and jaw with Ms. Ingrid Blomvik for five minutes. Part of him had known the coach guards wouldn't like him going up to the balcony, before God and all, and that doing so was bound to raise their hackles. And that same part, that same devil inside him, hadn't cared one bit if he and everyone else died tonight, so long as it was halfway interesting.

But they didn't have time for dwelling on the past. The wounded needed tending and he was the only surgeon on hand. Hayes cleaned the blade of his knife with a whiskey soaked rag and started with the worst case first.

"Lord Sweet Jesus."

"Hang on, Clem. I need to find the bullet."

"Sweet Jesus sweet Jesus. I think I can feel you scraping against my arm bone, El. You hear that scraping?"

"Hush. This ain't the first time I've dug a bullet from your hide."

"No, but it's the first time you had to dig like it was buried treasure."

Elwood smiled at the idea of buried treasure and pushed the tip of his hunting knife a little further into Stubb's shoulder. Roach had already flushed Owen's wound with whiskey and bound it tight with a bar rag. The two of them sat at one of the few tables still upright, watching Elwood work on Stubbs like they were watching a play. Owen was white as a sheet and hadn't said three words since the shootout.

Elwood nicked something with gristle to it and Stubbs howled.

"Give him some more whiskey, Roach. Give him all he

can swallow."

Roach handed over the bottle from their table. Stubbs took it with his good arm and swallowed a third of it in one long gulp, his fat gut pushing out against the fabric of his shirt.

"You ready, Stubbs?"

Stubbs lowered the bottle and let out a loud belch. Whiskey trickled down his beard and onto the floor.

"Fiddle shits," he shouted, handing the bottle back to Roach. "Have your way with me, Doc Pain."

Hayes renewed his digging until he found the slug tucked under a strip of muscle and popped it out with the tip of his knife. The slug made a hollow plunking sound as it dropped to the floor. Owen leaned to the side in his chair, coiled up, and retched heartily.

Stubbs laughed through the tears in his eyes. "Sweet Mary," he sputtered. "Aren't we all a pretty sight."

"Fit for Paris," Elwood agreed. "Now, don't move while I wrap your arm."

"Why? You going to shoot me sideways, too?"

"If I have to."

Stubbs laughed again, but looked him over as if he wasn't sure it was a joke. Elwood kept his face straight and staunched the flow of blood with a shirt taken from a dead guard. He wrapped the shirt round the big man's arm and tied it off with a leather belt, which he'd also filched from the dead guard. Stubbs shuddered from the pain but held off from more bellyaching—either the whiskey was doing its work or poor Stubbs was starting to feel it for certain.

Ingrid Blomvik stepped out of the crowd and set her hand on Owen's shoulder. "Here. Drink some of this."

Elwood blinked and raised his head.

"Owen."

His brother stared into the distance, a brown spot of vomit still on his cheek.

"Owen, Miss Blomvik is talking to you."

Ingrid pulled a silk scarf from her pocket and dabbed at the spot of vomit. Owen sat there and allowed himself to be attended to, more docile than he'd ever been for their mother when she'd tried the same at church. Roach shook his head and removed his spectacles to consider the cracked lens. His wiry body looked smaller than normal, as if Roach had drawn himself in during the shooting and hadn't quite let himself puff back out yet.

"Owen's spooked, El. That leg graze is the least of his wounds."

"He'll come back round. He's just never traded lead before. You always get a good jolt, your first shootout."

Ingrid cupped Owen's chin in her hands, helping him pry his jaw loose. She held the glass to his lips and tipped it back, sending the water into his mouth. Owen sputtered, spitting out half the water and swallowing the other. His eyes regained some clarity and he took another drink, looking up at the whore with the big brown eyes of a grateful pup. "That's my brother," Elwood said, his voice too loud and abrupt in his own ears. "That's Owen Hayes."

Ingrid smiled, her teeth clean and even and white.

"Howdy, Owen. So you're this gunslinger's little brother? Must have had a rough time of it growing up."

Owen nodded, still staring up at Ingrid like a flower into the sun.

"He fought anybody about anything."

"Did he now?"

"He'd fight you over how many stars were in the sky. He threw me out of a tree once and I broke my arm."

Elwood laughed, remembering the day. His brother flapping his arms and hollering his lungs out. The feel of their father's belt against his back, later that afternoon. Cracking the air like thunder.

"Well, I say. Is that true, Mr. Hayes? Did you throw Owen from a tree?"

"No, ma'am. He was trying to throw me out and got the wrong end of it. He was mad a girl liked me and not himself."

Stubbs, who'd sunk into his chair until his beard touched his belt, groaned and slid to the floor, lying down on his good side. Elwood rubbed his face in his hands, wondering how they were going to fly town now. And that sheriff would come back from the mine, sooner or later, asking more questions. They could deal with him, maybe, but if they killed a company lawman you could bet the Dennison Mining Company would be twice as likely to pursue them across the States, maybe all the way into Mexico.

"What you doing, Stubbs?"

"My arm hurts."

"You shouldn't lie down after you've been shot."

"Why the hell not?"

"You need to get good air. Down on the ground is where all the bad, musty air settles."

"I never heard that before."

"Yeah, but that doesn't make it wrong, does it?"

Stubbs sighed and sat up.

"I wish I were smart like you, Elwood. Like how you snuck up on those shotguns sideways like that. Bang, bang. Fight's over go on home, everybody. That was fine reckoning."

"I got lucky, is all."

"And you're quick, too," Roach said, settling his spectacles back on his face. "I never seen anybody move that swift."

Stubbs nodded.

"I'll say. I'd prefer to be speedy, myself, but my weight don't allow it."

The Madam had regained her wits and started ordering her doves around, tasking them with returning the saloon to order. She examined the man Hayes had shot between the eyes, the knife man, with a pinched look of distaste and clucked her tongue. She sailed across the room and brought her large, round frame right up to Elwood's chest.

"Look! Just look!"

"I'm sorry about the mess, ma'am—"

"You kill our customers—how will we make money tonight? No miners and now no coachmen, either."

"I can pay for the damages."

The madam's eyes softened. She looked from Elwood to Stubbs, who was still sitting on the floor as his bandage darkened.

"Really? You can pay?"

She held out her hand. Elwood shifted on his feet and glanced at Ingrid. Her face had gone blank, as if they'd never spoken a word between them.

"Well, not right this moment. But before we leave town."

The madam laughed, a high, trilling sound that reminded Elwood of barbed wire and caused him to turn away and inspect the saloon. He saw the poorly dressed girls lifting tables and chairs back to their feet, their backs curved like old women, their movements cautious and sore. He saw three dead men who needn't have died that evening lying on the ground, waiting for their coffins. He saw Roach Clayton with a cracked spectacle lens and Clem Stubbs lying like an upturned turtle on the floor and his brother, pale and hollow-eyed, with a wrap around his thigh. Most of all, though, Hayes saw Ingrid Blomvik, watching him with those damn blue eyes of hers, hoping this would all turn out good, hoping that she'd hitched her wagon to the right horse. It was a look like that made a man regret losing his temper, even if the ill-mannered bastards he'd shot had deserved it more than most.

15

The gunfire across the street lasted longer than Revis Cooke expected, an impressive symphony of noise and chaos, and the longer it went on the more squirrely Hollis Wells grew, pacing up and down at the front of the house like he was bent on wearing a groove into the floor, his nose twitching as he sniffed the air.

"Really, Mr. Wells. Look how agitated you've become."

Wells scowled and returned to the front door, sliding the viewing slot open and peering outside for the twelfth time since the shooting had started.

"I should be with my men. I should be in that saloon."

"Life does not always make way for our intentions."

Wells turned back round.

"You are acting in a prissy manner, Mr. Cooke. Are you really so scared you cannot, for a moment, open this goddamn door and let me out?"

Cooke smiled and studied his fingernails. "You can rant and rave and call me names, Mr. Wells, but company policy is firm. I cannot, in good conscience, open that door until I feel certain the scene outside is secure and there is no danger of a holdup."

Wells snorted and turned back to the door. Cooke got up from his chair, circled around the accounting table, and crossed the room to the bookshelf against the wall. He was about to recommend a volume on patience and fortitude when something crashed into him from behind, knocking him into the shelf. It was Wells—the coachman had sprinted across the room and bull-rushed him. Cooke whirled round, thrashing as white lights burst across his vision.

"Just give me the key, Mr. Cooke."

Wells' reach was greater, but Cooke was able to free one of his legs, pull it back, and land a solid kick to his assailant's groin. Wells groaned and fell back, allowing Cooke just enough space to grab a heavy volume off the shelf and smack it across the side of the guard's head with a satisfying thud.

Cooke scrambled to his feet while the other man, clutching himself, tried to recover.

"I haven't fought another man in years, Mr. Wells, but I think you'll find me suited to the task."

Wells opened his mouth to reply, but Cooke threw the heavy book at the knot in his throat. The coachman coughed and gasped, grabbing at his larynx, and Cooke delivered another weighty kick to his groin, dropping the National man to the floor. More white lights popped in accountant's vision as he staggered toward the room's unlit fireplace. He grasped the iron poker leaning against the brick chimney, untouched for the past few summer months, and felt its solid weight in his hand.

"You're not so different from the rock trolls here in town," Cooke said, turning back round to face his fallen opponent. "They have little patience as well. You should see them, shifting from one foot to another as they wait in the line on payday, fidgeting as if their boots were filled with red ants."

The guard was on his knees now, reaching for his belt. Oh

yes, he was wearing a long-knife. Every good stagecoach man carried a knife.

"I am sorry, sir," Cooke said, landing the iron on Wells' arm with a crunching force that caused the coachman to drop the blade and holler. "A knife is not included in a fair fight."

Wells raised his head, his eyes flashing as he clutched his forearm.

"Goddamn you. You broke my arm."

Cooke laughed.

"I don't doubt it, Mr. Wells."

Tears filled the coachman's eyes, his chest heaving like a bellows. He swallowed and spat on the floor.

"You think you're so high and fancy in this stone shack, don't you? Well, you ain't. You ain't any better than any other man in the town, or any other. You're just a bagman for Mr. Dennison. No different from any of the miners you pay out, except they come by theirs through honest sweat."

Cooke nodded, tightening his grip on the iron.

"Is that your true opinion of me, Mr. Wells?"

The coachman drew a hissing breath between his teeth.

"Yes, sir. It is."

Cooke smiled and brought the iron down with all his might, landing it on the coachman's right shoulder. Wells cried out and toppled back, exposing his body to any angle Cooke decided to take.

He'd take his time working the coachman over. Patience was a virtue, was it not?

Billy Atkins watched the shootout in the Runoff Saloon from the porch of the general store down the street, moon-eyed and delighted, his mission to bring his father home for dinner long forgotten.

Actually, there wasn't much to see, since the gunfight was indoors, but he could watch the pretty ladies on the saloon's front porch watching the fight, how they crouched real low and peeked inside the building while the shots went CRACK CRACK CRACK, still loud even from down the street. The ladies were so excited that they forgot to keep their short dresses down and he could see their bloomers showing, red and pink and white, and the sight made him giggle and rub his crotch.

Finally, two shots rang out, cracking so fast they almost sounded like one, and the gunfire stopped inside the saloon. The ladies got up off the porch floor, straightened their dresses, and went inside. Men poured out of the Copper Hotel and started mingling in the street. A minute later more folks showed up from both ends of town.

"Hey! Boy!"

Billy turned and looked into the general store. It'd gotten darker, both outside and in. He could barely make out the man sitting at his pa's desk, chained up to that metal ring in the floor.

"What the hell is going on out there?"

Billy wiped his nose with the back of his hand, wondering if he should answer or run back home. Either way, he'd probably get a whipping for how long he'd dawdled. He could picture that juniper switch his ma kept beside her dresser.

"Answer me, son."

"Why should I?" Billy hollered back into the store. "You're a criminal, ain't you? I don't have to say nothing to you."

The man didn't respond. Billy took a few steps toward the doorway and peered in, wondering what he was up to. He saw him hunched over his pa's desk with his face in his hands. His pa sat like that, too, when he was tired.

"There was shooting."

The man raised his head and scowled.

"I figured that. Where was it?"

"At the saloon down the street. The Runoff."

The man nodded his head like he'd been expecting that, too. Billy stepped inside the doorway to see him better, toeing the doorway with his foot.

"You see anyone get shot?"

"No. Just the ladies watching from outside."

The man sat back in his chair, rattling the chains around him. "My friends were in that saloon," he said in a soft voice. "I wonder if they took it to those shotguns, or if the shotguns took it to them."

Billy squinted and scratched the back of his head.

"You have friends?"

"Yup," the stranger said. "One punched me out cold, too. But I reckon he had his reasons. I shot a man who spilt beer on my knee."

"Shot him dead?"

"Dead as a stuffed cougar."

"And that's why you're chained up and sitting in my pa's chair?"

"That's right, kid," the man said, nibbling on one of the metal bands on his wrist. "You're figuring it right out."

Billy rubbed the instep of his foot with his other foot. He'd never thought much about criminals having friends or losing their tempers. The only trouble they ever had in Red Earth was fighting, and that was usually only between the miners, who his father said were just drunk and ignorant. The man in chains didn't look drunk to Billy, though he did smell like beer.

"What's you name, boy?"

"Billy. Billy Atkins."

"Well, Billy, my name is Johnny Miller and I'm hungry. Haven't ate all day, but I'm thinking my dinner is low on your father's chore list tonight. Would you agree with that, boy?"

"I guess."

Johnny Miller yawned and nodded his head.

"So, Mr. Billy, think you could fetch me something to eat?"

"From my ma?"

"No, you don't need to run all over town. Just grab me something from behind the counter over there."

Billy looked over to the store's counter, which he'd never been behind his entire life. Only the Jamesons were allowed back there. He could see cobwebs covering the store's two back windows.

"It'll be square, son. I've got money. I'll pay for the food when the men get back to the store. I only need you to fetch it for me." Johnny Miller held up his wrists and gave them a shake, rattling the chains. "I can't eat these, can I?"

Billy looked back to the door again, feeling another urge to fly outside and run into the street. He was tired of talking to this man, even if he really had killed somebody for spilling beer on his knee. He was tired of how the man's eyes stayed on him every second, in a way no grown-up had ever watched him before. Just standing in the store with him made Billy feel unsettled.

"You ever been hungry, Billy? So hungry it feels like something's chewing on your guts, making them ache?"

"I don't know."

Johnny Miller sat forward, settling his hands flat on the table and he stared into the boy's eyes. "You don't know? Well then, I'd say you ain't never been hungry enough to know what I'm talking about."

"I guess not."

"You don't know a goddamn thing about a goddamn thing, kid. You ain't lived long enough to know what it's like to grow up. The pressures that build in a man till his head feels like it's going to burst."

Billy took a step back.

"You think life's all home cooking and warm blankets. How your pa's cheek smells nice after he shaves." Johnny shook his head like an invisible fly was buzzing around him. "But you wait. You just wait and see. Someday you'll run into something bad, something real bad, and you'll wish it was just being hungry and maybe you won't feel so high and mighty anymore, with that stubby nose of yours all stuck up in the air."

Billy turned and bolted for the door. Chains rattled as the criminal jumped from his seat and thrashed about, pulling at the ring in the floor. Billy ducked his head, pumping his arms and legs. More ugly words came from inside the general store and the boy tried to outrun those, too, dodging the dim figures of more adults as they gathered in the fading light.

16

A new breed of weariness seeped into Hank Chambers' soul as he stared into the dark barrel of Milo Atkins' revolver, a vast and all-encompassing fatigue that had nothing to do with the horrors he'd witnessed in the mine below and everything to do with the number of fools in the world. So many fools, covering so much of God's fertile creation. What could their purpose be? And in what poorly-lit hour had they been conceived? Throughout his entire mining career—heck, throughout his whole damn life—fools had been dogging Chambers at every turn, weighing him down like rocks in his pockets. They'd nearly killed him a hundred times beneath the ground—not minding their chisels, their hammers, the tightness of their knots—and now one more fool was trying to get him killed. It was enough to drive a man plumb crazy.

But he had to keep his head on straight. Bonnie was expecting him home for dinner and to drink as much water as she saw fit. He would drink whole jars of water, one after the other. He'd fill himself with so much water his body would puff out and gurgle when he walked—

"Lord, Hank. You stink to high heaven. What are you

covered in, anyhow?"

Chambers spat on the ground, trying to regain his senses. Harder now. They wanted to run off like wild horses, all skittish with nerves and fever.

"It's gore, Milo. Something in the mine killed my men."

"I heard. Three of them, is that right?"

Chambers looked past the sheriff and counted four others, including Leg and Henry Jameson. Nobody had a gun except the sheriff.

"More than that, Milo."

"How many, then?"

Chambers turned around, looking for the sun. It had already set behind the hills, throwing the whole town below in shade.

"About all of them, I'd say."

The sheriff's jaw went slack. Chambers could hear the cogs grinding inside the young man's brain, needing a bit more lubrication in the July heat. The sheriff lowered his gun a bit and let out a big guffaw, glancing at the men behind him. Leg Jameson tittered with him, but his mute son Henry and the two old loafers, Butch Hastings and Larry Nolan, did not make a sound, their somber eyes glued on Chambers. Some men expected the worst, some did not.

"All of 'em, you say? Huh. That fever you're running is worse than we all thought."

Chambers shook the fuse cords in his hand, wishing he could light them with the power of his mind alone. Every second that passed was one more second toward the death of them all. That Charred Man would find his way to the mine's opening sooner or later, like water finding a hole in a dam.

"Don't mistake my sweat for madness," Chambers said, taking a step toward the sheriff's gun. "I know what I saw down there. Some creature got loose, tore into the men, and killed them all. I'm blowing the mine so it doesn't do the same down in camp. Every second you hinder me you risk your own imminent death, Sheriff."

Atkins smirked and motioned at him with the revolver.

"You stay where you are, Mr. Chambers. I like ghost stories myself, but I've never heard of anything killing seventy some men. Nothing except what you're attempting here."

Butch Hastings, one of the old general store loafers, cleared his throat. He had rheumatism in both hands and it made them shake as if they had a mind of their own.

"What about the two adits? It'd get out through them, wouldn't it?"

Chambers nodded at the crate of extra dynamite and fuse caps.

"There's enough sticks left to close those, too, if we get lucky and have the time. I figured it would follow me up to this entrance first, though. I felt it hunting me."

A fly lifted off the ground and circled round Chambers, intrigued by the slickness and odor to his clothes. The wind had died down. The hillside was so quiet you could hear the fly buzzing and everyone breathing, including the horses tied to a post outside the dry house. Atkins was squinting like he had a headache and a toothache at the same time, his eyes darting from Chambers to the mine entrance and back again.

"What's really going on, Hank?"

"I told you already, Sheriff. I'm not to going to make up a lie to make you feel better. The truth is strange enough already."

Atkins frowned and scratched his chin.

"Why don't you set down that cord and we'll check out the mine together? You show me the seventy men murdered, as you say, and I'll let you blow the mine, even if it costs us both our jobs. We'll create a big old tomb for your crew. We'll even get Father Lynch to bless the whole affair."

Chambers swatted the fly away, which just looped around

and came back again. Like the conversation they were having.

"Fine, Sheriff. Let's do it your way."

The foreman dropped the blasting cord on the ground and stepped back, holding his hands in the air. It was growing clear to him that there was no good way out of this situation, that he'd finally run into the King Fool himself, and that he might not survive this last foolish encounter.

"Thank you, Hank. I know—"

The sheriff stopped in mid-sentence, whatever grating thing he was about to say suddenly wiped clean from his mind as he looked over Chambers' shoulder, eyes widening at what he saw there. The foreman swore softly and closed his eyes, apologizing to his wife in his mind.

The sheriff lowered his gun and Chambers turned around so he was facing the mine's entrance. He couldn't make out anything except dark.

"You saw it, didn't you?"

"I might have. I might have seen something walk past."

"Big hands, like claws?"

"I don't know. Could have just been a shadow. Or a regular man."

Butch Hastings shook his head.

"I saw it, too. Wasn't no regular man. Never seen anything that moved like that."

Chambers bent over and picked up the pile of cords again, hoping they still had time. Atkins licked his lips, eyes still fixed on the mine's entrance.

"Maybe you got me spooked, too. Maybe you spooked everybody."

"The Charred Man. That's what I call him, Milo." Chambers touched the end of the cords to the lantern's open fire. They smoldered for a moment, then caught in a dozen sparking strands.

"You should all get back now."

Atkins broke from his paralysis and looked down at the fuse cords, which had already burned a foot down.

"Jesus Christ, Hank. This is going to kill the town. We lose the mine, the whole show is going to close up. We'll be a ghost town by fall."

"There'll be other towns, Milo. Now, you and Henry grab that crate and haul it around to those adits. If it's truly up here with us and we seal it in, I doubt it'll make it to those adits faster than men on horseback."

Chambers handed the lantern to the sheriff, who looked like he was finally catching on. The foreman started forward, moving before he could think too much. He caught up to the burning section of cord, passed it by, and headed unarmed into the mine. He thought about how any day you worked underground could be your last. How every miner knew it and accepted it as a risk he could not get around, not with prayer nor luck nor goodness.

Still, it felt strange, knowing you were entering a mine for the last time, realizing you would not emerge to see the stars again. The feeling pushed Chambers' summer fever away and flushed it out of him. When he sprinted into that first big room of the Dennison Mine, hollering for the Charred Man to come out and fight, to fight him like a goddamn man, Hank Chambers felt stronger than he ever had in his life. Strong enough that when the Charred Man did find him, smelling like burnt copper and smoke, Chambers was able to wrap his arms tightly around the clawing devil until he heard an enormous blast, a thunderclap that brought the world to an end.

17

The street outside the Runoff Saloon was filled with curious residents of the Copper Hotel and a dozen mining wives who'd come downtown to find out why their husbands had not yet returned home though it was nearly eight-thirty. The men stood clumped together in one group discussing the shootout while the women stood in another and speculated about the whereabouts of their men. The saloon's owner, Madam Petrov, had already come out to speak with both groups, assuring everyone that not one miner was currently in the saloon, either in bed or on a barstool.

Bonnie Chambers stood among the women, trying to ignore the idle chatter around her and eavesdrop on the men.

A hand touched her shoulder.

"Bonnie?"

She turned, heart fluttering, but it was only her friend, Susan Logan, mother of the loudmouth, red-headed Jess Logan, spreader of gossip and alarm.

"Did Hank say anything to you about the men working late?"

"No," Bonnie said, wondering if he'd said something she'd

missed. "I can't say he did."

Susan shook her head as if she'd expected as much. She was a thick-shouldered woman who wore her dark hair in a tight, nest-like bun.

"Maybe they found a new seam?"

"Could be."

"That'd be nice," Susan said, her round face brightening. "More work for everybody."

Bonnie nodded, as if she cared two bits about more work. As far as she was concerned, they could run out of copper tomorrow, close shop, and head directly for the Rawlins' train station.

"Still," Susan said, "it's getting late, even for that."

Bonnie's gaze drifted past her friend toward the hillside south of town. The evening light was going from blue to black, yet she could still make out the Dennison Mine's dry house and storage shed, small as they appeared from such a distance.

"You think they—"

A flash lit up the hillside, followed by a loud bang. Everyone in the street turned their head in the direction of the explosion, the women around Bonnie gasping in unison. Dust blanketed the hillside, obscuring the mine's entrance and the buildings outside it. Bonnie felt her heart squeeze in her chest, a painful, aching contraction, and then she found herself pushing through the crowd of dumbfounded women and men as if propelled by a great wind.

By the time she'd moved beyond the gawkers, Bonnie had come to her senses enough to realize she'd need a lantern if she wanted to hike the half-mile to the mine, perhaps some proper footwear as well. She stopped at the general store, which was dark and empty. As she'd expected, both Leg and Henry Jameson had both run off half-cocked, likely out of their heads in their excitement to join the sheriff's little expedition. Bonnie, who knew her way around the store as well as anybody else in town, made her way to the counter in back, found the lantern, and lit it with one of the white phosphorus matches Leg kept beside it in a little tin box.

The lantern bloomed like a sun being born. Metal rattled at the front of the store, making Bonnie jump. A stranger sat at the sheriff's desk, his wrist and ankles wrapped in chains.

"Howdy, ma'am."

Bonnie, who didn't have time for pleasantries, declined to respond. She went around the counter and examined the shelves, which could have used a good scrub. She plucked an oil lamp off the shelf, checked it for fuel, and lit it from the counter lamp. In the increased light she noticed a pair of boots on a bottom shelf. She took off her shoes and tried on the boots—a little big, but they'd do.

"They haven't fed me dinner yet."

She tightened the laces on each boot and knotted them.

"You mind bringing me something to eat? I can see they've got some ham on that middle shelf there."

Bonnie picked up the second lantern and went back round the counter.

"Ma'am?"

"I'm sorry, but good men are in trouble out there. You're going to have to wait for your dinner."

The stranger lowered his head.

"My luck has not held today."

"Yes," Bonnie agreed, "but you are not the only one."

And she was out the door.

The air cooled now that it was fully dark and the stars had come out. The surrounding hills, a shade lighter than pitch black, absorbed the growing starlight and sat hunkered against the sky. Bonnie crossed the valley floor as fast as she could, watching the rocks at her feet so as not to trip or step on a rattlesnake. Enough time had been wasted without more bother like that.

A cloud of dust from the explosion drifted down from the mine's entrance, rolling across the valley floor. Bonnie coughed and bowed her head, covering her mouth with her free hand while the lantern flickered in the other, the flame struggling with the thick air. The dust limited her sight so much she did not see the figure until she was plowing into his chest with the crown of her head.

"Ooof."

Bonnie shielded her eyes against the grit and raised the lantern.

"Randy Bale?"

The boy sniffed and wiped at his mouth. His eyes looked red and wet and scared.

"Yes, ma'am."

"What happened?"

The boy dropped his gaze to her feet.

"They blew the mine shut."

Bonnie clucked her tongue and peered up the hillside.

"On purpose, you mean?"

"Yes, ma'am. Mr. Chambers had me stay at the dry house while he went down into the mine. He was gone a good while and I fell asleep on a bench in there. When I woke up, I saw Mr. Chambers talking with Sheriff Atkins and Leg Jameson and some other fellas. They was looking into the mine kind of strange like. Then Mr. Chambers was torching a pile of fuse cord and the other men were running down the hill like scattered hens, taking their horses and a crate of sticks with 'em."

Randy Bale paused to swipe at his nose again. Fresh tears were running down his cheeks.

"Then Mr. Chambers ran back inside the mine."

"Back inside?"

"Yes, ma'am. Right into the entrance, past the burning

fuses. And then the whole thing blew to Kingdom Come."

Bonnie swallowed. The cloud of dust had rolled past them and the air had cleared.

"What about the other men?"

"They never came out after their shift, far as I know. Not a one."

"And the sheriff? Where's he at?"

"They ran off soon as the mine blew. They weren't headed toward town, though. More like to the south. I hollered after them, but they didn't heed."

Bonnie passed Randy Bale and started up the hillside, bending forward to adjust for the grade.

"The mine's shut, Mrs. Chambers. The ceiling dropped right in."

"Yes, I heard."

"You want me to go back up with you?"

"No. You've done enough today, Randy. You head back into town."

"I'm sorry about your husband."

"Go on, now."

The boy took off like a jackrabbit across the valley floor. Scree tumbled down as Bonnie climbed higher, peering up the slope. She hadn't been to the mine since the previous spring when she surprised her husband with a stein of beer, but she knew the hillside well enough to see the blast had changed its face. If she hadn't had the dry house to aim for, she might not have been able to place the mine's entrance at all.

Because the entrance was gone.

Blown up and buried in rock.

Tremulations crept up Bonnie's legs. They worked their way up her thighs and stomach like a bunch of prodding fingers and they made it hard for her to breathe. By the time she reached the dry house, she had to set her lantern down and lace her fingers behind her head to find her air. Even the flat grade beneath the mine's entrance was gone, the patch where the miner's hung out before their shifts, laughing and bragging with each other while their lunch pails swung about in their hands.

The tremors moved higher, to her lip, to her quivering eyelids. Why would her husband have done such a thing? Why—

A rock broke loose above and rolled down the hill, knocking loudly against others. Bonnie wiped away her tears and looked up. A second rock broke free and tumbled down, and then a third. A spot had opened on the hillside, darker than the chalk-white rocks around it.

More rocks tumbled down. The spot of darkness grew.

"My Lord," Bonnie whispered, starting back up the hill. Something was burrowing out from under all that rock.

Someone.

"Hank! I'm here, Hank!"

She could see a head pushing through, then shoulders. She started to run, heedless of the loose rock underfoot or the lantern she'd left behind. She thanked God from the depths of her poor sinner's soul and started to laugh and then the man rose, pushing himself up from the ground and standing tall against the night.

Bonnie froze mid-stride, smelling burnt flesh.

"Hank?"

The man cocked his head, taking note of her. He appeared to be covered in dirt, or soot, with a few patches of white glowing off his body in the starlight. He started toward her, his strides long and smooth, his footing unnaturally steady on the loose rock. He moved like a piece of the mountain itself come to life.

Bonnie stepped back, the tremors in her body grown tenfold. She was like a leaf, ripped from its branch and taken by the wind.

PART THREE

What the Priest Saw

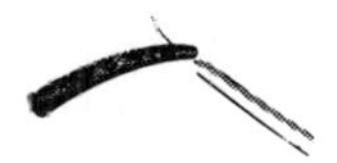

18

The men fumbled in the dim light, cursing the cold and the dark and the tremble in their hands. They'd ridden hard to the mountain's south end, where one adit entrance sat twenty feet beneath another, and somehow the dynamite strapped to the back of Milo Atkins' horse had not gone off during the rocky journey. The whole ride had possessed a syrupy, dreamlike quality for Sheriff Atkins, as if it had been going on forever and would outlast the mountains themselves. He kept picturing Hank Chambers, arms pumping as he picked up steam and sprinted into the mine's entrance, hollering for a fight.

The Charred Man.

"Come over here, Milo. We've got a batch for ya."

Leg Jameson, Butch Hastings, and Larry Nolan were hunched over the two crates they'd brought along, capping sticks of dynamite and unspooling fuse wires in the faint light provided by the foreman's lantern. They'd left town in a hurry, while the day still held some light, and hadn't thought to bring a light with them. Young Henry Jameson had already walked off from the group with a pile of capped and strung dynamite in his arms, headed for the upper adit.

"Now you just set these in as many nooks as you can," Leg wheezed, placing a crop of dynamite in the sheriff's arms. "We don't have time for a pretty blast, but you need to get them dug in enough so they tear rock out when they go."

"Sure."

"And when you've got those sticks ready, run that wire back to us and we'll set the whole mess off."

Atkins nodded, already walking away from the old man. He bristled at the store owner telling him what to do, like he didn't know full well already. It didn't take a genius to see how blasting was done, even if you weren't some old coot of a forty-niner. You had your sticks and your fuse caps and your wire—stick it all together, light a match, and watch the rock fly.

But damn if it wasn't getting brisk now, the stars coming out and no moon. Downright cold in these mountains, even in the middle of July. Atkins climbed the slope toward the lower adit, his jaw clenched so his teeth didn't chatter while the fuse wires tangled around his feet, trying to trip him and his load of capped dynamite. Wouldn't that be a fine way to die. Out here with Leg Jameson and his strange crowd, while his wife and boy were back in town expecting Atkins by the fire. Blowing himself to bits would just cinch the day's events with a big satin ribbon.

Rocks dribbled down the hillside. Atkins looked up and saw Henry Jameson struggling with his footing.

"Easy there, Henry."

Henry answered him with a sort of half-choked grunting, about as much noise as Atkins had ever heard him make. The young man was climbing the last and steepest slope before he reached the level ground circling the mouth of the upper adit. The dynamite in Henry's arms was weighing heavy on him, causing the young man to recline at an alarming angle.

"You go on now, Henry," Atkins shouted up, his own troubles momentarily forgotten. "You keep pushing that goddamn heap."

The mute wavered on his heels another moment, still fighting gravity's pull, before finally making the last few yards and disappearing from Atkins' sight. Henry would have had an easier time going up the switchbacks the haul wagons used, but that path took longer than scrabbling directly up the hillside.

And they didn't have much time, did they? Not if the Charred Man was still seeking a way out.

Atkins reached the lower adit and set his bundle of dynamite outside the tunnel's opening. Leg Jameson hollered something from below that Atkins could not make out nor cared to. His eyes had grown accustomed to the weak starlight and he was able to see just enough to pluck a few sticks from the pile and start plugging them into crevices around the adit. A gust of air, warmer than the chill night, blew out from the tunnel. Atkins sniffed it for anything suspicious, like powder smoke, but all he got off it was the smell of water and stone, about as innocent a scent as you could wish for. He returned to his pile of sticks, took up another load, and brought them inside the adit's entrance.

He could make out two steel rails, faintly gleaming along the tunnel's floor and disappearing into the dark. He turned his head but couldn't hear anything beyond the wind and his own breathing. He imagined the Charred Man, walking out of the tunnel in that odd, choppy manner....

Something rustled outside the tunnel entrance. Atkins blinked and poked his head outside. Henry Jameson had scrambled down the hillside, already finished with his own load of sticks. He stood with his fists at his side, watching Atkins in that loud silent way he had. "Just a few more," Atkins said, and went back inside. He finished his work in a hasty, unsafe manner, plugging in the dynamite with too much force, and brought the tangle of fuse lines back out with him.

The mute had already straightened the other fuse lines, added them to his own, and was running the lines down to where his father and his cronies were standing around the one lantern like a bunch of old witches with their favorite bubbling cauldron. Atkins brought the remaining lines down the hillside, no longer feeling the cold as much.

"You want the honors, Sheriff?"

Atkins glanced around at the men, surprised by the rare show of respect. Nobody in Red Earth had offered him honors before.

"Let your boy do it, Leg. He was the one that near broke his neck climbing up to the higher tunnel."

Leg Jameson nodded and stroked his beard.

"Go ahead, Henry. Touch 'em off."

The mute took up the lantern and put its flame to the fuse wires. With each wire sparked, a new line of hissing red was born, its color and beauty made all the more spectacular by the near dark. The horses whinnied and toed the ground, not liking the hissing, and the men grabbed their halters, stilling their whipping heads.

"Hard to believe all this," Atkins said, watching the wires burn. "Today, I got up and ate my breakfast like it was any other day."

Leg cleared his throat and spat on the ground.

"That's how the bad ones start. Same as the good ones."

The hissing of the wires grew fainter. Atkins glanced at Leg to see if the old miner was worried by the quiet.

"You don't think those wires—"

A terrific flash of white lit up the hillside, interrupting Atkins with a booming thunderclap. Atkins covered his ears and ducked his head as a spattering of pebbles and dirt rained down upon his shoulders and his horse fidgeted beside him, wanting to bolt.

A long second passed.

Then another.

Another flash of light followed by its own thunderclap. This time all the horses reared up, tearing at the sky with their hooves and forcing their handlers to wrangle them back into submission.

"That was a fun one," Leg Jameson shouted above the ringing in everyone's ears. "Forgot about that charge you get. It's one thing to watch a blast, another to help set 'er up yourself."

Hastings and Nolan grunted in agreement. Henry ran back to make certain the two adits were collapsed fully and returned, nodding yes. Atkins patted the neck of his horse and looked back up the hillside. "That mine is sealed tight as a bunged keg," Leg said, following the sheriff's gaze. "Hank and the other men can rest easy and that damned creature can stay with them."

Atkins brought his horse around, put his foot in the stirrup, and swung up into the saddle. The leather creaked beneath his weight, gone rigid in the cold. The other men mounted as well and they started riding for town as a group, picking their way slowly through the treacherous dark, each man absorbed in his own thoughts. This was trouble for certain. The kind Atkins' father had warned him might come to a lawman's door someday.

They rounded the mountain and headed north across the valley floor. The horses snorted and you could see the steam rise from their nostrils, lit white by the starlight. The sky was black and the stars so plentiful it was like they were riding through them, not just beneath them. Atkins tried to focus on the terrain, his mind still uneasy. He felt he might be uneasy the rest of his life, no matter if he lived another seventy years, and he'd think of the discomfort as simply the price you paid for being allowed to go on living.

Atkins noticed a light on the hillside, near where the mine's entrance had been. "Whoa now," he called out, both to the group of men and his own horse. "Look up the hillside, fellas."

The others drew up their horses and turned. Sure enough, a smallish fire was flickering in the wind.

"I reckon that's a lantern."

Leg Jameson smacked his gums and mumbled something.

"What was that, Leg?"

"I said, my sight ain't so good. I guess I see something up there."

"Right. I suppose we should check it out."

Atkins dug in his heels and his horse took a few stutter steps forward. The other men hung back, however, looking at each other like nervous hens.

"Well?"

"The rest of us are getting hungry and cold, Sheriff," Leg Jameson said. "We just want to go home and sit by the fire."

"Sit by the fire?"

Leg nodded and looked to Hastings and Nolan for support.

"We're old men, Milo. We've already had about as much as we can take out here. Any more and our hearts might give out."

Atkins waved the men off.

"Fine, then. Go on back."

"Thank you, Sheriff. We'll buy you a round at the saloon."

Atkins smirked at the other men and spurred his horse. He sat hunched forward in the saddle as the horse picked her way up the hillside, eyes straining to see in the starlight. It took him a moment to realize Mute Henry was riding beside him, a few feet off in the dark.

"Well," Atkins called out. "I'm glad to see there's one Jameson who still has guts in his belly."

Henry looked over and nodded. Didn't say anything, of course.

They reached the lantern and found the body a few yards

beyond. A woman, stretched out on her side, with her head lying against her arm as if she'd fallen asleep there. They dismounted and approached the body slowly, scree tumbling down the hillside with each footstep.

Atkins took up the lantern and held it over the dead woman, wincing from what his eyes told him.

"Lordy. That's Mrs. Chambers."

Henry nodded, the glassy whites of his eyes poking out from the coating of dirt on his face. Atkins squatted to get a closer look at the dark ribbon across the dead woman's neck. "Her throat's been ripped open," he said, his voice soft with wonderment. "Something with claws got at her."

Henry took a step back from the corpse, kicking more scree loose. Mrs. Chambers' eyes were open to the night sky.

Atkins straightened above the corpse and wondered if he was going to vomit. He turned his head to the side, prepared, but his queasy stomach held its peace—lunch had been a long time ago, and he'd missed dinner. Violet would not be happy with him when he got home.

Henry snapped his fingers and pointed up the hillside. Atkins followed the mute's gesture and climbed a few yards further.

"What is it? What'd you see?

Henry snapped his fingers again, still pointing, but Atkins had already found what was getting him so worked up. A hole had appeared in the hillside, centered over the rubble covering the mine's entrance.

Atkins stood over the hole. Something large had burrowed through the loose rock, something as big as a man.

"Shit."

A gust of air wafted up from the opening, but it didn't smell like deep earth. It smelled like smoke and char.

"He wasn't headed for the adits. He didn't need to."

Atkins and Henry turned toward the lights of Red Earth,

which looked faint and small from the hillside. Atkins set the lantern down and returned to the spot where he'd left his horse nibbling on a pile of uprooted brush. "We need to get to town first, Henry. Before he does."

Mute Henry nodded and they rode out, kicking more scree loose as they galloped to the valley floor and toward the lights of town. The earthly remains of Bonnie Chambers watched them depart from the hillside without comment, the emerging stars reflected in her eyes. Around her, the hills had already returned to their endless, windblown calm.

19

Father Lynch watched as the men who'd carried a coffin into his church earlier that day were lowered into three of their own. Chester would have plenty of company now—apparently his friends were as bad at keeping themselves out of trouble as he'd been. "At this rate," Lynch announced to the crowd assembled in the street, "Leg Jameson's going to run out of coffins."

"He has," somebody in the crowd replied. "Those cleared him out."

Lynch scowled and waved off the gawkers, trying to make the whole lot scatter with a swipe of his hand. He came up to the first of the coffins, made the sign of the cross above the dead, and prayed for his soul to find its peace. Then he did the same for the second man, then the third. He could feel the crowd's eyes upon him and heard a few mumbled prayers echoing his own. Never had such a large, interested crowd assembled in his own church, not even on Christmas Eve or Easter Sunday. He figured it was death that drew them together this cool summer evening, the racy spectacle of it, and the idea alone made him feel raw and old and useless.

The drunken loafer Owen Hayes and a second man came out of the saloon and looked over the line of coffins. Owen looked pallid and damp, with a cloth bandage wrapped around his left thigh. The other man, who was clean shaven and hawk-eyed, looked untouched except for a ragged cut across the front of his jacket and shirt, where the blade of a knife must have passed through.

"Father Lynch, this is my older brother, Elwood Hayes."

The priest eyed the pair closely, seeking out the family resemblance. Owen's face was round and soft, with the ruddiness of a habitual drinker, while Elwood's skin was taught and deeply tanned, like a man who spent most of his time outdoors. Yet you could discern a certain likeness to the set of their jaws, the ample breadth of their foreheads.

"You two are brothers?"

"Yes, sir," Owen said, nodding vigorously. "He was just coming to town to pay me a visit."

Lynch ignored the obvious lie and scrutinized the older brother further.

"So this is how you look out for your little brother, Mr. Hayes? By involving him in the first gunfight Red Earth's ever known?"

Elwood Hayes returned the priest's stare.

"They had it coming, Father. They stepped to us first."

"We all have it coming, Mr. Hayes. But no man shall say when that time has come for another."

"That something Jesus said?"

Lynch nodded.

"Yes. In a manner."

The priest turned back to the coffins, considering them. The Hayes brothers remained where they stood, also considering. The murmuring of the crowd grew louder as people began to lose interest in the coffins and the killers standing beside them. Two explosions, one after the other, sounded in the distance.

"Goddamn," Owen Hayes cursed, unmindful of the priest or his proximity to the resting dead. "How much more blasting they bent on tonight? Must be past nine o'clock."

"Something's gone wrong in the mine," Lynch said, speaking as much to himself as the Hayes brothers. "Men died there earlier today, and I fear more have died since."

"They're sealing her up," Elwood said. "Has the mine played out?"

"No," Lynch said. "Not how you mean, anyhow."

Caleb Rollins and Madam Petrov came out of the bar. The madam looked as angry as slapped bull, her bulk all hunched up into her shoulders. Father Lynch would not have been surprised if she'd lowered her head right then and charged the nearest man.

"What was that explosions?"

"They were down at the mine, ma'am," Owen said, removing his cap. "We don't know what they're about yet."

The madam's cheeks filled with air and bulged. "I knew, I knew! I knew they would blow this town to high heavens!"

"Please, Madam Petrov," Father Lynch, raising his hands. "There's no need—"

"I told you this afternoon, Father," the madam shouted, stepping forward and poking Lynch in the chest. "I told, but you did not listen!"

The priest looked around him for help. The crowd had stepped back, including the Hayes brothers. The madam made to poke Lynch a fourth time and he caught her fingers in his own.

"I had dream! I had dream this would happen!"

"Please, Madam. Calm yourself."

"Calm myself? Four men killed in my saloon in one day, a fifth with a shot knee, and you want me to calm myself?"

"I'm sure these men here will be more than willing—"

"You see men here? I see nothing but dogs. Ugly dogs fighting for no good reason in my bar."

"Please, Madam. I'll be happy to house the deceased in my church until their remains can be sent to Rawlins."

Madam Petrov closed her mouth and eyed him. She dabbed spittle from the corners of her mouth with a linen handkerchief and took several breaths, her considerable bosom rising and falling with each lungful. Beyond her, Lynch could see Elwood Hayes grinning like this was fine theater.

"Thank you, Father," Madam Petrov said, stepping back. "Your help in storing coffins would be fine."

Father Lynch gave the madam a small bow and turned around to the crowd of men and women.

"Okay, men," he shouted above the din. "Who's willing to help us move these coffins?"

The crowd quieted. Three prospectors from the Copper Inn, all past fifty, stepped forward. Father Lynch felt a presence over his shoulder step up as well.

"I'll lend a hand," Elwood Hayes said. "Being that I was the one that put'em there in the first place."

They carried the coffins across the street one at a time, a man to each corner, with Father Lynch overseeing the affair and holding the church door open. By the last coffin, the crowd sensed the show was over and returned either to the Runoff Saloon or the Copper Hotel's dining room. The dozen or so women who were still waiting for their men to return from the Dennison Mine chose the Copper Hotel over going home to fret, entering the hotel as one large, formidable mass, unified in their worry and taking their small children along with them. Their numbers gave the ramshackle building a holiday atmosphere—the buzz of their voices carried through the hotel's walls and into the church, even with its windows shut.

"You'd think it was a wedding party," Elwood Hayes said, peering through the church's south window to take in the scene. "Only needs a bride dressed in gauzy white to set it all off."

They'd placed the final coffin at the back of the church, bringing the number of stored dead to four. The other pallbearers had left already, eager to join the festivities. Father Lynch imagined a fresh round of drinking, followed by a fresh round of brawling, with more drinking shortly after. Anything was possible on a day like this—on the day they sealed the Dennison Mine.

Red Earth was already dead; it just didn't know it yet. And they'd built this serviceable church not a year before.

"And the light shineth in darkness; and the darkness comprehended it not."

Elwood glanced at the priest. "That must be from the Bible."

Lynch nodded, feeling old and tired.

"Don't know how many times I tried to read that darn book, only to fall asleep by the second page."

Lynch tugged at his clerical collar, loosening it. "You should try again. The holy scripture might do a man in your position good."

"Because I killed all these fellas."

"Yes."

"I am a killer," Elwood said, knocking on the nearest coffin lid. "I'm a killer and I'm going to hell when I die. Is that right, Father?"

Father Lynch rubbed his cheek and sighed.

"I need a drink."

"Go on. Don't mind me none."

Lynch went into his little room at the front of the church and retrieved his gin, along with two glasses he wiped clean with a rag. When he returned to the sanctuary, he found Hayes seated in a back row pew and staring at the wooden cross hung at the front of the church. Hayes, who sat with his back to the room's only lantern, might have been any congregant from any of the past forty years Lynch had served the Catholic Church.

"Thought you might have run off while I was back there," Lynch said, walking down the middle aisle. "The company of an old priest and four dead men is not particularly enticing."

"I don't mind the dead. It's the living that cause me trouble."

Lynch sat in Hayes' pew and set the glasses between them. He poured the gin carefully, not wanting to spill it in the sanctuary. He gave one glass to Hayes and took the other in hand. They drank in silence, listening to the wind rap against the windows and the babble coming from the hotel next door. The priest recalled parties he'd been to as a young man in Philadelphia, the feverish, rosy glow people took on when they gathered to dance and drink and listen to music. That loud, gauzy world had been shut to him for a long time, yet Lynch didn't miss it, except in sudden bursts that fell upon him with the suddenness of a lightning strike.

But that was just the Devil, whispering in his ear. Telling him to be not satisfied.

The bench creaked as Hayes shifted his weight.

"We've a farm, back in Nebraska. Wheat and corn and cows. Not a bad spread."

Lynch sipped at his gin and felt its warmth slip down his throat.

"You and your brother?"

"No, sir. It's our father's farm. Owen and I just did what we were told, at least until we were old enough to leave. Neither of us ever have been much for peaceful living. Could hardly sit still, even in a good situation."

Lynch turned his gaze to the ceiling. "Mr. Hayes, that sounds like nearly every man in Wyoming."

Hayes chuckled and shifted again. "Wandering has been in my bones as long as I can remember. Like a whirlwind. Like a whirlwind that's carried me around from job to job and fight to fight. Three years ago, I accidently killed a man with my fists. I hit his nose too square and he dropped like a hay bale kicked from a loft. I kept waiting for him to get up, but he never did."

Hayes emptied his glass. Father Lynch filled it up again.

"I didn't want to kill him, Father. It was just stupidness. Not drunk stupidness, either. Just the stupidness that rises up in me sometimes, wanting to hurt something no matter what else."

Somebody whooped outside and was answered by laughter. The party had started to gain steam—perhaps the miners had finally returned for the evening and joined their wives at the Copper Hotel.

Father Lynch set aside his glass and rubbed his palms upon his knees.

"Mortal men, such as you and I, are imperfect creatures. We are bound to be so—we cannot escape that fate. The best we can do is temper ourselves. Temper our rage, our sins, our urge to destroy for the sake of destroying."

"And then we'll get into Heaven? If we temper ourselves?"

Father Lynch turned and looked at his visitor's profile. The young man's gaze was fixed on the cross at the front of the room.

"I don't know about Heaven, Mr. Hayes. But it might keep you from the wrong side of a jail cell."

A short while later, somebody knocked on the back door and let themselves into the church. Father Lynch turned to see Owen Hayes, standing hat in hand.

"Excuse me, Father. I came to get Elwood."

The older Hayes brother sighed.

"What is it, Owen?"

"Roach sent me. He wants to know what we're doing next."

Lynch and Elwood looked at each other. Elwood shrugged.

"I'll be over."

Owen nodded and exited the building as quickly as he'd entered. Elwood set his glass on the pew and they shook hands.

"Thank you for the gin, Father. I believe that is the first time I've ever drank with a man of the cloth."

"Temperance, Mr. Hayes. Remember temperance."

Elwood nodded and rose to his feet. As he left the church, he ran his hand across each coffin lid he passed by, his movements easy and loose. Once the church's door had shut behind him, Father Lynch got up and turned the lantern down. Suddenly bone-tired, the priest went into his bedroom, stripped to his underwear, and lay down upon his cot. When sleep arrived, it fell hard upon him, turning him into an immobile figure not much different from the four men lying in the next room.

20

Somehow, despite the chains and his ever-gnawing hunger, Johnny Miller had fallen asleep sitting at the sheriff's desk. When three old men entered the general store, stomping their boots and rubbing their hands like it was the dead of winter, Miller raised his head and opened his sleep-heavy eyes.

"Took you boys long enough. You have to lie with those three dead fellers to make sure they was dead?"

The old men looked at each other. The store's owner, who they called Arm or Leg or Armpit or something queer like that, cleared his throat and pointed a wobbly finger in Miller's direction.

"You shut your mouth."

"I will, soon as you fill it."

Armpit lowered his finger and blinked his milky cow eyes. "What do you mean by that, boy? Some perversion?"

"I mean I'm hungry, goddamn it. You ran off without leaving me a speck to eat and chained to this damn ring. I've got to piss, too. I'm fit to rupture."

Armpit walked back to the counter. He got an empty jar off the shelf, unscrewed its lid, and brought it back to Miller, setting it before him on the sheriff's desk.

"There's your piss pot, murderer."

"Don't get all fancy on my account, Mr. Armpit."

Armpit laughed and looked back at his pals. "You won't have to worry about fancy in my store, boy. Maybe in Rawlins, you will. Maybe they'll show you a little fancy before they hang you high in the street."

Armpit's wooly-looking pals whooped at that, but even their laughter seemed strange and unnatural. Their eyes kept darting to the windows, like they expected something out there in the dark.

"What's going on with y'all? You're acting funny."

The old timers looked at each other again.

"Was those miners real ugly when they found them?"

Armpit sniffed and shook his head.

"That's none of your business, boy. Gentlemen, if you'll follow me. I have bottle we can uncork in the back."

Miller sneered at the old timers as they shuffled past, wondering if they were close enough he could stick out a leg and trip one up. Armpit led the way, guiding them around the back counter and through a doorway Miller couldn't see.

"Hey! What about that dinner?"

"I don't feed murderers in my store," Armpit called back, slamming a door. Miller groaned and laid his head on the table, wishing he had a better way about him. Even when he wanted something and wanted it bad, he still couldn't put honey in his words.

Muffled talk came from the back of the store. The old-timers were keeping their voice low, like they were worried about being overheard. What in the hell were they being so secretive about? They were as bad as schoolgirls, whispering to each other while the teacher's back was turned. Mayhap it was a murder they discovered down there and not an accident. A murder, yes, and they'd decided to cover it over with a layer of bullshit.

And then they come back here, calling him a murderer. Wasn't goddamn fair at all, was it?

"I'm hungry!" Miller bellowed, rattling his chains. "I'm starving up here!"

The talking paused as the old men laughed.

"Goddamn it," Miller said, considering the piss jar on the table. "Goddamn all you stinking bastards."

Especially Elwood Hayes. Damn him most of all. Laying him out like that with a sucker punch, turning him over to the damn stagecoach guards. One minute they were all thick as thieves, ready to rob the Dennison payroll, and the next Miller might have been Jesus Christ himself, so eager was Elwood Hayes to betray him.

Well. He'd get his comeuppance soon enough.

Miller would see to that himself.

The piss jar must have been twenty years old. The lid was screwed on so tight Johnny Miller practically had to bite it with his teeth to get the stubborn piece of tin to budge. But, at long damn last, it did give and he was able to screw off the lid and watch it go spinning across the floor, like a tiny wagon wheel gone mad.

"That's right, liddy. You run and hide before I stomp you twice as flat."

The jar itself, which looked to hold a quart, clunked as Miller set it on the floor, every movement made more difficult than necessary because of the shackles. His wrists were starting to burn with new, bone-deep pain and his lower back ached as if he was close to being snapped in half—he'd always hated stiff, proper furniture like this, preferring all day in a saddle to an hour at a dinner table.

The chains also made fumbling with the buttons in his pants a damned chore, rattling with each poke and tug, and

Miller could feel the pent-up piss inside him welling up, ready to break through with or without his orders. Too easily, he could picture Armpit and his pals popping out of the backroom to find him sodden in a pool of his own urine. They'd all have a good holler over that, he was sure. Whenever they discovered another soul in misery, men never accounted for being in the same circumstance themselves someday, further down the road. No, sir. They just laughed and pointed like ugly, two-legged jackals.

The last button popped open and Miller stuffed his hand inside his underwear, retrieving his pecker and pulling it out into the cool air. A hot stream of piss rushed forth immediately, magnificent in its warm force, and shot loudly into the jar. Miller sighed and closed his eyes, thanking the Good Lord that he'd made it in time.

He was only half-finished when the store's front door opened, letting in a fresh batch of cold air.

"Hey there, Sheriff."

The lawman didn't stop and gape at Miller relieving himself at his desk, sitting in his very own chair. He didn't even give Miller so much as a second glance, blowing right past him. Next came Armpit's boy, following the sheriff inside. The boy stopped to look at Miller's pecker, scowled, and continued to the back of the store.

"You fellas must be used to men pissing around here. With all this fine hospitality and such."

Neither man answered. Miller finished his business, shook off the last couple of drops, and tucked his pecker back into his pants. Hot piss smell rose from the jar on the floor, which he'd half-filled.

"Well, don't that smell pretty."

Again, no response. The sheriff and Armpit's boy were laying rifles, shotguns, and knives out on the counter, followed by shells and bullets. Armpit Junior fed the sheriff ammunition while the lawman loaded the guns, working so fast he might have been under fire that moment. Miller counted five shotguns and three rifles in all.

"What the hell you all planning to hunt? A herd of buffalo?"

The sheriff looked up from the guns and across the room, focusing on Miller as if he'd just noticed him sitting there.

"Johnny Miller, how'd you like to go free?"

Miller frowned and wiped at his nose with a shackle cuff. The sheriff's eyes had gone bright and hot, like he was running a fever.

"How do you mean?"

"I mean, how'd you like to have that murder charge dropped clean away? How'd you like to escape that old hangman's noose?"

Miller licked the back of his teeth, thinking.

"I'd like that."

"I thought so," the sheriff said, plugging two more shells into a sawed-off ten gauge and snapping the action shut. "There's just one condition you have to agree to, Mr. Miller. As soon as we take off those chains, I want you to fetch your horse from the livery stables, mount it, and ride right out of town. No circling back, no plotting a bloody revenge, no further stupidity. You're going to ride right back into those mountains and never return to Red Earth again."

The sheriff gestured toward him with the shotgun's end.

"You agree to that, Mr. Miller?"

Johnny Miller straightened in his chair, feeling the touch of grace upon his head. He didn't know why, but his luck was finally changing toward the better. He was going to be spared a while longer from those fires of Hell.

"Can I have my gun back?"

"Yes, but unloaded."

"And some food and water to take with me on the road?"

"Sure."

"Hell's bells," Miller said, rattling his chains. "I'll ride out soon as you get these damned things off me."

The sheriff reached into his pocket and handed Armpit Junior a brass key. "Please free our prisoner, Henry. I'll prepare his provisions for the road."

The old men came out from the backroom while Miller was rubbing feeling back into his wrists and ankles, staring at the chains piled on the floor and wishing he could, in some showy way, destroy them fully. The sheriff had loaded up an old saddlebag with tins, bread, and a canteen of water, still moving as fast as a man under fire, and now he was emptying Miller's revolver on the counter, paying no heed to how the bullets dropped and rolled off. Armpit Junior was keeping a shotgun trained on Miller, his pale face flat and without expression.

"Don't talk much, do ya?"

"He's mute," Armpit Senior said, puffing out his chest. "What you doing with this one, Sheriff?"

The sheriff shoved the emptied pistol into the saddlebag, came out from around the counter, and tossed the bag to Miller, who caught it and staggered backward under its weight.

"I'm sending him on his way."

"His way?"

"You heard me, Leg. We already have enough trouble on our hands for one night and I can't watch over this fool bit."

"Mr. Cooke won't be pleased to hear that. He killed a coach guard."

"Mr. Cooke can go fall in a well." The sheriff picked up a shotgun from the counter and waved it at the ceiling. "Go on, Miller. Git."

Miller sneered at the old men and the mute and turned for the door. "Have a fine evening, gentlemen."

The old men muttered under their whiskers and Miller

kicked his foot out, toppling the piss jar as he headed for the door.

As he fetched his horse from the livery and saddled up, Johnny Miller considered Elwood Hayes, revenge, and circling back into town. He could find bullets in that hotel across from the saloon, he could buy 'em from a broke prospector or some other rundown vagrant. It wouldn't be too hard, so long as he avoided the sheriff—men would be in their cups and less watchful. Sooner or later, the Hayes gang would attempt their big robbery and he could be there, too, waiting to get the drop on them while they were loaded up with money.

But the night was cold, the wind was starting to howl, and the men back at the general store had been acting so damn odd. Odder than any mining accident should have allowed for, odder even than men covering up murder. Elwood, curse his treacherous soul, had taught Miller to watch for such strangeness, had trained him to look for jittery hands and where a guard's eye drifted during a holdup.

If the moment ran odd, you ran, too. You tucked tail and ran and lived to rob another day.

"Plenty of gold and silver out there," Miller said to his horse, bending over in the saddle to stroke her neck, "but you've only got one life." The horse picked up speed, thinking he was trying to cajole her. Miller smiled at the wind in his face and pulled a chunk of bread from his saddlebags. They passed the edge of town and rode across the valley floor, the starlight revealing a faint, silvery trail for them to follow into the hills. Miller chewed his bread and looked at the mountains all around, swaths of pure darkness against the white dotted night sky. He felt like giving a large, mighty whoop and slapping his horse's hindquarters with his hat, running her even harder, but he held his tongue and settled for more bread, every pore in his skin breathing newfound freedom.

21

Peace settled over the Cooke house after Hollis Wells stopped his sputtering and had the good sense to expire. The National man was harder to kill than he'd looked, with more life clinging to his bones than Revis Cooke would have allowed, just looking at him. Perhaps it was living on the road that coarsened a man like that, the sun beating down all day long and the wind curing your skin until it was like hide on a cow. The stagecoach rolling along beneath you, every bump jarring the teeth in your jaw while you watched the trees for road agents, a shotgun set out across your lap.

But even hard road living was no match for a good fire iron applied with leverage and appropriate vigor.

"Isn't that right, Mr. Wells?"

Revis Cooke laughed, turning onto his side to properly view the corpse. Cooke had fallen to the floor after administering the beating, winded yet exhilarated. Even after his chest was half-caved and both forearms shattered, the National man had begged for his life. The words "no" and "please" rising from his lips like brief, useless prayers.

"But your men didn't come running to save you, did they?

All that fuss and they're probably still in that damn saloon, drinking themselves into a stupor. And tomorrow, after they wake up rough beside some faded whore, they'll stumble out into the warm light of day while you'll be stiff as a board."

Mr. Dennison wouldn't be pleased, of course. Cooke understood that. He understood that Mr. Dennison was a businessman, first and foremost, and that as a businessman he was interested in his operations (even a backwater one such as this) running as fluidly as possible. Men in the employ of National Bank, an institution which Mr. Dennison did a great volume of business, were not supposed to be reported dead after safely arriving at their destination, their bodies robustly beaten by his trusted accountant. Even if that accountant had been physically attacked, while his back was turned, for no logical reason whatsoever.

Happily, the wheels had already begun to turn in the finely tuned mind of Revis Cooke. The bludgeoning had cleared his thoughts, flushing out all the boredom and ennui of dwelling two years in Red Earth like a hard rain washing the soiled streets of San Francisco. Yes. He would lump Wells' death in with that of the other shotgun killed in the Runoff Saloon. All it would take was some coin placed in the right hand—Sheriff Atkins was a young man with a family. He'd be glad to earn some fat on the side for altering his report and testifying to the court in Rawlins. A few weeks from now, the whole messy event would be swept out the door.

Cooke crawled across the floor and brought his face near to the dead man's. The shotgun's eyes were open and aimed toward the ceiling, still wide with shock. Cooke scratched the stubble of the dead man's cheek with his fingernail, a hooked grin playing at the corner of his mouth.

"You probably thought you mattered, didn't you? You probably thought the world itself would cease when you died. That bell towers would ring out across the world as women rent their clothes, wailing your name at the top of their lungs while their children lit candles for you in the darkest, most forlorn corners of their rooms. Alas, the world has lost a glorified messenger boy! Another stagecoach guard, taken from this mortal coil too soon!"

The dead man smelled like blood but Cooke's nose had garnered other scents as well. Wells had soiled himself, filling his trousers in his death throes like a frightened infant, and several internal organs had burst as well. The gastric organs, Cooke supposed. Perhaps the spleen—that was said to process bile and other waste, was it not?

Cooke pulled himself up into a sitting position, careful to avoid the blood pooling beneath the body like a small red lake. He'd seen dead men before, but he'd never encountered one in such an intimate manner.

"I have to say, Mr. Wells, you certainly are a mess. Even compared with the dregs of humanity currently ambulating around town tonight, looking for something wet to stick their pricks into."

Revis Cooke giggled, appreciating his own joke even if the dead man could not. He reached across the shoreline of pooled blood and brushed at a curl of hair that had settled out of place on the dead man's forehead. The curly lock, matted with blood itself, had hardened and gave way reluctantly. Wells' face was actually more or less intact—by the time Cooke had finished cracking the rest of him, it was already apparent his job was complete.

Cooke licked his lips, realizing that he was thirsty, possibly as thirsty as he'd ever been in his life. He looked back at his desk, which was still piled with coins and bills. His glass of water was sitting on the desk's far edge, beside the tallying books. A long distance to cross—

Someone knocked at the front door.

Not the bashing of a drunk's fist, as you might expect from

one of the stagecoach guards, or some grimy miner come to collect his wages a day early, despite the company's firmly stated policy. No, the knocking was a soft rapping, hesitant yet eager.

"Hello?" a woman's voice called through the door. "Mr. Cooke?"

The accountant rose from his spot on the floor, groaning from the needles he felt floating in his legs. He'd been sitting on the floor longer than he'd thought, chatting with the dead man as if they were old school pals. It was strange how you felt after murdering a man, like you suddenly knew him better than anybody you'd ever known in your life.

"Mr. Cooke? It's Ingrid. Ingrid Blomvik."

"Yes, yes," Cooke called back, shaking his legs out as he went round to his desk. "Just a moment." He drank the rest of the water in his glass and poured himself another from the clay pitcher beside it. His hands were sore, the flesh tender where he'd gripped the fire iron with such ferocity. They felt more like gnarled claws than the hands of a well-educated bookkeeper.

Cooke grinned and brushed the hair from his eyes. He took his time crossing the room again, going up to the iron front door, and sliding back the view slot. A draft of cold air blew in through the slot.

"Good evening, Miss Blomvik."

"Good evening, Mr. Cooke. I hope I am not disrupting your work."

The accountant leaned closer toward the door. The Norwegian whore was standing alone on his doorstep, hands clasped together. She was dressed in a low cut dress he'd never seen before, possibly borrowed from one of the other saloon girls, and the frock revealed an enticing amount of cleavage.

"That remains to be seen, Miss Blomvik. What do you need from me?"

The whore nibbled on her plump bottom lip.

"Did you hear about the shootout, Mr. Cooke?"

"Yes. One of the coach guards was killed by some transient. A tragedy, to be certain, but the sun will still rise tomorrow."

"That was only the first," the whore said, frowning. "You haven't heard about the others?"

Cooke blinked, his eyes made teary by the wind. He recalled the exchange of the shots that had riled his visitor to the point of attack, how each dry pop had made Wells' fists ball ever tighter.

"Oh, yes. The second round of shots. How did that turn out?"

"Not well," the whore said, stepping closer to the door. "Three more guards were killed and a fourth was shot in the knee. You can hear his moaning still—we've set him up in a room for the night."

"Three more killed?"

"Yes, sir."

A throaty laugh rose from Cooke's throat. He shook his head and wiped his eyes.

"Hell's high tower. That makes for a heavy one-day loss for National Bank, doesn't it? Three more. Who killed these? Don't tell me Atkins released that hot-tempered boy from earlier."

"No, it wasn't Johnny Miller. It was his friends. They didn't take well to Miller going to jail."

A fresh gust of wind ruffled the whore's scanty dress. She shivered and hugged herself, pushing her breasts together beneath the flimsy fabric.

"Would you mind if I came inside, Mr. Cooke? It's cold out here and I'm hardly dressed for it."

Cooke stared a moment at the whore, registering the question. He looked back into the house where Hollis Wells was lying in his own blood, still quite dead. The color had drained from Wells' face, leaving it as pale as a trout's belly.

"I'm sorry, miss, but I cannot currently accept visitors."

The whore's red lips pursed into a pout, her eyes so blue and clear they dazzled even in the dim light. "Please, Mr. Cooke? I was hoping you could comfort me after the day's events. I saw three men die with my own eyes."

"Yes, I am sure that was very disconcerting, Miss Blomvik, but I'm afraid that I am not allowed to unlock this door the same evening I hear a great quantity of gunfire exchanged. As you well know, the stagecoach that arrived earlier delivered the company's payroll to my office. I cannot take any chances with its security."

The whore looked back toward the Runoff Saloon.

"But the fighting's over, sir. The men have all taken a girl and gone upstairs—they've reserved the entire second floor to celebrate their victory. They were already soused when I left."

"I am sorry, madam. I do not dictate company policy."

The whore sniffled and rubbed her shoulders. Her cheeks glowed pink from the chill—another minute and she'd catch ill.

"You're a hard man, Mr. Cooke."

The accountant nodded in agreement. A series of lewd images, most involving the Norwegian whore and the fireplace iron, flitted through his mind, each image more arousing than the next.

But he'd already indulged his base urges enough for one day, hadn't he?

"Good evening, Miss Blomvik."

Cooke closed the viewing slot with a satisfying flick of his wrist, its dark bar obscuring the whore as if she no longer existed at all. He returned to his man on the floor and nudged him with his foot.

"Did you hear that, Mr. Wells? It appears that Red Earth

does not have an affinity for men of your profession."

Cooke bent nearer to the corpse, lowering his voice to a stage whisper. "Personally, I'm beginning to think these hills do not appreciate our presence here much at all."

22

The Dennison man closed the little peek-a-boo slot in his fancy iron door. Ingrid Blomvik remained on the front steps a few moments longer, shivering and hugging her shoulders. She looked small, and young, and Elwood Hayes had never felt a stronger urge to fold a woman into his arms. He wanted to give her his own warmth, like a gift for her to have, and take all her coldness onto himself. To act as a counterweight to Revis Cooke and his strange, warbling voice that had sounded near mad.

Instead, Elwood held back in the shadows along with the other thieves.

"He's not buying it," Owen whispered, breathing too loud. "He knows we're out here waiting to pounce."

"He don't know bull," Roach Clayton whispered back. "He's like all them other stubborn company men. They follow the company line, not their peckers. The shooting scared him to ground."

They had their guns out, ready to make the rush as soon as Cooke opened his door. Clem Stubbs was back at the Runoff Saloon, drunk and resting his hurt shoulder. The plan was to take care of the accountant first, pack up the money, and hole up the night in his stone house. In the morning, once Stubbs had sobered up enough to ride, one of them would get the horses and they'd all ride out of town, hopefully before anybody, including the sheriff, caught on.

Ingrid looked toward them, three grown men peering around the corner of Cooke's house like Peeping Toms. Elwood straightened and stepped out into the front yard, waving her over. He put his gun away and signaled Owen and Roach toward the street. Ingrid crossed the yard swiftly, rubbing her arms.

"The bastard wouldn't take me in."

"It's fine. We'll go back and rethink it."

"Am I still going to get my cut?"

"Sure. You'll have a part, too."

Owen and Roach glanced at him, their eyebrows lifted. Elwood hadn't told them about Ingrid's cut yet—they thought he'd just charmed her into getting through Cooke's door. They didn't understand much about women.

"Why don't you go back to the saloon and warm yourself," Elwood said, touching Ingrid's elbow. "We'll be back shortly."

Ingrid looked from the other men to him. Her pale skin had a tint of lavender to it in the starlight.

"You gave your word, Mr. Hayes."

"I did. I will stay to it."

She broke from them after one last piercing glance and crossed the street. They watched her walk up the street and go into the saloon.

"You offered her a cut?" Roach said in wonderment. "A full cut?"

"I don't mind," Owen said. "She can have a cut of anything she wants."

"You're still off from that shootout earlier. You both are."

Elwood held his tongue. Roach may have been right. Every time he tried to think, the whore appeared in his thoughts and turned them into a swirling fog. They'd been out in the woods too long, sleeping on the ground and eating game. It made the first woman you saw in town seem an angel sent from heaven above.

South down the street, four men stepped onto the front porch of the general store and looked out into the night. One of them said something and they went down the porch steps and started up the street. They carried rifles and shotguns two or three apiece, as if going to war.

Roach whistled softly.

"Sheriff's got himself a posse."

Owen shifted from one foot to the other, a nervous habit he'd had since he'd been a little boy.

"I don't want another shootout, Elwood. And it's three against four."

The men were marching with purpose, coming up the street fast. They should have been fanning out but they kept close together, their guns pointed at angles impractical for shooting.

"Keep quiet," Elwood told the other two men. "I'll speak with them."

The men neared so you could make out faces. Sheriff Atkins was leading the posse, sure enough, but his face remained blank when he saw Elwood and the two other men standing in the street, huddled outside the Cooke house with no apparent purpose.

"Town meeting, Mr. Hayes," the sheriff called out. "We'd be pleased if you all attended."

Atkins and his posse marched past without stopping. Elwood noted the stiffness to their gait, the purpose. Something was happening beyond the normal business of a sleepy camp town. Something bigger than the shootout earlier and the dead men lying in the church.

"Should we go?" Owen asked, hopping from foot to foot.

"Might be a trap."

Elwood glanced at Roach, who shrugged and looked up the street.

"Owen, you go on back to the saloon and tell Stubbs we're heading to the meeting. If we don't come back in an hour, you boys will have to spring us free."

"Spring you free?"

"That's right. You wanted to be an outlaw, didn't you? Well, outlaws spring each other free."

Owen rubbed his hands and blew into them.

"Right. Spring you free. I'll go tell Stubbs."

They watched as the younger Hayes brother lurched down the street, shot thigh and all. Roach removed his spectacles and wiped the one good lens.

"He won't be coming to our rescue, El."

"I hope not," Elwood said, straightening his hat. "We'd all get shot then."

The lobby of the Copper Hotel was packed, with more folks assembled along the second floor railing to watch the proceedings below. Elwood and Roach managed to wedge themselves through the front door and find a place at the edge of the crowd, backed up against the hotel's front bay window. Almost as many women were in the crowd as men. They'd gathered around Sheriff Atkins, who'd raised his hand for silence, and shouted questions about the miners still not back from their shift. Atkins made no effort to respond, simply holding his hand in the air like a school boy waiting to be called upon. Gone was the puffed lawman Elwood had encountered earlier—there was no strut to the way he held himself this evening, no cocky gleam to his eyes.

Eventually, the sheriff's gesture for quiet worked, as eerie and uncommon as it was, and the shouted questions trailed off into silence. Atkins lowered his arm and looked around the room.

"You all aren't going to like what I'm going to tell you, but it's the truth. Leg Jameson and his boy will tell you the same as I'm about to."

Atkins crossed his arms.

"They unearthed something in the Dennison Mine. Something wicked."

The crowd broke into a racket again, everybody turning toward their neighbor to shoot off their mouth. Atkins waited out the first wave of yammering and shouted over the second.

"It killed the miners down there. All of them. It killed Hank Chambers, too, when we tried to seal the mine."

The racket tripled this time, louder than a dozen hens crammed into a barrel with a hungry fox. Elwood and Roach glanced at each other, wondering at this news and whether it would help or hinder their own scheming. The crowd shouted a barrage of questions until Sheriff Atkins, lips tightening, took out his pistol and fired it into the air, causing the folks along the hotel's second floor railing to start and draw back.

"We don't have time for jawing and hair pulling. If we're going to live out the night we need as many men armed as possible. If you've got a gun, make sure it's loaded and ready to fire. We blew the mine shut, but it broke out anyway. Burrowed right through the loose rock."

"But what is it?" a man called out. "Bear?"

The sheriff shook his head and holstered his pistol.

"No. Not a bear. Looks like a human, but its skin is burnt up and it's got hands like claws. Hank Chambers called it the Charred Man."

A thoughtful silence fell over the crowd as everyone tried to picture this creature in their own minds. Hayes tried to figure it himself.

"That's why you blew the mine shut?" a man on the second floor called down. "Because you're 'fraid of a goddamn critter?"

The sheriff looked toward his critic on the second floor. Elwood noticed a disturbance in the crowd at the far back of the room, in front of the hotel's kitchen door. It looked like somebody had stumbled and taken a few others down with them. Then a woman screamed, and the crowd turned into a scrambling, hollering mass as something charged through it.

Elwood stepped up on the bay window's sill for a better view. He saw a spray of blood erupt like water from a geyser and a tall, soot-colored man clawing his way through the crowd, tossing bodies like a farmer harvesting wheat. Elwood looked down to Roach, whose mouth had dropped open.

"Well, I reckon that's what a demon looks like."

Most of the town, except the dead miners, was in the Copper Hotel when the Charred Man entered. Men, women, and a handful of children surged back in terror as he tore among them, slashing at their vulnerable spots with his clawed hands, crushing their skulls as if they were made of eggshells. The crowd trampled each other in their mad terror and clogged the hotel's two exits. The few armed men fired their weapons without having the time or proper stance to do so—elbows flew into their backs, tossed bodies sailed at their knees—and their shots went wide, missing the Charred Man and hitting other folks instead. When the armed men tried to reload, their shaking fingers failed them and the Charred Man knocked away their guns and fell upon them with uncanny strength.

For the second instance that day, time slowed for Elwood Hayes. The crowd, wild as it was, receded into the shadows of his vision as he focused upon the unnatural thing in their midst. It was shaped like a man, with arms and legs, but it wore the form like an ill-fitting skin. A damaged skin—somehow the creature had been badly burned, but it'd been too stubborn and unnatural to die.

The creature lifted a man off his feet, bit into his neck,

and ripped out his throat. Amid the spray of arterial blood, Hayes noticed patches of clammy white poking through the creature's blackened skin.

The Charred Man was growing himself a new hide, like a snake.

"God almighty," Hayes shouted above the din, reaching behind his back and removing his revolver from its holster. "Roach, try and aim for the white spots. They might be weaker."

"Hell," Roach shouted back, leveling his gun and spreading his feet. "I think we're just going to rile it further."

Roach Clayton was right. They emptied their pistols at the Charred Man, but either they missed him as he whirled about or the bullets had no effect. He kept tearing through the crowd, knocking folks down and going at them. The hotel's floor was covered in bodies and gore and, as they watched, a scrambling fat man, not minding himself, stepped onto an infant as she lay flailing, caving her chest in as he plowed mindlessly forward.

"Nothing we can do," Roach said, grabbing Elwood's arm. "You saw how those shots didn't do nothing."

At the back of the room, two women fought over a pistol until it went off, shooting a third woman in the back. The shot woman dropped to her knees and keeled over while the other two kept up the fight.

"We need to git," Roach shouted in his ear. "Right now."

Elwood turned to his friend, his mind still fogged. Roach's eyes darted in their sockets like hummingbirds. Behind him, the hotel's bay window reflected the whole bloody scene. The smell of piss and blood and smoke filled the room, a scent somewhere between slaughterhouse and coal fire.

Elwood shrugged off the fog and raised his pistol above his head.

"Mind your eyes, Roach."

The bay window shattered beautifully as Elwood brought

the butt of his gun down on the wide and expensive pane, closing his eyes as shards of glass laced the air. A cold draft of air rolled into the room. They jumped over the windowsill and into the night, already running as they touched the ground. Elwood sprinted with his head down, as if he was being shot at, and when he looked to his side he saw Roach doing the same. The juiced feel of escaping after a robbery had come over him, shooting through his veins like heat lightning. "Runoff," Elwood shouted, though they were both already headed there anyhow. He could see his brother standing on the saloon's front porch, looking confused in the spill of torchlight.

Elwood pulled up at the porch, gasping. Owen stepped down.

"Good hell, brother. What's happening over there?"

Elwood turned to look at the hotel. Folks were breaking windows on the second floor and jumping out while the Charred Man, a choppy blur, swept behind them. Those who'd managed to escape stood scattered in the street, watching like he was. Several had fallen to the ground, badly hurt, and their moans competed with the cries inside the hotel. Nobody seemed to know where to go or what to do.

Owen came over and stood beside him. Roach was bent over beside the saloon's porch, dry heaving.

"What is it, El? What?"

Elwood took a breath and tried to pull the strands of his mind together. A light was snuffed out on the hotel's second floor, then another. More screams erupted behind the broken windows—tortured, ugly screams. He was still holding his pistol upside down, his hand frozen around it.

"We had a meeting," Elwood said, finding his voice. "We had a meeting and a demon showed up."

Roach heaved again as more lights were snuffed out and the hotel's entire second floor went dark. The screams came less frequent now, but Elwood could hear a repeated snapping that reminded him of breaking dried branches for kindling.

"A demon?" Owen said, turning a shade paler than he already was. "Like preachers go on about?"

"That's right, little brother. And he's an ugly son-of-a-bitch, too."

Elwood holstered his gun, climbed up onto the saloon's porch, and turned to the folks in the street. "You want to live, get in here right now," he hollered. "You see somebody hurt, carry them along."

Heads slowly turned his way, each lost in their own fog.

"You tarry, you die."

23

He'd tried. He'd tried to warn everybody, to let them know what the town was dealing with. He'd called a meeting and brought all the guns and asked Leg and Henry Jameson to guard the hotel's front door and Butch Hastings and Larry Nolan to guard the back. He'd spoken loudly and with purpose, like he'd been a lawman for twenty years instead of just two, and he hadn't taken any bull about any of it. He'd done everything within his worldly powers that he could.

But the Charred Man had still come calling. Too fast and too strong and now they were all dying, dead, or about to die, and you couldn't blame Milo Atkins for running for home. No sir, nobody could blame him for that. Not the groaning man he'd just passed, crawling in the dirt with his guts torn out, or the woman who was just standing there in the middle of the street, covered head-to-toe in blood and mumbling to herself as if speaking in tongues.

At a time like this, a man needed to look after his family.

He'd known they were in for it when the faces around him changed from confused and angry to surprised, plumb surprised, like all the steam in them had leaked out all of a sudden. He'd known before he heard the screams at the back of the room, before the first bone snapped and the smell of burnt flesh reached his nose. He'd known and he'd recalled the face of Hank Chambers, covered in grime and furious at the sheriff's disbelief.

Luckily, belief was not a problem for Atkins anymore. Soon as he realized the meeting was over, and more folks were about to die, a lot of folks, he'd ducked low and sprinted through the room, barreling his way through the crowd before any of them could think to do the same. He'd been the first out the door, in fact, and had tripped over the bodies of Leg and Henry Jameson on the Copper Hotel's front porch.

Their eyes bulged from their sockets, almost popped all the way out, and black bruises circled both their necks. Atkins imagined the Charred Man lifting them off the ground, one in each clawed hand, and squeezing the breath from them until their feet stopped kicking and their bowels loosened, Leg falling as mute as his son.

"I'm sorry, fellas," Atkins said, scrambling to his feet. "You did your duty as best you could."

The screaming started in earnest inside the hotel. The first couple of escapees burst out of the hotel and tripped over the Jamesons, as Atkins had done. They fell hard, before they could brace themselves for the impact. Atkins moved to help them up, but suddenly more folks sprinted out, knocking him into those he was trying to help, and then a third wave of escapees added to the heap, the whole tangle of folks roaring in terror. Atkins cursed the pile at the top his lungs, picturing his wife and boy weeping over his grave.

At last, a few sensible heads prevailed and the heap began

to untangle itself. Atkins extracted himself from the crush and started pulling others out as well, grabbing any hand he found outstretched and pulling with his heels dug in.

"Settle yourselves," he shouted, recalling himself and his position in town. "Everybody cool off and we'll get you safe."

The shouting helped. The pile was unpiled, each person freed staggering to his feet and running off into the dark.

It wasn't so simple in the hotel's doorway, though. Big Reggie Stills had somehow gotten himself wedged sideways against the doorframe, like he'd been running for the door, tripped, and fallen that way, only to have the surge of folks behind him press him into the frame before he could right himself. Atkins couldn't see Reggie's shoulders or legs—only his round gut, protruding through the door as the crush of folks shoved into his spine, bowing it out.

Big Reggie's screams were something special, even compared to those coming from further inside the hotel. Two men, still on their feet, were crammed right behind Reggie, their faces reddening from the forces working at their own backs. Atkins took a breath, figuring the problem. He picked up Leg Jameson's shotgun, checked to see if it was still loaded, and fired both barrels into Reggie's gut, aiming right where his body was bent the most.

A scattering of insides flew into the air. Big Reggie screamed double, his whole body shaking. Atkins wiped the mess of pulp off his face, picked up the other shotgun, and emptied it into about the same spot. This time Reggie split open, snapping like a branch bowed too far. The two men behind him fell through the doorway, landed flat on their faces, and were trampled under by a dozen more folks scrambling for their freedom.

Those at the back of this group were caught by the demon at their heels and yanked back into the hotel, howling murder. Atkins removed his pistol from its holster, fired all six rounds into the hotel without taking particular aim, and took off at a sprint, relinquishing his role as the town sheriff right then and there.

He slowed to a walk, his side burning. The north side of Red Earth seemed quiet and strange after what Atkins had seen downtown. The cabins and shacks were dark. No lamps burning, no squabbling, no cries of rough lovemaking. Only a few whip-thin dogs, curled and sleeping against shut front doors as they waited for dinner scraps.

Atkins prayed his wife was home. He looked up at the stars and begged them from the pit of his stomach. He hadn't seen Violet at the meeting but everything had happened so fast, so fast and then the Charred Man had appeared, tossing folks left and right. His wife might have been at the meeting the whole time, holding Billy by the hand and waiting to speak to him.

Atkins broke into a run again as he reached the north end of town.

"Vi? You home, Vi?"

A light was burning in their cabin. A shadow moved behind the window and Atkins felt his heart bump.

"Hey!"

The door opened. Two figures, one tall and one short, stepped out into the night. The shorter one dove forward and tackled Atkins around the waist.

"Pa!"

Atkins grabbed the boy and lifted him into the air, sending his little feet swinging. He hugged him to his chest and breathed in the fresh hay scent of his hair.

"What are they having downtown?" Violet asked. "Some kind of miner's ball?"

Atkins took another breath, savoring it, and looked at his wife. Violet had her white apron on and her hair tied back with a ribbon. "We heard the blasting earlier," she said. "They find a new seam of copper along with those killed miners? Is that why they're so riled up tonight? Billy said there was gunfire in the saloon."

Atkins set his son down and pushed him toward the cabin.

"Go inside, Billy."

"We ate supper without you, Pa."

"That's fine, Billy. Go on in."

Atkins took his wife in his arms. He nuzzled her neck and kissed its softness. He could feel her smiling, even with his eyes closed. An owl hooted up in the hills and the wind rustled the pine trees. She tasted like salt with a faded bit of soap to it. He wondered what his father was doing back in Wichita tonight, if the ornery old lawman would ever believe the stories that came back to him from this small company town.

"I love you, Violet," Atkins told his wife, cupping her narrow shoulders with both his hands. "I sure do."

24

Father Lynch fought against waking, even as the noise next-door rose to a babbling clamor. He'd only slept long enough to enter a deeper phase of sleep—the gin he'd drunk before retiring still warmed his blood, soothing, and the feather down in his pillow was soft and yielding beneath his skull. He'd lived in Red Earth long enough to expect additional noise on a Saturday eve, the one night the miners would be allowed to sleep in the following day, and whatever was happening at the Copper Hotel reached him only as a natural attendant to the usual revelries.

Until the gunshots and the screams. They roused him from bed as if he'd been fired from a cannon, sending him stumbling across his dark room in bewilderment. For a moment he could not recall where he was, or what time it might be, and listened at stiff attention as more screams filled the night, wondering if he'd gone mad.

A new round of gunfire rang out—shotgun blasts, one followed shortly by another, and then six rapid shots from a revolver. Lynch rubbed the sleep from his face and yawned.

"Lord. Another brawl?"

The priest searched the floor for his pants and shoes. He slipped the pants on one leg at a time, struggling to keep his balance, and sat back on the cot to put on his shoes. He took his time with the lacing, his vexation rising as he grew more alert. Sixty-two was too old to be woken so abruptly to such noise. Really, any age was too old to be woken so rudely. If the sheriff couldn't keep the miners reasonably in line perhaps it was time the camp found herself a new sheriff. One less given to strutting and primping, somebody with a seasoned voice and the respect of hard men.

The floorboards creaked beneath his weight as Father Lynch opened the door to the sanctuary and strode down the aisle, still buttoning his shirt. The gunshots and the screams had both died off, as if he'd been dreaming them all along. Lynch opened the back door, winced at the chill, and stepped outside. As he came round the church's south side, he halted in his tracks—bodies lay piled around the Copper Hotel, both on its front porch and beneath its shattered front window. The upper floor was totally dark and, as Father Lynch watched, the last light on the first floor was snuffed out as well.

Lynch crossed himself and turned his head. Across the street, the Runoff Saloon was shuttered and dark and the street before it was littered with bodies lying face down or upon their sides. In fact, a woman had fallen only a few yards from the church, her neck torn open and one arm outstretched toward the church as if in supplication.

The priest searched his mind for some possible explanation for all this, something to do with the violence earlier that day, but could find none. He wanted to call out, to step into the street and see to the fallen, but instinct held him back in the shadow of the church and told him to wait a moment.

He did not have to wait long. A tall, spindly man stepped through the Copper Hotel's doorway and tilted his head toward the night sky, listening. The spindly man's posture was strange, both stiff and slightly off-kilter, and he wore ill-fitting clothes as well—his white shirt sagged off his shoulders and his overlarge pants billowed around his legs. Lynch shivered, glad the wind was blowing toward him, and then wondered at his gladness.

Perhaps it was the stranger's hands. The right was much larger than the left, the fingers elongated and almost claw-like, like the pinchers of a crab. Was this because of a sickness of some kind? A defect of birth?

The stranger lowered his chin and scanned the street. He had a large, scab-like patch on his cheek—the scab appeared to grow and recede in size steadily, as if it had a pulse of its own.

The priest's breath caught in his chest.

This man was the reason for the gunshots and the screams. This stranger was the cause of the dead lying in the street.

Father Lynch forced his body to stillness while the tall stranger turned his gaze toward the church. He did not wonder if the porch's shadows shielded him from the stranger's gaze or pray to the Lord to be passed over. He stopped thinking altogether. He was an emptiness...

until...

finally...

the stranger turned away again, heading south down the street, his stride awkward and unsure, as if he were still learning to use his spindly legs.

Father Lynch remained immobile until the stranger disappeared into the dark. Then, and only then, did he allow himself to breath once more, to slip slowly back into the church and lock the door behind him.

25

None of the girls came back from the town meeting. They'd all gone, all of them, hoping for excitement and gossip, and they'd wanted Ingrid to go along. They'd gotten all fancied up in their best going-to-town clothes, like proper ladies, with their hair combed and ribboned and their mouths rinsed with salted water. They'd all gone and begged her to come along, too. "I do not believe anything can be accomplished by men, or by any meeting involving men," she'd told them, still stung by Revis Cooke's rejection. "You ladies go on without me."

Anita and Gertrude and Sarah and Ruth and Elizabeth and Agnes and Alexandra and Rachel and Daphne and Odette and Grace and even Madam Petrov, the old iron-skinned Russian herself, hadn't made it back from the doings at the Copper Hotel. Ingrid had a hard time imagining anything, man or bear or haunt, tougher than that woman—Madam Petrov drank nothing but hot black tea that tasted like tar, ate nothing but meat and potatoes, and could haul a keg of beer on her shoulder like it was a scrap of cloud.

Now it was only her and Caleb left to run things. Well, her and Caleb and Elwood Hayes, who'd taken over while everybody else looked about the saloon stupefied and shocked. He ordered the folks who were badly hurt to be taken to rooms on the first floor and everybody else to start stacking furniture against the saloon's front and back doors. He'd nailed the wood down as best he could, both into the walls and the floor. He also had Caleb turn all the lanterns low and shutter the windows—Ingrid had never seen a man so unsettled and sure of himself at the same time.

When all the moving and hammering was over, she came up beside Elwood and touched his elbow.

"You think he's going to leave us be if we keep the lights down low?"

"I don't know. Never dealt with a demon before. Their reasoning is as strange to me as any woman's."

Ingrid smiled and met his eyes. "We're not that hard to figure, Mr. Hayes. We just want fair treatment and a look now and then."

"I'll keep that in mind, Miss Blomvik."

"Actually, I'm Mrs. Blomvik, Mr. Hayes. I was married once, but he passed on a few years back."

"Is that so? I'm sorry to hear that."

Ingrid looked across the room at the three miner wives, all of them newly minted widows, who were sitting in a circle, pale with shock and drinking coffee without a table between them. Counting the widows and four prospectors who'd been lodging at the Copper, they numbered twelve healthy bodies on the saloon floor and five wounded in the rooms, including the National man Elwood had shot in the knee. Everyone else in town had either scattered back to their cabins or had already been killed.

Ingrid crossed her arms, frowning at the furniture nailed to the walls.

"I'm going to be seeing my husband soon enough, I suppose."

Elwood curled his arm around her shoulders and smiled. "Naw. We'll get this figured, sooner or later."

"Like we figured robbing Mr. Cooke?"

Elwood laughed.

"Well, there's no accounting for a company man. Once they've swallowed the hook, you can't get them off the line for anything."

Ingrid leaned closer into Elwood. She liked his strong arm around her shoulder, his warmth.

"How long—"

"They're dead," somebody shouted, making everybody in the room jump. It was Owen Hayes, as pale and glassy-eyed as anybody she'd ever seen, even the girls she'd known who'd taken laudanum.

"The three folks wounded at the Copper are dead. Their wounds turned black."

Elwood took his arm back and crossed the room.

"What about Stubbs? Is Stubbs dead?"

"Hell no, I ain't dead." Clem Stubbs stepped through the doorway to the hall, keeling to the side a bit and holding his wounded shoulder with his good hand. "I'm soused as hell, though."

Stubbs exhaled loudly, rumbling his lips together like a horse. His hat had gotten lost somewhere and his red hair was a tangled and wild as his beard—he reminded Ingrid of an overgrown lilac bush.

"You should be in bed, Stubbs," Elwood said, fetching a chair and lowering the big man into it. "That shoulder will howl at you for a week."

"Let it howl. Besides, how's a man supposed to sleep with all that hammering?" Stubbs nodded at the tables they'd thrown over the doors and windows. "Looks like a poor attempt at the Alamo."

"This is the Alamo," Elwood allowed. "Our own."

Elwood told Clem Stubbs about what'd happened since they'd pried the bullet from his shoulder, occasionally looking to Owen or Roach Clayton to confirm what he was saying. The whole room listened to Elwood talk, like they were hearing the story for the first time themselves, and when he finished it was so quiet you could hear the wind outside. The story seemed just as wild to Ingrid as she heard it for a second time, like something out of a tall tales book you read to children before bed.

"Jesus, that's something," Clem Stubbs said, scratching his bearded cheek. "That reminds me of the skin-walkers the Navajos talk about." Elwood glanced around the room.

"Skin-walkers?"

"Yup, except they're more like witches. They can turn themselves into animals when they feel like it. Bears and wolves and such. That Charred Man doesn't sound like any kind of animal I ever seen."

"Maybe he was a skin-walker a long time back," Owen said, "but the Indians in these parts found him out."

"Or maybe he's a pure demon," one of the widows said, staring into her coffee cup. "Sent by the Devil to take us all to Hell."

The room was quiet another moment, till Stubbs laughed.

"Well, if that's so, I'm not going easy. How many guns have we got, El?"

"We tried shooting him already," Roach said, his voice soft and far away. "Elwood told you that part."

"You must have missed him, that's all. Look at those sorry spectacles you're wearing."

Roach sighed and looked at the ceiling. One of the widows shifted on her chair, making it creak. They all looked her way.

"We just need to figure this out," Elwood said. "Anything can be figured if you chew on it long enough."

The night passed slowly in the dim light of the turned-down lamps. Four times they heard a scream outside, but none of them lasted long. The men checked and rechecked their guns, making sure what little they had was loaded and ready. Elwood, Clem, Roach, and Owen each had a revolver, Caleb the scatter gun he kept under the bar, and Ingrid the small one-shot pistol she'd found in Madam Petrov's dresser. Elwood had placed the armed men so that each faced a corner of the room, with their backs to the bar and a second man at their side to help keep them awake. The widows had gathered up their own chairs and set them behind the bar counter, so that when they sat again only their heads showed above the bar. Ingrid sat on the landing halfway up the stairs, with the one-shot in her lap and a good view of the saloon floor.

Elwood Hayes didn't sit, though. He kept pacing the room and bothering the furniture they'd nailed across the windows and doors, testing it for weakness and muttering to himself. He was like a dog chewing its tail, wondering at the pain but still willing to give it another try. Everybody watched him cross back and fourth like he was a stage show, hoping that every pursing of his lips hinted at a breakthrough, at a thought nobody else had come up with yet. Something good to save their lives.

Right at one A.M., the coach guard with the shot knee woke in his room, bellowed his pain and confusion, and passed out again. "Jesus," Clem Stubbs said, shuddering. "I think I need to start drinking again. I can handle my shoulder—it's the waiting that's special agony."

"I'll go check on him," one of the widows said, rising from her chair. She looked at her two friends in a meaningful way, wringing her hands. They both sighed and agreed to go with her.

"Thank you," Elwood said, going round the bar again. "I appreciate that."

Owen Hayes turned in his chair to look at his brother. "What about upstairs, El? What about the windows in those bedrooms?"

"I shuttered those, too," Caleb said, yawning and stretching out his arms. "Locked them tight."

"But they're not boarded, are they?"

"No," Caleb admitted. "I didn't get to that."

"I'll do it," Elwood said. "You stay with Roach and Clem and see to it nothing gets through down here."

"Yes, sir," Owen said, straightening in his chair and snapping his hand in mock salute. "Yes, sir, Mr. High and Mighty General, sir!"

Elwood ignored the sass and made up a pile of boards, setting a hammer on top of the pile and jamming a fistful of nails into his pocket. He was relieved to have something to focus on, something that wasn't pacing round the room and figuring. He picked up the stack of boards and started for the stairway.

Ingrid rose on the landing and smoothed the front of her dress. "I can help," she said. "I'll hold the boards."

The stairs creaked as Elwood climbed the first flight. "Could use the help, now that you mention it."

The outlaw set the boards at the top of the stairs and drew his gun. "You hear anything funny, run back down and call the others."

"What—"

"Wait here a moment."

And like that he was headed down the hall and opening the door to the first room, gun at the ready. He poked his head in, looked around, and stepped back.

"Still empty, shutters locked."

"Well, I am glad to hear that—"

He was already gone again, poking his head into the second

room. He said the same thing when he came out of that room, too, and five rooms after that. His mind seemed to work like a train, moving steadily, sure, but one track at a time. After the last room, he picked up the hammer and some of the boards.

"He's not up here. Not yet, anyhow."

Ingrid nodded. Hayes took out a handful of nails from his pocket and hefted them in his hand.

"Well, let's start down at that first room."

"Sure. You're the carpenter, Mr. Hayes."

They didn't have much light to work with, only what came from downstairs. The first room, like all the others in the Runoff Saloon, had only one window, neither large nor small, which a board could easily be fitted across.

"This was Madam Petrov's room."

Elwood stuck a few nails in his teeth. Ingrid held the board across the window and he hammered a nail into the board's upper right corner, taking only two knocks to send it home.

"Smells like powders and perfume in this room."

"They all smell like that here," Ingrid said, shifting her grip on the board. "Except Caleb's, I suppose."

Elwood hammered a second nail into the board's upper left corner.

"Madam Petrov was scared of smelling like an old woman," Ingrid said, releasing the board and letting it hang on its own. "And she only fifty."

Elwood grunted, holding on to his thoughts. Ingrid blew a puff of warm air into her bangs.

"You think we're going to die tonight, Mr. Hayes?"

"Can't say, but I hope not. Haven't raised near enough hell to suit me. Figure I got a good ten more years in me yet."

Ingrid smiled and got a second board ready. When they'd boarded the window tight they moved on to the other rooms.

They took their time, doing the job well. Ingrid went to the railing and checked on the saloon a few times, but nothing had changed down there except the widows had fallen asleep behind the bar, wrapped in blankets and huddled together. When they finished boarding the last window, the one in her own bedroom, Ingrid came up and hugged Elwood Hayes from behind. He stiffened at her touch, then exhaled and leaned into her grasp. She hugged him tighter, squeezing her eyes shut.

"I don't want Revis Cooke to be the last man I shared a bed with, Mr. Hayes."

"That so?"

"Yes, sir. It is."

They stood like that for a long moment, with her arms around him, both wavering slightly on their feet, as if they could fall in about any direction. He turned and she let him go, opening her eyes. He was a dark outline against a darker room, a hammer swinging loose from his hand.

"You're a lovely woman, Mrs. Blomvik. A pure beauty."

She flushed at the compliment. He leaned down and kissed her, his lips rough and cracked. She reached up and laced her hands behind his neck, drawing him toward her, and returned his kiss with a longer, more open one. A heat she barely recalled rose into her cheeks, something she had not thought she'd feel again. Not after putting Erik in the ground like that, dressed in his black Sunday best, a bouquet of cattails and sunflowers clutched between his stiffened fingers. The heat that drew you to a man like a pull you had no control over.

She closed the door and lifted her dress over her head, pulling the cotton over her breasts and head in one swift, fluid motion, leaving her standing in her slip alone. Elwood reached behind his back, pulled out his gun, and set it carefully on the dresser.

"Should keep that handy."

Ingrid smiled and reached for his belt, unbuckling it. She pulled down his trousers and he wavered on his feet again, stepping out of the pants one leg at a time.

"You ladies don't fuss around, do you?"

"We don't get paid for fussing, generally."

She ran her hands up his right leg, then the left. She ran her hands over the bulge in his drawers and slipped them beneath his shirt. She took that off, too, lifting the fabric over his head and pulling it off his hands. She kissed his chest, making him shiver as she took his right nipple in her mouth and bit down, softly.

"Mercy."

His hands cupped her ass and squeezed. Ingrid felt the silken fabric of her slip rub against her skin and the warmth in his clutching fingertips. She remembered Minnesota in May, the last of the snow finally melting and the budding trees and the chilled but warming days, the farmers planting in the fields, shouting their oxen on. The dogs running unchecked across the farm, eager to scent it all, and the cats yowling in heat. The roughness of the straw on her bare back, the feel of Erik Blomvik on her body and between her legs and the knots in the wood above and the loft, creaking, while her mother was out there somewhere, working at something. She recalled how everything seemed to have excitement about it, even the long visits to their neighbors, how the future was somehow both likely and unlikely at the same time.

Elwood lifted her slip off as she pulled down his drawers. They moved to the bed at the same moment and Ingrid lay beneath him, kissing at every inch she could reach. His body had such warmth to it, and felt so good.

Afterward, they lay naked beneath the covers, watching the crack of light that shone beneath the door. Ingrid had burrowed her blond head into the crook of Elwood's arm, draping one arm and one leg across him, enjoying the hot pulse coming from her loins.

"Hard to believe I went so long without it."

Elwood shifted beneath her, turning his head.

"Without it?"

"Without enjoying it, I mean."

Elwood exhaled and she could hear the wind leave his lungs. She could hear his heartbeat as well, and the gurgling down in his stomach.

"Must be hard, lying with men you don't feel for. You must have to make yourself go blank, like when you need to shoot somebody."

"It is. And toads like Revis Cooke don't make it any easier, believe me. Even the lightest touch from him is like ice."

Ingrid squeezed Elwood harder, warding off the memories. He kissed her forehead and touched her hair. "You're done with all that. No matter what happens from here on out, you're done with that."

Ingrid nuzzled deeper into Elwood's chest, trying the idea out in her mind. She was done. Done with all that.

"Goddamn."

Elwood bolted up in bed, causing her head to slide off his chest and drop to the mattress.

"Fire."

Ingrid sat up beside him, letting the sheet drop from her breasts.

"What?"

"Fire, sweetheart. What we need is fire."

26

Safely tucked away in his house, Revis Cooke listened to the screams, shots, and hollering that rose throughout Red Earth, sounding as if they were rising up from some ancient, black-hearted place. As the town shrieked and shot itself into drunken fragments, Revis looked at the dead National man on the floor and felt assured that whatever was going on tonight was far larger than the death of one man, an unimportant man who would not be greatly missed, and it set his feverish mind at ease.

For the past few hours, he'd been counting and recounting the payroll for the Dennison Mining Company and wondering how far he could get, and for how long he could live, on $2,810. About seven years salary for an average working man, wasn't it? He wouldn't live like a king, or even a politician, but a savvy individual with few expenses could get along well enough on such a sum, at least until such time they relocated to a new environment, such as New York City, that more favorably suited their disposition.

"What do you think, Mr. Wells? Should I abscond from this ghastly place and start anew?"

Flies buzzed about the dead man's face, intrigued. How they'd gotten into the house was a mystery to Cooke, who kept the windows shut and locked no matter the weather outside. He bore no great love for insects, birds, bats, or rodents. Their place was out of doors, his was in.

Cooke rose from his chair and circled round his desk. "Did you ever think of a comparable plan, Mr. Wells? The temptation must have been great, I am certain. Thundering about in that stagecoach of yours, loaded down with lockboxes. All that money riding with you, quite close yet quite out of reach. Out of your reach, I should say. You were allowed to carry it, yes, but you were paid the same meager wages any delivery boy is paid, and if you would have taken a single dollar for yourself they would have strung you from the highest tree."

Cooke laughed and bent over the corpse.

"You must have dreamt about that money as you drifted in and out of sleep, Mr. Wells. Perched on top of your jouncing coach, yearning for hot food and hoping to make the next town in good time—that money must have haunted you as much as any beautiful, untouchable woman."

The lake of blood had congealed around the dead man, creating a sticky surface similar to the covering of skin on a pail of milk. When the flies landed on it, their weight was so insignificant that they were able to walk across it, like Jesus striding across the Sea of Galilee. Unable to restrain his curiosity, Cooke poked his finger through the blood skin and took a sounding. "One-eighths of an inch, I'd say," he said, holding his blood stained finger toward the lantern light. "By morning, the whole lake will be dried through."

Cooke examined the dead man's face. His skin had taken on a decidedly purplish hue, as if he'd been strangled to death and not bludgeoned with a fire iron. Yet, perhaps Wells had been strangled, in a way. His chest and ribs had taken a fierce beating—one of those ribs, which had snapped with such a pleasing crack, could have pierced his lungs, causing him to suffocate from the inside out.

"Was that it? Was that what killed you, sir?"

Cooke placed his knees onto the floor and crawled forward, so that his face hovered inches above the dead man's. He could feel the chill of death rising off the skin. Transfixed, he lowered his head and kissed the dead man's purple lips with his own, parting them with his tongue and breathing hot air into the lifeless mouth.

When he drew back, Cooke's entire body was vibrating, as if strung through with electric current. The flies buzzed about his face, now drawn to him as well. The wind had dropped outside. The town was quiet.

"Your taste, Mr. Wells. It—"

Someone pounded loudly at the door. Cooke exhaled, his gaze still fixed upon the dead man.

The visitor pounded again.

"Just a moment."

Cooke reluctantly rose from the floor and brushed off his knees and shirt, his heart thumping in his chest. An image of a dark river filled his mind, its coal-black waters flowing rapidly along its curving, serpentine banks—

The visitor pounded a third time, louder still.

"Yes, yes," Cooke shouted, striding to the door and opening the viewing slot. "What is it?"

He expected Ingrid Blomvik on his front step, back again to mew for attention. Or perhaps Sheriff Atkins, hat in hand with some fresh tale of mining camp stupidity ready for the telling.

Instead, the figure on his step was a stranger, one as tall as Cooke himself. The stranger's face was a pale outline in the dark (how had it gotten so dark? Even in the middle of the night, the Copper Hotel and the Runoff Saloon habitually left a few lamps burning). The stranger's eyes, sunk back, were two black slits, his mouth was a tight line above his pointed chin. Black patches, scab-like, spotted his cheeks and forehead.

Revis Cooke frowned, a new current of thrill arcing through his shoulders and into his gut.

"Cooke," the stranger said in a low, rasping voice.

"Yes, what is it? What do you want?"

The stranger closed his eyes and a slight, curling smile rose on his lips. The accountant flinched and stepped back from the viewing slot. The smell of burnt meat had seeped in through the door, fouling the air.

"Go home," Cooke shouted through the slot. "Go home, drunkard, and sleep off whatever rot you've been swilling!"

The accountant slammed the viewing slot shut and stepped back, his chest heaving. Somehow the stranger had managed to unnerve him. What had happened to the ruckus outside, the hooting and hollering? It wasn't that late—only one in the morning. Usually the stoutest drunks lasted well past two, especially on a Saturday night.

Cooke looked at Hollis Wells lying on the floor. The dead man suddenly appeared so obvious, so nakedly exposed. What had he been thinking, allowing the National man's body to remain in the middle of the room like this? They would catch him, he would be found out. He'd killed a man in rage and would now be punished for his brute indulgences.

"This is what you wanted, isn't it, Mr. Wells? Did you somehow call out to this prying stranger and bring him to my door?"

A fresh pounding on the door, each blow reverberating through the house.

"That door is made of iron," Cooke called out. "Pound all you like, but I'm not opening it."

A rain of blows pummeled the door. A buckled dent appeared in the door's surface as it strained inward against its hinges. The accountant picked the fire iron off the floor—it was still covered in the National man's blood and felt solid in his hand.

"I am warning you, sir—"

One mighty, concussive blow and the door tore from its frame, whistling through the air and sailing inches above Cooke's head. He froze in mid-sentence, stunned silent as the door struck the rear of the house and clanged to the floor. A gust of cold, smoky air blew into the building and ruffled the stacked bills on his desk.

The stranger stepped inside through the open doorway, his scabbed face blank as he studied the body of Hollis Wells.

Cooke licked his lips and squeezed the fire iron's handle.

"This building is the property of the Dennison Mining Company. Not only are you attacking me, sir, you are attacking its interests."

The stranger smiled insolently and stepped forward on his long, bony legs. He spread his arms apart and raised his palms.

"Revis Cooke, you are but a drop in the ocean."

The accountant stiffened, feeling the white heat of his earlier rage returning. Cooke charged across the room, swinging the iron with every sinew in his body, certain of victory. Then he was lying on the floor beside Hollis Wells, gazing upward as something warm pooled beneath him.

27

They did not tell the boy about the Charred Man. Billy, only seven-years-old, frightened easily, and nothing good would come from adding another boogey man to the forest of nightmares that rose up each night beneath his bed. The encampment of Red Earth was already filled with enough terror for one night—terror you could feel in the air and hear in the occasional distant scream.

Milo Atkins did not explain the blood. He simply stripped down to his underwear and threw his stained, pulp-flecked clothes into the fire and stood there, watching them catch fire and burn through.

Violet came up beside him and set a kettle of water over the fire.

"Should heat shortly."

Atkins looked over his shoulder. Billy was sitting at the kitchen table, playing with his straw dolls.

"Are you hungry, Milo? There's soup left."

An image of Big Reggie wedged in the Copper Hotel's doorway came unwelcomed to Atkins' mind.

"No. I'm not hungry."

Violet touched the small of his back and it was all he could do not to flinch.

"That bad?"

"Yes. It was."

Billy murmured something at the table and made crashing noises with his mouth. Atkins picked up his holster from where he'd dropped it on the floor and brought it over to the table, sitting down across from his son. He drew out the pistol and spun the chamber open. It was empty.

"That's right," he said aloud. "I fired them all before I tucked tail and ran."

Billy looked up from his dolls.

"You ran, Papa?"

"Yes, sir. I did. Like a scared rabbit."

Billy smiled and made his dolls bounce along the table, their dry straw legs crunching on the wood.

"Rabbit, rabbit, rabbit. Hoppity, hoppity, hop."

Violet dropped a cloth pouch on the table.

"Your father did exactly what he should have, Billy. He fled from a bad thing and returned for his dinner. To his family."

Atkins untied the ribbon from the pouch and dumped its contents onto the table. Two dozen bullets rolled across the table, bumping into each other like metal logs floating down a river. He picked one up and held it to the light.

"Might as well be air."

Violet crossed her arms.

"They're not air, Milo. They're bullets."

"Can I hold one?"

Atkins looked at his son.

"Please, Papa?"

Atkins handed the bullet to the little boy. Billy held it up to his eye, so close it brushed his long eyelashes.

"I can see me in it."

"Your reflection, that's called."

"My reflection. I can see my reflection."

Violet tucked a loose strand of hair behind her ear and went back to the fire. She tested the water with her finger and stirred it about.

"Say, Milo. Finish with that gun and get over here."

Atkins held out his hand. Billy pouted and cupped the bullet.

"No. I want it."

"What for?"

"I like it."

"Don't work without a gun."

"I don't care. It's pretty."

Atkins picked up a different bullet and loaded it into his pistol's chamber. Some of the blood had dried on the back of his hands.

"Sure, son. You can have your pretty bullet."

Billy smiled and held the bullet out to his father. "Here. I want you to have it for your gun."

"Thank you, sir. I appreciate that."

Atkins plucked the bullet from his son's warm palm and thumbed it into the second empty chamber. Then he filled the other four, too, and slapped the chamber shut. Billy laughed and made his dolls dance some more on the table, giving them all a show. Atkins slid the pistol back into its holster and brought the belt with him to the fire, where Violet was dipping a rag in the kettle water.

"That's your side of the family he takes after," Violet said, smiling as she wrung out the steaming rag and rubbed it with soap. "No one on my side is as odd as that."

Atkins set his belt on the floor and dragged a chair away from the wall to sit before the fire. He sat sideways, so he could watch the cabin door. The door had no lock on it, had never needed a lock, and he supposed there was no point locking it now. He'd seen the Charred Man pick up two large grown men at the same time and hurl them twenty feet like they'd been filled with nothing but cotton. No way to block something as strong and determined as that, even if they heaped everything they owned against the door, bed and all.

"What about your ma? She thinks she talks with Jesus in her dreams."

Violet touched the wet cloth to his face. The heat felt good as she scrubbed, her thumbnail scraping through the fabric.

"How do you know Ma doesn't talk to Jesus?"

Atkins closed his eyes.

"Guess I don't."

"That's right. You don't."

She wrung out the rag in the pot and moved on to his hands. Atkins cracked open one eye—he could not remember the last time his wife had tended to him like this. Her rough hands had gone soft and kind as they worked his skin over, rubbing out the blood.

"I love you, Vi."

"I know. You said so earlier."

Atkins rubbed his hands together, smelling the soap in the air. "I just wanted to say it again, is all."

"Yes, well. Thank you, Mr. Atkins. I love you, too."

Billy made kissy noises at the table, mashing the faces of his dolls together. Atkins turned to get a better look at his son, who was sitting with his back turned to them.

"I suppose that even goes for you, boy. Though it wouldn't hurt anything if you put those dolls away and went to bed."

Violet smiled and handed Atkins the wet rag. "Why don't you scrub the rest of yourself, Milo, and I'll dig out a pair of clean trousers. You need something to buckle that gun belt around, don't you?"

Atkins ran the rag across his chest and under both arms,

enjoying the heat.

"I don't know, Vi. I thought I might go about town naked."

His wife snorted and went into their bedroom. "No thank you, sir," she called back. "There's already been enough fearsome happenings in camp for one night."

Atkins lowered his gaze to the gun belt on the floor and the puddle of pink-tinted water around his feet. As usual, his wife was right.

With nothing else to be done, they went to bed. They had a proper bed, with a cot in the corner of the bedroom for Billy. They had a proper bedroom, too, separate from the rest of the cabin. Violet had demanded the room, arguing that sleeping shouldn't be done in the same place where you spent all your days awake. She liked things separate like that, each part of their lives in its own box. She thought if you were going to live in the wilderness, with no city finery or enjoyments, you might as well do it right.

Before they'd snuffed the lantern, Atkins had removed his pistol from its holster and set it on the table beside their bed, where he could reach it if he needed to. He'd also boarded up the bedroom's sole window along with the two others in the main room, fitting the boards together so tightly he'd be surprised if a crack of light shone through in the morning. He knew the boards wouldn't do much, but he hated the idea of the Charred Man lingering out there, peeping before he came inside.

Billy and Violet fell asleep quickly, their breathing steady and reassuring in the dark. Atkins lay curled around his wife and allowed the day's events to play across his mind. Johnny Miller shooting that coach guard over spilt beer. The ride out to the Dennison Mine with Leg Jameson and his crew. Hank Chambers covered in gore, his eyes wild and serious, ready to torch the whole mine. And that first glimpse of the Charred

Man, a murky outline at the far back of the entrance—like a man, but not. How they could all tell, even at a hundred yards, that he was an unnatural thing, something right out of a child's nightmares.

They should have believed Chambers right off. They should have let him put fire to those fuses as soon as they'd seen that blood on his clothes and the fear in his eyes. Instead, they'd held him up with their foolish chatter, still worried about the mine and the goddamn copper.

Atkins sighed and turned onto his back. His mother said the past was like the stars in the sky—you couldn't change either, no matter how much you worried them in your mind. Nothing to be done now until morning, when they'd have to see to the dead and living and make preparations for leaving town. Atkins started going over the long list of things that would need doing, the supplies they would need and what they could leave behind. He started drifting above himself, rising above the bed and the dark room, and a fine silt of sleep came over him without his notice.

Next he knew, Milo Atkins was sitting up in bed, wide awake and listening. Somebody had come into the cabin—he could feel him in the other room, waiting.

"No," Atkins whispered. "Lord, no."

He reached for the pistol on the bedside table but it was gone. The room smelled like smoke.

"No, no, no."

He put a hand out and touched his wife's shoulder—she was still warm and breathing. Thankfulness flooded his heart and he swung out of bed, his strength returned. He pulled on his pants by feel, then a shirt. He padded barefoot to his son's cot and stood over him, listening to his whistling breath.

"You're a good boy, Billy."

The rhythm of his son's breathing paused, started again.

Atkins went out of the bedroom and closed the door behind him.

They had a visitor at the kitchen table.

Their visitor had set a lantern in the middle of the table, providing the cabin's only light. Atkins swallowed the fear that threatened to overwhelm him and sat across from the Charred Man, his legs tingling with an urge to run as fast and as far as they could. He set his hands on the table and felt the wood grain beneath his palms. The Charred Man was wearing a different suit than before, a finer getup that fit him better. His pale skin was clearer, too, with only one middling black patch on his right cheek. He smelled like a smokehouse.

"Thought you might show," Atkins said, his mouth dry. "Hoped you'd pass us by, but I suppose not."

The Charred Man tugged at the emerald cufflinks on his jacket and grinned, the corners of his lips receding with unnatural stiffness.

"No, Milo. No one gets passed by."

Atkins nodded, suddenly feeling very tired and very heavy, as if his body had been stuffed with clay.

"Is that Revis Cooke's suit?"

The Charred Man's tight grin faded. He leaned forward in his chair and set his hands upon his bony knees.

"Milo Atkins, you shall bear witness to what has happened here."

"I will?"

The Charred Man appraised Atkins with dark and uncanny eyes. Their visitor was old, Atkins realized. Very old.

"What about my family?"

The Charred Man reached into his coat pocket. He drew out a pearl-handled straight razor and set it on the table.

"A prophet travels faster alone."

Atkins looked around the cabin. It was like he'd never seen it before, any of it. Not the fire or the rocking chair or the straw dolls scattered on the floor. He picked up the straight razor with a hand that did not feel like his own. He unfolded it and studied the keen, square-headed blade. He recalled the screams from inside the Copper Hotel, the sound of bones cracking and flesh tearing. The sense, deep in his gut, that something was feeding inside the hotel—not on flesh and blood, but on the agony itself.

Atkins licked his dry lips. His bones felt hollow and cold. He rose from his chair and went into the bedroom where his wife and son lay sleeping. He floated above himself, drifting through the roof of his home and into the night sky, rising so high it was as if he were looking down on their cabin from the heavens, with a field of endless dark all around him.

28

The night had grown so cold and silent it was tempting to peel back a few layers of hammered board, straighten your hat, and step outside to look around and breathe in some fresh air. You could almost convince yourself the whole thing had blown over, that the demon set loose on the camp had moved on like a fast-rolling thunderstorm.

Of course, you'd probably get your head ripped off before more than three seconds passed. Elwood Hayes had no doubt of that, no matter how peaceable things appeared both inside the Runoff Saloon and out. The Charred Man was growing a new skin–he'd need all the food he could get and Red Earth was the closest town for fifty miles. The demon could hunt wild animals, sure, but they'd be nearly as much trouble as they were worth, stringy and fast as they skittered around the mountains. No. The Charred Man would make sure he'd picked Red Earth clean before he moved on and he'd have caught their scent hours ago, their fear and sweat and piss, as they holed up in the saloon. The Charred Man was just biding his time, picking folks off one or two at a time, till he felt strong enough to assail the Runoff.

Which was why Elwood had run back downstairs, still buttoning his pants as he took the stairs two at a time. He turned the hanging lanterns back to full flame, stoked the fireplace high, and brought out three bottles of moonshine from under the bar, careful not wake the widowed ladies sprawled on the floor. A fierce, eye-watering smell wafted up as Hayes uncorked the bottles, but the shine was clear and didn't have much grit floating in it.

"That's nothing but rotgut," Caleb said. "Not much better than turpentine, I reckon. You could probably use it to strip paint off the side of a barn. Some wild-eyed prospector traded me three bottles for three shots of good whiskey. I talked him down to two shots and he was happy to deal."

Elwood took a cotton bar rag, wetted it with shine, and plugged the rag into one of the bottles.

"You must be crazy, wasting good alcohol like that."

Elwood glanced at his brother, who was watching him while Roach and Clem and Caleb and the prospectors were all still dutifully watching their respective corners of the saloon, as instructed.

"You mind your business, Owen, and I'll mind saving our hides."

"My business? Is that what you're calling this empty corner I've been staring at for three hours?"

"Hush," Clem Stubbs said. "Your piping voice is making my head hurt."

"You're soaked twice over, that's why."

"He's got a point there, Clem," Roach said, turning in his chair. "You've been sucking on that whiskey bottle like it's water. How you expecting to shoot straight when you need to?"

"The Good Lord shall be my shield, Roach, and my aim he'll guide true."

The men all laughed at that, breaking the strain. Elwood

pointed his younger brother back round again and returned to his work, wetting bar rags with the moonshine and stuffing one into each bottle. They weren't sticks of dynamite, but they'd do nicely once you touched the rags to flame and tossed the bottle—he'd read once that some hard case had done this same thing to start a fire at the back of a bank while he was standing out front. When the tellers had run out, carrying the bank's silver in their arms, the bandit had just kept his gun level and ordered them to hand the sacks right over.

Elwood took a step back from the bar and surveyed the room, wiping his hands on a clean rag. The fumes from the bottles had made his sight watery and blurred.

"Who here's good at pitching?"

Chairs creaked as all eight men turned to look his way. One of the prospectors, an old codger the others called Jim, scratched beneath his hat.

"Pitching?"

"Like rocks and such."

Clem scratched under his beard.

"You want us to throw those bottles at the haunt?"

"Yes. First you light them with one of the lanterns, then you throw. You need to be quick about it, too."

"Like touching off a stick of dynamite," Roach said, smiling and pushing up his spectacles. "You think we can burn this son-of-a-bitch out."

"That's right, I do. He's been burned before, ain't he? We just—"

Something pounded on the saloon's front wall. The men rose from their chairs as if they'd been bitten and raised their guns.

"That's him," Owen said. "That's the goddamn Charred Man."

The pounding stopped. Elwood glanced at the saloon's second floor railing but Ingrid hadn't come out of her room.

She was probably still in bed or getting dressed.

"Maybe it's somebody else," Stubbs whispered. "Maybe somebody is trying to hide out with us."

"If that's so, I don't give a damn," Owen said, whispering back. "They can find their own hidey hole."

The pounding started up again, louder now. The tables they'd overturned and nailed to the wall shook with each strike.

"He can't be that strong," said Stubbs, who hadn't been at the Copper. "That's solid oak—"

The nailed-up tables cracked, lines running through them.

"Jesus," Stubbs said, pulling back the hammer of his pistol. "I guess y'all weren't telling stories."

Elwood turned his back to the front of the saloon to look at the men. "Everyone go round to the far side of the bar and sight your guns. Don't fire till he's close and don't waste your shot. You might only get one."

The men stood frozen, looking past him. He could hear the wood splintering without having to see it.

"Move, damn you!"

That got the men scrambling, but they'd barely circled round the island bar when the barricaded wall gave way, exploding like a crack of thunder. Elwood reached for the nearest bottle on the bar, touched it to the flame of his lantern, and turned.

A tall, pale man in a fine dark green suit was striding through the breach in the wall, grinning as he unfolded a straight razor. His hands were no longer claws, but you could still make out the strange creature he'd appeared to be earlier in the tight way he held his shoulders, the darkness in his eyes. Elwood said a brief prayer, drew back his arm, and hurled the lit bottle at the demon's chest.

The Charred Man ducked as if he'd already known what trick was coming. The bottle crashed behind him, exploding in a ball of fire.

Elwood shifted back on his heel.

He'd missed, and the level part of the fight was already over.

Ingrid remained in bed after Elwood Hayes rushed out of her bedroom, mumbling queerly about fire. She was in no hurry to return to the vigil downstairs. She preferred to stay burrowed far down in her blankets, splendidly nude, retaining as much warmth as possible as lovely sleep tugged at her, calling her home. She could still feel the stubble of his chin brushing against her cheek, rough and welcome at the same time. The weight of his body—

Gunshots.

Ingrid pulled the blankets above her head. More gunshots cracked below. She moaned into the covers and turned onto her side.

She understood that she was supposed to get out of bed. She understood she was supposed to put on her clothes, run to the railing, and peer down to watch the pitched fight. Perhaps there was something she could do, some brave and clever way she could kill the Charred Man, like a girl in a fairy tale.

Yet, she did not care to do so. Her love was gone, gone for years and gone forever, and she did not care. Ingrid Blomvik preferred to stay in bed, cozy beneath the covers, and wait for the events downstairs to play out, one way or the other. She was spent and Erik was gone.

29

The priest retreated to his bedroom to guzzle as much gin as he could hold down. He was bent on getting blind drunk and falling back asleep until morning. His great hope was that when the sun rose above the hills, burning the morning dew off, that everything in Red Earth would go back to normal. There'd be no one dead, no coffins in the sanctuary, and no tall, spindly stranger walking about in ill-fitting clothes, sniffing the air like a bloodhound.

Sleep would take an ocean of gin, though. From his bedroom window Father Lynch could see two bodies lying in the street, both lying face down in the dirt, pitched forward like they'd been shot in the back. He kept staring at them, vague outlines in the starlight, but they made no move to stand on their own and they did not disappear. This was a firm nightmare.

"Rise," he whispered through the window. "Rise and walk again."

The wind caught at their clothes, whipping them about, but neither rose. One of the bodies was a man, the other a woman. The wind made the woman's skirt balloon over the back of her legs, revealing a patch of creamy white skin that would have been comely under other circumstances. Lynch found his gaze focusing on this exposed skin with the absorption of a lovesick youth gazing at the moon—the bare whiteness of it was somehow brighter than everything surrounding, including the fallen woman's bare neck and hands.

Fresh screams came from the south end of camp, down by the general store and livery stables. The screams didn't last long, sometimes only a half-second, but the shortest ones were the worst, like you'd heard some poor soul's final worldly utterance before it could even reach full-throat. Lynch took a pull from the bottle after each cry and said a prayer for the screamer's soul, willing it safely to Heaven with every liquor-warmed ounce of his body and asking it to forgive an old man his cowardice, his locked door, and the bottle in his hand.

After the south end screams, a quiet period passed. Lynch pulled his gaze away from the fallen woman's exposed thighs and tried to focus on the Runoff Saloon instead, from which he could hear the occasional hammering behind its shuttered windows. He wondered how many folks had taken shelter there, seeking the safety of numbers and firearms. He hoped their numbers were large—fifty, sixty souls—and that they had plenty of good men left to lead them. Perhaps they could last out the night, emerge at daybreak, and hunt the stranger down as a posse united.

"Hold out the night," Father Lynch implored, pointing his bottle at the window, "and we shall hunt the stranger together. We will hunt him down like a rabid dog, hang him from the highest tree, and bury him six feet under."

Lynch leaned toward the window.

"We'll bury all of them, together, and I will pray for their immortal souls. I will say my finest prayers."

As if in response to his plea, the tall stranger reappeared on the street, walking smoothly. He paused briefly to examine the two fallen bodies in the road, bending slightly at the waist for a better look. His coat seemed to fit better than earlier, more tightly, and the priest realized the stranger was wearing an entirely new suit.

Lynch lowered the bottle of gin and set it on the floor beside him. The stranger straightened abruptly and smelled the air. A terrifying pause, in which the priest could hear his own heart beating in his ears, and the stranger began moving again, his long legs scissoring as he continued toward the camp's north end.

A minute passed before Lynch realized two things: the stranger's hands had both resembled normal hands, with nothing claw-like about them any longer, and that Lynch had pissed himself more than slightly.

The priest changed into clean clothes in the dark, only bumping his knee once on the iron frame of his bed, a bump which he did not feel much as the gin began to take greater hold, asserting itself over his fear. Once he'd changed, Father Lynch opened his bedroom door and passed into the sanctuary, striding down the main aisle toward the four coffins lined together at the back. The floor creaked beneath his weight but Father Lynch didn't mind the noise—he welcomed it, in fact—and as he stood before the coffins, he felt like a general surveying his troops.

His dead, coffin-bound troops.

"Men," Lynch said, "You have not given your lives in vain."

The priest searched his memory, trying to recall exactly for what reason these four men had given their lives. Their arrival at his church seemed so long ago, a daylight affair unconnected from anything that mattered now.

And the lids—only one of the coffin lids was nailed shut.

"Lord Almighty," Lynch said, loudly. "That is no way to honor the memory of the dead. Any meddlesome fool could come along, lift your lid, and get an eyeful."

Lynch lifted one of the lids and peered inside the coffin. It contained a dead man, his hands politely crossed. He was no older than forty.

"Poor fool. You could have lived another two score."

Lynch dropped the lid and dusted off his hands. He was sweating now, his power returned. He strode back across the room, paused beneath the large cross hanging behind the lectern, and swiftly made the sign of the cross.

"Please, my Lord. Deliver us."

The priest went back into his bedroom and sat at the window. He heard more screams on the north side of camp, or howls (they could have come from a coyote, lonely for the moon) and the world spun beneath his chair. Then Lynch might have nodded off, or he might not have, and suddenly there across the street was the stranger again, knocking on the Runoff Saloon's front door. He battered it with such force the building's entire front shook from the impact, the door buckling till it finally splintered and gave way with a loud crack.

Lynch expected a barrage of gunfire to greet the stranger as he stepped through the doorway, moving as casually as any invited salesman. Instead, there was only a silent pause, followed by a sudden rise of flames in the saloon's doorway.

Then came the gunfire.

"My," Lynch whispered, watching the flames curl out of the doorway and rise up the saloon's front. The whole building was tinder-dry wood. If they didn't throw water on it straight off the entire structure would burn like it was filled with hay.

More gunfire. Nobody ran outside to throw water on the fire, or to escape. The gunfire stopped and the flames climbed higher, lighting up the whole street until it seemed like mid-day.

"No..."

The shutters of the second floor window drew back, revealing a woman cast in shadow. She looked down at the ground, back into her smoke filled room, and swung her legs out, so she was sitting on the windowsill. Lynch willed her to make the jump, prayed for it, and finally she dropped, landing awkwardly on one leg before the other. The priest flinched, imagining her pain as she laid on the ground clutching her knee.

"Keep moving," he said, as if she could hear him through the window and the distance. "The fire..."

The fire had risen to the building's roof and was avidly devouring the entire structure, its heat so ferocious Lynch could feel the glass of his own window warming. The woman began to crawl into the street, favoring her hurt knee.

Lynch squinted, studying the woman's face. It was one of the Madam Petrov's girls—Ingrid.

Sad, beautiful Ingrid.

Her dress was untied at the waist, as if she'd dressed hurriedly, and the fire behind her was so bright Lynch could see the rounded outline of her body through the garment's light fabric. The priest rose from his chair, ready to run and help pull her to safety, as the tall stranger stepped back through the saloon's doorway.

Father Lynch cursed, his hands balling into fists at his side. Ingrid noticed the stranger striding after her and rose from the ground, scrambling in her terror. She made it to the middle of the street before her knee buckled and sent her sprawling.

The stranger came on, brandishing his straight razor, and Lynch remained rooted to the spot, paralyzed by the scene playing out before him. Ingrid moved to rise again but suddenly the stranger was beside her, covering the distance in an unnatural blur. He grabbed at her blond, corn silk hair, lifting her head toward him, his face as blank as if he were considering a fence post, or a fish, while behind them the saloon crackled and raged with flame.

Twisting in the stranger's grasp, Ingrid drew a small pistol from the folds of her dress and raised it. Just as quickly, the stranger slashed down with his razor, opening the skin of her wrist and forcing the gun from her hand.

A moan rose up from the back of Lynch's throat as the girl considered her bleeding wrist. She looked from the wound to the razor and back again, as if unable to believe the connection between the two. The stranger kicked the gun away, wiped the razor on his pants, and hugged Ingrid against him, like a father showing his child how to tie her shoe. He set the razor beneath her throat, tightened his grip, and drew the blade across her yielding skin in a slow, easy arc.

A ribbon of blood appeared, trailing where the razor had passed. Ingrid's eyelids fluttered as her body quaked for several seconds, then stilled. The stranger released his grip on her long hair and let the girl fall to the ground. The scab on his cheek, already shrunk to the size of a nickel, pulsed once and then faded away entirely. The stranger smiled and touched his face. He shone like a new penny.

Father Lynch took an involuntary step back from the window, his foot knocking over the gin. Outside, the stranger's head swiveled as if he'd heard the bottle's clunk. He looked toward the church.

"No," the priest whispered, drawing back from the window. "Please, Lord. Please."

Lynch retreated to his bedroom door. He turned the doorknob and quietly let himself into the sanctuary. Whatever comfort the gin had brought the priest had now departed, leaving in its place a muddled terror that felt like a ball of ice in his gut. Lynch scanned the sanctuary, trying to picture a way out. He noted the coffins and crossed the room, raising the unfixed lids and studying each man. He chose the skinniest

National man and got in beside him.

"Don't mind me, son."

The priest dropped the coffin's lid and sealed them in darkness. The National man gave off a sour, gaseous odor. Lynch slowed his breathing and tried not to think about the smell. About anything. Somebody tried the door to the church, found it locked, and forced it open with one strong kick. Lynch didn't think about it. He didn't think about the sound of a man's footsteps going round the coffins and toward the front of the church. He didn't think about his bedroom door creaking open, or the long pause after that. He was a cloudbank of white. He was not there. He was dead, one dead man wedged beside another.

The footsteps returned and stopped at the coffins.

A cloudbank, pure and white.

One of the other lids was lifted. The coffin's contents examined.

Clouds. High blank clouds.

The lid dropped back in place.

Clouds.

Floorboards creaked as the footsteps slowly, ponderously, drew back, leaving the church. The living dead man waited, taking shallow breaths. He wondered when he could safely rise once more.

PART FOUR

The Last Souls in Town

30

When the sun rose again on Red Earth, Father Lynch was sitting on edge of his cot, fully dressed, with his worn Bible on his lap and his clerical color tight about his throat. He had not slept, read, or touched a drink since emerging from his shared coffin, the stink of decay in his nostrils. He'd simply sat on his bed, his mind both blank and feverish, anticipating the grim day before him. He believed he was the last living person in camp, the only lamb spared from the nocturnal slaughter.

Lynch had no idea why he'd been spared, why the Good Lord had chosen him alone to escape from the demon set loose upon His creation. Lynch did not believe he was a particularly good man, if he could be said to be good at all, and he was definitely not a brave man. He might have been spared by his calling alone—perhaps it was too much, even for the all-powerful Lord, to allow another priest to fall to the Devil.

Or perhaps that was not the reason at all. Perhaps the reason would never be revealed, could not be revealed. The ways of the Lord were mysterious, to be certain, and Lynch had not been present when the world's foundations were laid. He was only a mortal creature, raised from dust and to dust soon to be returned. In the time between, Lynch could only perform his duties as best he could, tending to the town's dead and easing their passage into the next life as best he could. What else could be done in the face of such wickedness?

"I will do so, my Lord. I will tend my butchered flock and ease their passage into the life beyond."

The priest rose from his bed, dropped his Bible into his coat pocket, and strode through the bedroom door. The church's sanctuary, which had been filled with such dark shadows throughout the night, was flooded with bright morning sunshine. The light caught the sifting dust motes hanging in the air and made the line of coffins resting behind the pews glow, as if the cheap pine was lit from within.

Father Lynch passed through the sunny room without lingering, pushing aside the broken front door and descending the church's back steps. Turning left, he was greeted immediately with the sight of the Copper Hotel next door, its front bay window shattered and dead bodies circling it on all sides. A wake of black feathered vultures had already found the piled dead—they sat perched on torn backs and split stomachs, their talons dug in and raking while their hooked beaks pecked at eye sockets and tore away strips of flesh. The ugly, enormous birds glanced up when the priest clapped his hands, eyeing him briefly before returning to their business.

Lynch approached the Copper Hotel, deciding to ignore the carrion birds. Some of the dead he recognized, some he did not. A great pile lay just outside the hotel's door, sticky with dried gore. The priest took a deep breath, placed a handkerchief over his mouth, and stepped through the hotel's doorway, which was splintered and beaded with buckshot. More bodies lay heaped inside, so many he had to push them aside to pass through. Each corpse was maimed in some way, with the most common wounds originating at the throat and chest, and a few were so badly gored their features were no longer recognizable. Only the center of the hotel's main room, which had been cleared of the usual tables and chairs, was empty, with the dead lining all four walls, while another large pile lay in front of the hotel's back entrance.

Father Lynch raised his head, reluctantly, and surveyed the hotel's second floor balcony. Madam Petrov stared back at him, her large, pale face wedged between two bars of the railing, her eyes glassy and flat. He couldn't see her wounds from where he stood but it was plain to see she'd been set on from behind.

"I am sorry, Madam," Lynch said, making the sign of the cross in her direction. "You were a true Christian woman and deserved a better fate."

As the sun rose higher in the sky the temperature, and the smell, in the hotel was increasing. Soon the stench would be unbearable. Lynch had thought to bury the dead, every murdered soul, but now he saw the work such an endeavor would entail with his own eyes and saw his folly for what it was. He said the Lord's Prayer through his handkerchief and made the cross over the entire room, one body after another, his free hand touching the Bible through the fabric of his coat.

"Rest in peace," he concluded, stepping out through the broken bay window and into the street. Ingrid Blomvik and the two other bodies, the man and the woman, remained prone in front of the church, with the still-smoking ruins of the Runoff Saloon behind them. The saloon's roof had collapsed entirely during the night, leaving its base exposed to the blue sky. Father Lynch found himself perversely glad for the fire—at least whoever had died in the saloon would not be left to rot slowly, uncovered to the vultures and the elements. They would have burned cleanly, hopefully quickly, their mortal bodies cleansed by flame as their souls fled to Heaven.

Father Lynch bent over Ingrid Blomvik and made the cross above her forehead. Her blue eyes—such a deep, wonderful blue—were open. The priest's chest hitched with a spasm of pain as he rolled the girl's eyelids shut. He would cover her with a sheet after he'd made his rounds through town. He'd bring a pile of sheets from the Dennison bunkhouses up the street and cover as many bodies as he could.

The vultures squawked behind the priest, fighting over a length of bare leg. Father Lynch straightened and continued his survey, circling round the smoldering saloon to get a closer look at the damage. What remained of the building's walls had blackened, as if roasted in a kiln. The priest had seen plenty of fires in his lifetime, but none that had burned so rapidly and so thoroughly.

Had the occupants set the fire intentionally? Had they decided to end their own lives before the stranger could perform the task more violently? How—

Lynch halted.

A body was lying in the grass, thrown twenty yards from the rear of the saloon. He could see its dark outline in the grass, boots up. Lynch approached the body and found a slim man covered in grime and blood, with an unsightly gash along his left cheek that ran to his jaw. It was the man Lynch had spoken to the night before, the one who'd told him about a fellow he'd accidentally killed in a street brawl. He had a brother. His family had a farm in Nebraska.

Elwood.

The cut man was Elwood Hayes, and he was breathing.

Hayes looked strong enough to be left alone for a few minutes. Father Lynch circled round the saloon in case anybody else had been thrown clear of the fire, but found nothing but scorched earth. It'd been a small miracle the fire hadn't spread to any of the other building's on the street, the bunkhouses on the south side or the shacks further north. Sure, the buildings had some space between them, but the fire had raged so fiercely earlier that morning it had seemed destined to spread across town, unchecked by the hand of man.

As he returned to the street, intent on gathering supplies for Elwood Hayes, the priest found Main Street eerily silent, the few buildings as still as the hills behind them. More bodies lay scattered up and down the thoroughfare. The priest eyed them uneasily as he headed down to the general store, not wanting to recognize anyone he'd known personally. The store's front porch was clear of bodies, which surprised him, and Lynch stopped short of the steps.

"Leg? You in there?"

No answer. The priest tugged at his collar, which always seemed to tighten as the day grew warmer.

"I'm coming in for supplies. Don't anybody shoot me."

Lynch climbed the general store's steps and showed himself inside, where it was cool and dark and smelled strongly of urine. He paused, letting his eyes adjust, and was relieved to find the premises empty. The shelves were in order, too, except for the empty spaces where Leg usually kept the rifles and scatterguns. Leg and Henry might have been in the backroom, still lying abed after a night of hard drinking.

"I need supplies, gentlemen." Father Lynch went around the counter and poked his head through the backroom's doorway. Both beds were vacant. Either the Jamesons had died on their feet or they'd cleared town. The priest looked around the store, its shelves still filled with stock, and decided he'd put his money on dead. "A shame, gentlemen," Lynch called out, pulling out the bottle of East Coast whiskey everyone knew Leg kept beneath the counter for fine occasions. He also gathered a tin of salve, a pile of linens, and a corked jug. He went outside with his supplies and circled behind the store, where he filled the jug with water from Leg's pump.

After a pause to catch his breath and wipe the sweat from his eyes, Lynch started back toward the Runoff Saloon. Hayes was in the same spot as where he'd left him, his chest rising and falling as he slept. Lynch splashed water on one of the towels and started scrubbing at the soot and grime that coated the wounded man like a second skin. The gash along his left cheek bled at the fussing, flaring red and sore. Lynch poured water on the wound directly, trying to flush it clean.

"You hear me, son?"

Hayes kept breathing without pause. He was deep under.

"This might hurt, but it needs doing."

Lynch uncorked the fine whiskey and took a swig. The liquor burned the back of his throat, cleaning out the sour. He hissed, took a second swig, and poured some into the sleeping man's wound.

Hayes' eyes opened and rolled in their sockets wildly while he thrashed about. "Whoa," the priest said, pushing the wounded man back to the ground. "It's over, it's over."

Hayes' eyes slowed their rolling and came into focus. Father Lynch smiled and patted his shoulder.

"I bet that stung as bad as ten hornets."

Hayes gazed beyond the priest's shoulder toward the sky. Then he turned his head to the side, as if he could not bear the sight of it.

"You remember what happened, son?"

Hayes said nothing.

"If you're strong enough to sit up, I got a jug of water here."

Hayes stared at the grass he was eye-level with. Finally, after a couple of minutes of this, he grunted and sat up. Lynch uncorked the water jug and Hayes snatched it away, pouring the water into his mouth and then over his head, sending rivulets of soot-blackened water down the front of his shirt.

"I'm no goddamned invalid, Father."

Hayes set the jug down between his legs, his chest heaving.

The gash on his cheek was bleeding anew.

"Your wound—"

"I can feel it. Don't worry about that."

Lynch handed him the tin of ointment and a clean towel. "You should rub some salve into it."

Hayes nodded, staring past him again at the ruined saloon. He took the cloth and the salve and unscrewed the tin's lid. A pungent, clean scent filled the air, reminding Lynch of gin. Hayes dipped two fingers into the white grease and smeared it across his cut cheek. He winced, folded up the towel into a thick square, and placed it against his face, still eyeing the blackened saloon.

"The Charred Man," Hayes said, "leaving behind more charred folks."

The priest straightened and crossed his arms. He felt like drinking more of the whiskey, but it was too early.

"That's what you call him? The Charred Man?"

"Sheriff Atkins referred to him as such."

Father Lynch turned, peering across the half-mile of valley toward the Dennison Mine. He could make out the dry house, halfway up the hillside, but the mine's dark mouth had disappeared.

"Was that what the blasting was about last night? The Charred Man?"

Hayes nodded.

"Sheriff Atkins said they tried to seal him in, but he got out anyhow. Atkins called a town meeting at the hotel but it was already too late for that. I reckon he's some kind of demon."

Lynch knelt down and took a drink from the whiskey bottle, deciding it was late enough after all.

"I saw them die," Hayes said, still pressing the towel to his cheek. "Clem. Roach. Owen. I missed with the fire and he came at us with his razor. Cut through the men like they were butter. Nobody got off more than one steady shot."

Lynch took another pull, imagining the scene. Fire at one end of the saloon, a retreat to the back.

"I tried a second bottle, got it lit and thrown. Missed with that, too, and the whole place was afire after that. He started tossing folks around. Even the dead folks, he tossed. I think he liked it. He liked watching us go flying like that. Like we was nothing but rag dolls."

Hayes looked around his spot in the grass.

"He tossed me after he lit into me with that razor. Must have thrown me through the goddamn wall."

A cloud drifted across the sun, dropping them in shadow. Hayes coughed into his lap, spitting up something black and wet.

"Did you see her, Father? You see Ingrid?"

"Yes. I did."

"She's dead, too."

"Yes. She died in front of the saloon, in the street. She got clear of the fire but not him."

Hayes doubled over further, until his forehead nearly touched his knees. He coughed and spat again.

"She fought him until the end. She pulled a gun."

Hayes looked up and searched the priest's face.

"You saw her die. From your church, you saw her."

The priest nodded, clutching his folded elbows with both hands. Hayes sniffed and wiped a smear of ointment from the corner of his mouth.

"I don't blame you, Father. If I was you, I'd have done the same."

Father Lynch turned his face to the clouded sky, feeling the wind on his face and how it blew through his gray hair. He could feel no blessing in it.

The day had warmed. Hayes' ugly cut stopped bleeding long enough for Father Lynch to apply more salve and slap on a fresh bandage, a swatch of towel that stuck to the greased wound on its own. Hayes claimed nothing broken but said his entire backside ached like one fearsome bruise. When he'd felt ready, Lynch helped Hayes to his feet, digging in with his heels as he pulled the younger man upward. Hayes cursed loudly and winced as he tottered about like a newborn deer. The priest couldn't help smiling and looked away.

"You find my suffering amusing, Father?"

"No, my son. Just your reaction to it."

Hayes laughed at that, but the laugh turned into a hacking cough as he spat out more soot.

"Goddamn. I must have swallowed half that fire myself."

They circled around the saloon. Lynch scanned the cabins toward the north end of town, deciding they'd need to head there next to check for more survivors.

"Jesus," Hayes whispered, stopping as they came to the street. A huge vulture had set upon Ingrid Blomvik's shoulders and was tugging at strands of her blond hair. Her face was turned toward them and her eyes had rolled back open.

"I'm sorry, Elwood—"

A gunshot rang out and the vulture dropped, shot through the breast. The priest looked to his side and saw Hayes with his gun fixed on the bird, as if he expected the vulture to rise again and attack. The young man's body, bruised as it was, had gone as straight and rigid as a flagpole.

Lynch held back as Hayes approached the girl.

"Damn buzzards," Hayes said, tucking his pistol away. He had some kind of hidden back rig for his gun.

"You got that one, for certain."

Hayes knelt in front of the girl. "Sorry we never got you out of town, Mrs. Blomvik. Looks like we should have forgotten about that fussy accountant and rode on."

Father Lynch looked down the street at the Cooke House. The front door was missing.

"I think Mr. Cooke was also called upon last night."

"Shit," Hayes spat. "Serves him right."

The other vultures, which had risen briefly after the gunshot, fluttered down from the sky and resettled on whatever fallen body looked juiciest. Lynch scratched his head, wincing at the sun overhead.

"You going to shoot some more?"

Hayes turned away from the hotel and started up the street. Lynch fell in beside him, matching his pace.

"No, Father. I'm going to need the bullets for later."

"Suicide is a sin—"

"I ain't talking about suicide, Father."

The priest closed his mouth, his brow furrowing as he considered what the other man was getting at. Hayes cupped his hands around his mouth and started shouting hello as they approached the miner shacks, a roughhewn assemblage of cabins and lean-tos that appeared to have about a year left between them. As they walked, they came across six additional dead bodies: three women, two men, and a little girl with pretty browns curls and a throat purpled from strangulation, her eyes nearly pried from their sockets.

Father Lynch joined in, shouting hello at the top of his lungs. Nobody answered or came running out of the shacks. They reached the end of town, where the road trailed to nothing and the hills sloped steeply upward. Lynch made out a shaggy mountain goat about halfway up the hillside. He was chewing on a clump of wildflowers that had sprouted from beneath a boulder like the tail of a cat.

"Quiet on this end," Hayes said, setting his hands upon his hips. "Everybody must have gone to the meeting."

"That's the sheriff's," Lynch said, pointing to a cabin. "Milo liked to live as far from the action as he could. He thought it got him hassled less."

"He have any family?"

"A wife and boy."

They headed to the cabin and found the door open. They found Milo Atkins inside, sitting at his kitchen table with an empty porcelain cup clasped between his hands. His eyes were fixed straight ahead, as if he could see through the cabin's walls. They thought he was dead, like the others, but then the sheriff turned and looked their way, causing them both to jump.

"Goddamn, Sheriff," Hayes blurted, looking from the priest to the lawman and back again. "You're alive."

Atkins blinked while the rest of his face remained set. Father Lynch placed his hand on the lawman's shoulder.

"Milo? You with us, son?"

Hayes whooped and slapped at his thigh, gawking at the sheriff.

"I can't believe it. Three of us. At least three of us slipped past."

Atkins turned in Hayes' direction.

"You know what this means, fellas? It means that son-of-a-bitch makes mistakes. He makes mistakes, like a regular man does, and something that makes mistakes can be killed. I'll be damned if it can't."

The right corner of Atkins' mouth twitched. Father Lynch felt the sheriff's forehead with the back of his hand—it was warm, but so was the cabin.

"You feeling peculiar, Milo?"

The sheriff's eyes flickered to something over Lynch's shoulder. Following the man's gaze, the priest felt an additional wariness settle upon his shoulders.

"Would you please look into the other room, Mr. Hayes?"

Hayes' grin faded as he turned around and sized up the cabin's bedroom door. "Sure," he said, lowering his voice. "I can do that."

The priest stayed beside Sheriff Atkins while Hayes went into the other room. He searched his mind for something comforting to say but found nothing that approached the situation. The sheriff's hands began to tremble around his cup.

Hayes returned to the cabin's main room, his face solemn and pale. "Throats cut," he said, swallowing. "Both of them."

The sheriff removed his hands from around the cup, clasped them together, and set them in his lap.

"I'm sorry, Milo," Father Lynch said, bending down so they faced each other. "I'm sorry about your wife and boy."

The sheriff closed his eyes and inhaled.

"They're with the Lord now, son, but the living still need your help. We need to find out if there's more survivors. We need to see to the dead."

Hayes crouched beside Lynch and set his hand on Atkins' shoulder.

"And when we're done with that, Sheriff, we're going to hunt him down. Hunt him till he's dead."

The crease in Milo Atkins' forehead smoothed.

He opened his eyes, returned to them.

The sheriff wouldn't answer their questions, or talk much at all, but he did rise from his chair and help them search the rest of town. Hayes took the shacks on the west side of Main Street while Lynch and Atkins took the shacks on the east. They found a total of twenty-two dead, nearly all of them women and children, with a few prospectors sprinkled in like rock salt. They swaddled each body in a blanket and dragged it out to the sunny street. Most had their throats torn or crushed.

Elwood Hayes checked the livery stables and came back scratching his head.

"Didn't touch the horses. They looked spooked, but when

I poured 'em their oats they fed well enough."

Father Lynch gazed across the valley south of town. "He spared the animals?"

"That's right."

"And nobody found teeth marks on the dead?"

"He doesn't feed like that," Atkins said, speaking for the first time since they'd found him. "It's souls that fed him. He liked the pained ones best."

Father Lynch stepped toward Atkins. "You think he's the Devil, Milo? Is that what you're saying?"

Atkins wiped his hands down the sides of his pants. "I don't know about that, Father. He's a devil, anyhow, and should have been left buried in those hills. I reckon he's headed for Rawlins now, where he can get at more folks."

Lynch imagined the Charred Man in a city that size, appearing regular to anybody who saw him. Rawlins, a town on the Union Pacific rail line. Hayes scratched under his hat and glanced at Lynch.

"He jawed with you, Sheriff?"

Atkins nodded.

"He said he wanted a witness to all this killing and figured folks would believe a lawman easiest. Some Indians put him to fire a while back. He's looking for revenge anywhere he can find it."

Hayes laughed and shook his head.

"Goddamn. If that don't beat all. Indians started all this?"

"No, I figure they tried to stop all this," Father Lynch said, glancing across the valley. "Was the Dennison Mining Company that got it started again."

Nobody said anything to that. The three men stood in the street while the crickets sang in the grass and the sun glared down. Lynch checked his pocket watch and saw it was already past noon. "Guess we should see to the dead," Hayes said, looking up at the sun. "I figure it'd be easiest to drag those in the street over to the Copper Hotel and let 'em go up together. We can't dig sixty graves."

"I am going to dig two," Atkins said, walking off and leaving them staring after. Hayes looped his thumbs in his belt.

"You think he'll be all right, Father?"

"No," the priest said, rubbing the sweaty back of his neck. "But as long as there's work ahead, he'll keep pulling that plow."

Lynch and Hayes started lugging bodies to the Copper Hotel. They ignored the vultures and hefted the dead into the hotel's front room, laying them side to side. The men were heavy, the women lighter, and the smaller children they could carry one apiece. What limbs had been removed from their original source were collected, matched, and reunited with their owners. They found Revis Cooke hacked into ribbons with one of the National men lying beside him, his own face and body thoroughly crushed.

"That National man's the first beaten on like that," Hayes said, stuffing a pile of dollar certificates piled on Cooke's desk into a leather satchel. "Why do you think the Charred Man dwelt on him?"

"Don't know," Lynch said. "Maybe he fought back the hardest."

"Yeah. Shotguns are always ornery old coots."

Hayes finished stuffing the bills and moved on to the silver coins.

"What are you going to do with that payroll, Mr. Hayes?"

"Exactly what it looks like, Father. I'm taking this as payment for services rendered, the death of my brother, and the death of my men. If Mr. Dennison don't like it, he's welcome to come find me."

"You're just inviting more trouble, Mr. Hayes."

"Yes, but I am reconciled with that."

Flies harried the two men as they continued hauling bodies. Father Lynch, who'd worked in his share of pestilence tents, fell into a familiar, mind-numbing reverie. The work needed doing, so he would do it. He was a servant of the Lord and did not shirk work merely because it was unpleasant. Better for it to be unpleasant, for it brought him closer to the purity of the spirit of Christ, who had not heeded the sores of lepers, who'd touched the untouchable. Better these biting black flies than the crack of the Devil's whip, snapping through the air as it lashed his hide for all eternity, the wicked and the damned lamenting their fate in one awful, united wail.

After they finished the south end of camp, they scared off the vultures and dragged the dead surrounding the hotel back inside it. When they'd finished with that, they started on the north end of camp, glad they'd already dragged the fallen into the street and could work outside where the smell was not as fierce. Atkins joined them a few bodies in, himself covered in dirt and sweat, and the three of them were able to work more quickly after that.

The priest's watch read four-thirty when they set the last body inside the hotel and splashed a whole bucket of kerosene over it. Hayes fashioned a torch and Lynch brought out his Bible. "Dear Lord," the priest called out, "please bless these souls, who died in such agony, and see to it they are rewarded in Heaven for their pain here on Earth. Many of them were women, and many of them were children. None, I am certain, deserved to die in such great terror."

Father Lynch pointed to the hotel and Elwood Hayes obliged, throwing the torch through the shattered front window. The fire caught immediately, with a loud thump, and rose so quickly the three men were forced to stand back to avoid the worst of the heat.

"Amen," Hayes shouted, his voice carrying above the fire

and into the hills. "Amen, amen, amen."

The fire crackled and climbed higher as a dark, foul-smelling smoke rose above the hotel. "I will not sleep in this place tonight," Atkins said, his voice low and so soft Father Lynch turned away from the burning hotel to make certain he'd spoken.

"You think we should leave for Rawlins straight off?"

"Yes, sir," Hayes said, answering for the sheriff. "He's already got near a day on us. No sense in dawdling here."

Lynch lowered the layers of handkerchief from his mouth. "No. I suppose not."

Hayes grinned and slapped Atkins on the arm. "We've gone through the mill, boys. Now it's our turn to hunt."

They saddled up four good horses and turned the rest loose from the livery. The fourth horse was piled with supplies from the general store and led on a string by Elwood Hayes, who guided two horses more gracefully than Father Lynch did one. The priest hadn't ridden a horse in years—his joints ached by the time they'd crossed the valley and started up the steep mountain path.

Hayes noticed him lagging and announced they only had an hour of good light remaining. "I'm riding my best, Mr. Hayes," Lynch replied. "The way you're leading that horse, I'm wondering if you've had some experience thieving."

"Some," Hayes called back, picking up the pace.

As they climbed the hillside, Red Earth grew smaller and the Copper Hotel continued to burn, giving off an ugly, rising smoke the color of tar. Father Lynch felt as if the fire were watching them depart, both enraged by their abandonment and consumed by the dirty work it had upon its hands. The Church would not be happy with such a mass burial—they'd not only find it a pagan blasphemy, they'd argue that destroying the human body in such a way denied the resurrection, that as an instrument of the Lord receiving sacrament, the human body itself was a sacred, sacramental object, and that to put it to flame was an insult.

Yet, plagues had come before in which burning the bodies were necessary, and plagues would come again. What had happened below in Red Earth was simply one more test of the Lord. Lynch had no plans to join the other men in their hunt once they reached Rawlins—he was not made to be an instrument of vengeance, even if such a thing was possible. No. He was sixty-two years old. He would simply test the winds and move on to a new town, where the living still prospered and sought the comfort of the Lord. To live a few more years in peace would be enough.

At dusk, they went over a rise and the path started to decline. They lost sight of Red Earth and would not see it again along the road. They rode until twilight turned to black night and made camp just off the road in a small clearing, each man relieving himself in the woods and dragging deadwood back. They built a small fire in a natural hollow in the ground and laid their bedding around it. The air felt chilled but was not near as cold as the night before, the wind having dropped to naught. The sky was clear and filling with stars, with a thin sliver of a new moon rising above the mountains. They collected more deadwood and stacked it at the foot of the fire.

"Should last through the night," Elwood Hayes said.

Milo Atkins stepped back and glanced at the worn-out horses.

"I'll water them back at that stream."

"Sure."

Atkins walked off into the dark, carrying no lantern. Lynch heard the horses snort at the sheriff's approach and drift down the mountain road. He turned to Hayes, who was sliding into his blankets with a whiskey bottle and a hunk of bread.

"You may not have known him long, but Milo Atkins is a changed man today."

"That right?"

"Just yesterday morn, he was strutting about camp like a rooster."

"Yes, sir, there might have been something of a strut to him when I first met him," Hayes said, tipping the whiskey bottle back. "This ugliness has taken the starch right out of him."

"You think it's only sorrow?"

"What else would it be?"

"I don't know."

Lynch bent over their saddle bag of provisions. He dug out a block of hard cheese and a stump of venison and slid inside his own blankets, glad for the fire. He took turns chewing the cheese and the venison, mixing the flavors in his mouth. "Didn't realize I was so hungry," he said when he'd finished both. "Didn't think I'd ever be able to eat again."

"Yeah," Hayes said. "But you did. And someday our buddy Atkins will find himself hungry, too, and he'll be eating."

"You're saying life moves onward, even after terrible events."

"That's right. It does."

Father Lynch lay back to regard the stars. "I am sorry for the loss of your brother and friends, Mr. Hayes."

Elwood laughed and turned onto his side.

"Jesus. What am I going to tell my pa? That old bastard will never forgive me, no matter what I tell him. There's no right way to tell any of this."

An ember popped in the fire. A spruce owl called from the trees. Lynch imagined Milo Atkins leading the horses down to the mountain stream and watching them drink, the thought of his murdered wife and child like an anchor tied round his neck.

The horses would know their way back, Lynch supposed.

Even in the dark.

"Elwood."

"Yes, Father?"

"When the Charred Man killed Ingrid, the last patch of scab fled from his cheek. I saw it go with my own eyes."

"Fled?"

"Disappeared, like. One second it was there, next it was gone. He gave off a shine, too. Like a new penny in the sun."

The spruce owl started in again with its inquiries. Lynch closed his eyes, blocking out the stars yet still feeling the firelight warm against his cheek. He hadn't slept out of doors for a long time. The crispness of the air resembled ice shavings in his lungs and the hard, rocky ground felt like a wooden plank. The mountain spun gently beneath him, lifting him toward the sky.

Atkins returned with more wood for the fire. Some time after that, Father Lynch heard the lawman sobbing softly beneath his bedding. The sobs came from deep in the young man's chest, rising up all cracked and stifled. Lynch felt his left arm turning numb, though he was not lying on it. The priest was on his back, burrowed under a heavy mound of blankets. He felt the numbness grow quickly, passing through his arm and into the other aching corners of his body, shortening his breath and making it come in little gulps, then not at all.

And the young man, still weeping.

Not understanding how this too would pass.

31

They buried the priest on the mountainside. The soil was shallow and pitted with stones and all they had to hack at it with were sharp rocks and sticks. They ended up covering the priest with pebbles and piling rocks on top of that, rock after rock, until Father Lynch looked like he'd become part of the mountain itself. "We should fill the cracks," Elwood Hayes said. "So the buzzards won't get at him."

Milo Atkins, who didn't care one way or the other, started scooping handfuls of sand. He took his time pouring it down into the cracks, covering the small patches of black cloth that showed between the rocks. Far as he was concerned, they could spend all day burying the priest. They could spend the rest of summer adding to the mound, building it up into a tower of rocks and sand until it reached fifty feet high.

When they'd packed the rocks tight, Hayes brushed his hands off and stood back to inspect their work.

"That's a comely tomb, ain't it?"

Atkins nodded, staring over the rock pile and into the woods beyond. He'd found the spot for the priest's burial that morning when he'd returned with the horses to the mountain stream they'd watered at the night before. The horses were at the stream yet, tied to the trees as they drank and mulled about, nibbling at grass and wildflowers.

"Funny how he kicked like that," Hayes said. "Survived a goddamn massacre only to go in his sleep a day later."

Atkins kicked a stone and sent it tumbling into the ravine below. Violet and Billy had gone in their sleep, too.

Well, Billy, anyhow. Violet had come to as he dragged the razor across her throat, opening her soft skin like it was soft cheese. Her eyes wide and scared and fast awake, as if she'd been expecting the razor, even in her sleep.

Expecting it, yes, but not from him.

A roar filled Milo Atkin's mind, making it hard to hear whatever Hayes was saying now. He was reading from Father Lynch's Bible, his mouth forming words as his eyes glided across the onionskin pages. This was the funeral: the two of them, standing over a pile of rocks covering the body of a good man. The July sky clear and blue above the trees, the sun rising in the sky, the birds singing in the trees, the horses watering at the stream, the air smelling like spruce needles and dirt. Slight rattlings in the forest as the squirrels jumped from branch to branch and the deer followed their old, well-worn trails to feed and bed.

Atkins touched the pistol holstered on his hip, seized by a strong urge to fire into the piled stones. He'd found his gun returned after he'd finished his work in the bedroom. He'd expected to find the Charred Man still at his table, grinning and death-eyed, but he'd already departed. Nothing else had changed in the room except for the reappearance of Atkins' revolver, glowing silver as it sat on the kitchen table.

Hayes said amen and set the Bible on top of the stones.

"Hope you can ride fast, Sheriff. We've got some catch up ahead of us."

Atkins dropped his hand and started toward the stream,

pushing the roar to the back of his mind.

"I'll fetch the horses to the road."

"Good man," Hayes said behind him, like he meant it.

The road climbed to one final summit before dropping steeply again, revealing a grassy plain that stretched into the horizon. Rawlins was forty miles to the north, an easy ride if they stuck to beat down cattle trails. They rode as fast as they dared coming down the mountain, keeping in mind they had two extra horses. Atkins allowed his mind to return to the steady roaring, letting his horse do the work, seeing but not seeing Hayes riding in front of him and the road beyond that, the corners of his eyes filling with tears he did not bother to wipe clear.

Past noon they reached the bottom of the mountain, leaving the last patch of the Sierra Madres for a level dirt road. The horses scared a flock of grouse into running, their brown and white feathers fluttering with agitation. Hayes threw up a hand, slowing his horse and the horse he was leading. Atkins slowed as well, noticing the stream curling up to the cattle trail for the first time. Its waters were muddy and low and it turned east again almost as soon as it reached the trail's edge, as if ashamed of its poor quality.

"No clear mountain stream," Hayes said, dismounting. "But parched horses ain't so choosy."

Atkins swung his leg around and dropped from his saddle. They led the horses to the stream and dropped the reins, letting them dip into the water at their own pace. Hayes dug into the saddlebags and pulled out a can of peaches.

"Might as well feed the fire," he said, prying the can open with his knife. He skewered a slice of peach with the tip of his knife and stuck it in his mouth. Atkins could see Hayes' jawbone working as he chewed, the skeleton beneath the skin. Hayes speared another slice of peach and offered it to Atkins.

"No. I ain't hungry."

"You don't like peaches?"

"I like peaches fine. I just don't feel like eating them."

"How about some hog? We've got salted."

Atkins shook his head and lowered his gaze to the horses, who seemed content with their muddy stream and the flies circling their heads and the sun beating down on their shiny, dun-colored hides.

"You can't live on air, Sheriff. Believe me, I tried that for a spell last winter. Did nothing but make my stomach hurt and my legs weak."

"I'll eat when I see fit," Atkins said, scowling. "If I do so or not is none of your goddamn business."

Hayes laughed and tipped the rest of the peaches into his mouth, no longer bothering with the knife. He chewed the mouthful like a prized cow, juice leaking from the corners of his mouth as he smiled.

"You're right, Sheriff. It is none of my business. I don't want you keeling over on me like the good father is all. I figure two is better than one when you're tracking down hell's own."

The horses lifted their heads from the stream, as if they heard something the men could not. Grasshoppers buzzed through the air, slinging themselves back and forth with mindless abandon. Atkins wiped the sweat from his forehead with his sleeve. He'd changed into another fresh shirt before they left Red Earth—this was his third and last.

"We're not going to track him down, Elwood. You're just spinning a tale."

"The hell we aren't. He's headed for Rawlins as sure as I'm standing here. All we need to do is follow the trail of dead and keep our guns ready. He won't be expecting us to come after him."

"Rawlins is a big city."

Hayes snorted. "Hell, it ain't that big. It ain't like Denver or Chicago."

The horses, having gotten their fill of the muddy water, returned to the men and stood beside them in expectation. Hayes chucked his empty tin into the air and they watched it flutter back down like a wounded dove. He dug into the saddle bags and came out with two flat cuts of cured ham. He handed one to Atkins and started gnawing on the other, frowning as he watched the younger man. "If it'll shut you up, then," Atkins said, tearing off a hunk with his teeth and chewing on it. The ham expanded on his tongue, sliding slowly down his throat and dropping into his empty stomach. It was the first thing he'd eaten since returning from the slaughter at the Copper Hotel, covered in blood and trembling from the shock of it. Violet had heated water for him. She'd scrubbed him clean with hot water and soap and the sharp tip of her thumbnail.

Atkins took another bite. Hayes nodded his approval and they stood on the plain, eating their lunch while the sun-baked horses hassled the high grass.

They rode throughout the long afternoon. The sun arced slowly through the cloudless sky, revealing every prairie dog, every draft gliding hawk, and every blade of Wyoming grass. Around five, they noticed a four-in-hand stagecoach on the horizon but rode for several miles more before they came upon it, sitting motionless in the center of the trail, the horses still harnessed and standing.

Atkins stayed in the saddle while Hayes dismounted, letting the reins of his horse drop and hang free. Atkins hailed the coach, but no reply was given from the passenger compartment.

"Unsettling sight, ain't it?" Hayes said, drawing his pistol. "I wonder where the driver's got to."

Hayes went round the stage and pulled back the passenger hold's curtains.

"Four dead. Two ladies, one feller, and a girl."

Atkins dropped his head.

"Throat's cut?"

"Throat's cut."

Hayes went round to the four coach horses and stroked their necks, murmuring sweetly to them. "He must have dropped the driver first, then come round for those in the hold. Don't look like they put up much of a fight."

Hayes started freeing the coach horses from their harnesses. Atkins' horse shifted its weight, curious.

"So he didn't linger to give them a proper carving?"

"Don't appear that way." Hayes unbuckled the last harness, lifted it off the horse's neck, and gave the horse a swat on its flank. The horse, a big white Appaloosa with a patch of brown spots on its right shoulder, swished its tail and joined its friends, the whole lot looking confused and disconsolate in their sudden freedom.

"Git," Hayes shouted, waving his arms. "Go find a sweet tasting stream and mind the coyotes."

The horses drew back and scattered, running off in a herd toward the west. Hayes remounted his horse and spurred it on, drawing his second horse behind him. They rode only a half-mile further before coming to a body lying in the grass. It was a man, slim with his skin reddened from the sun. His face was crushed, the forehead caved and jaw hanging loose like he was still screaming. They rode in a circle around the corpse, both men leaning from their saddles for a better look. If the body smelled yet, Atkins couldn't tell. His nose was still stuffed with Red Earth.

"The horses pulled for a half-mile without a driver?"

Hayes shrugged.

"Maybe they caught our friend's scent. I don't know about

you, Sheriff, but that burnt smell alone would send me running a mile or two."

"Stop that," Atkins said. "Don't call me Sheriff."

"Why not?"

"'Cause I ain't the sheriff anymore. Nobody is. You can't sheriff for the dead."

Hayes laughed and spurred his horse.

"I can't argue with that, Mr. Atkins."

They returned to the trail, allowing the bodies of the stagecoach driver and his passengers to remain where they lay. It was three or four miles further along before Atkins wondered, briefly, if they should have buried them.

At dusk the cattle trail they'd been following merged with a dirt road. They halted at the joining and ate a cold dinner of venison, hard tack biscuits, and blackberries they found growing near the crossroads. They watered the horses at a small, clear pond, hand fed them from a sack of oats, and let them crop a short while before remounting, switching their weight to the fresher horses. They started down the dirt road, which was the official southern road into Rawlins, while the last of the pink and gold light faded from the sky and the stars came out. Atkins focused on breathing the cool night air, the wind against his face, and on Elwood Hayes, riding before him with his second horse on a short lead. He let the weariness of the long, sun-cooked day flow through him, muddling his thoughts. He tried not to think of his lovely wife, rocking by the fire, or his boy playing on the cabin floor, giving life and noise to his cornhusk dolls.

But when he raised his head to the stars, Atkins could see their faces in each white-dotted patch. Their names rolled onto his tongue and burned there like hot coals. He wanted to shout them into the sky and have them taken by the wind. He wanted to be rid of their names and faces, the memory of their touch, and he understood that his love for them was like a curse, a great, eternal curse as strong and wicked as anything a demon could devise. He could have fought. He could have been struck down right there, in his own kitchen, but how quickly he had given in to the Charred Man's unnatural will, going so far as to carry out his own heinous duties for him.

He could only imagine what his father would say, if the full story ever reached him in Wichita.

They arrived at Rawlins in the blue light of false dawn, approaching from the south. The city had grown since Atkins had last been through two years before—more homes had grown up south of the railroad tracks, more businesses to the north. A handful of yellow lights burned in the middle of town, glowing like steady June bugs.

"I'd heard they'd got electricity here," Elwood said, slowing his horse to ride at Atkin's side. "Give a man a clear stream and the railroad and he'll hunker down anywhere, I reckon."

To the east of them, past the houses, was the smelter where the Dennison Mine had shipped its raw ore in haul wagons for refining. The copper that came from that got packed into a boxcar and shipper further down the line, where they'd make something useful out of it in Denver.

"How long you figure it'll take them to figure out the mine's shut?"

"Few days still," Atkins said. "Last haul wagons went out on Friday."

They passed the outskirts of town and crossed the railroad tracks, the horses stepping carefully over the steel rails, the sound of their clopping hooves loud in the morning hush. They turned down Front Street, passed a livery stable, and circled back to it. An old Mexican was sleeping on a stool inside the livery's entrance, leaning back against a wall. A kerosene lamp burned near his feet, ripe for the kicking, and the dirt ground was covered in straw.

They woke the Mexican and paid him to look after their horses for two days. "Why don't you get electricity put in?" Atkins asked him. "You're like to burn the whole town down with that lantern sitting there."

The Mexican shook his head, his eyes narrowing. "No, sir. I don't trust those lights. The wires hum like bees."

"You rather burn up?"

"*Sí.* Fire, at least, I know."

Hayes nodded.

"You might be right. Say, can you point us toward some grub?"

The Mexican pointed to the east. Hayes thanked him, shouldered his heavy saddlebags, and headed out the livery's entrance, turning left onto the street. Atkins gathered his own bags and followed behind.

"Shouldn't we visit the sheriff first?"

"Naw," Hayes said, eyeing the storefronts. "Sheriff's in bed still. Deputies, too, most likely. Might as well get settled."

Most of the stores were dark and locked. They stopped under a sign that read

City Restaurant
MEALS AT ALL HOURS

and went into the narrow one-story building beneath it. The room inside was lit by a single light bulb and filled with a half-dozen tables that looked more like school desks. A bald, red-eyed man was sitting at one of the tables, reading the paper and smoking a cigar. He was dressed in a cook's apron turned brown from use.

"Ten cents for breakfast."

Hayes crossed the room, dropped his saddlebags beside a table, and sat down with his back to the wall.

"We'll have two."

"Biscuits and sausage?"

"Sounds fine."

The bald cook grunted and stood up, leaving his paper on the table as he went into the kitchen. Atkins felt no interest in the paper's headlines—nothing could equal what they'd come from. Nothing at all.

"Have a chair, Milo."

Atkins adjusted the saddlebag's strap on his shoulder. "I ain't hungry. We should go to the law."

"I told you already. The law's sleeping."

"They won't believe us."

"No, they likely won't. Not until somebody checks on Red Earth and reports back. Till then, we'll hunt our friend as we please."

Iron clattered in the back room and the cook swore loudly in Polish. Atkins stared at the chair Hayes had pushed out for him, frowning. He felt his wires humming, humming like angry bees.

"How can you be so sure he's in town? He might have headed straight for Cheyenne or Denver. They're on the rail line, too. And they're bigger. He'll be able to hide like a pebble in a stream."

Hayes laced his hands behind his head and leaned back in his chair. "He doesn't want to hide, Milo. You said it yourself—he wants everybody to know about him and be a-feared. Rawlins is a good size for that. Enough folks for a proper massacre, but still on the rails when he feels like making a getaway. He looks like anybody now. He can hide right in the middle of the street."

The saddle bag's strap had started to cut into Atkins' shoulder, turning it numb. He sighed and let it drop to the floor.

"Damn it all, Hayes."

The older man nodded. "That's right. Damn it all."

The cook swore again in the kitchen, but the rich smell of sausage gravy was already leaking out through the doorway, promising heat and a packed stomach.

After breakfast they went a block over and checked into a hotel, where they deposited their bags and took advantage of the wash basin in each of their rooms, scrubbing off as much of the road as they could. The clock in the hotel's lobby read eight when they stepped back out into the wide street, which had filled with pedestrians mulling about in the early morning sunshine, visiting the bakeries, the short orders, the druggists, the tailors, the attorneys, the dry goods, the liquors, the meat markets, the dentists, the insurance agents, the goddamn Masonic hall. After two years sequestered in Red Earth, Atkins felt irritable and enclosed in such dawdling traffic and scowled at anybody who looked his way. His hands kept clenching, too, like they wanted to tear into something. The children bothered him especially, the boys and girls laughing and chasing after each other like curs set loose. Their smiling, bonneted mothers and indulgent, fat-chinned fathers, letting them rush about as they pleased.

By the time they got to the jailhouse, Atkins was ready to tear right out of his skin, set it on fire, and hurl it at the world. Hayes turned around at the door, as if he sensed the younger man's eyes burning through his back.

"You feeling well, son? You look a touch rabid."

"I'm dandy, Elwood. Let's get this over."

Hayes paused, studying him.

"You know, I've seen that sort of look before."

"Yeah?"

"Yeah. That's how a National man looked at me right before I shot his knee and killed three of his pals."

Atkins dropped his gaze and turned his head, pretending

he was looking at something down the street.

"Should I take that revolver of yours before we go in?"

"I'll be fine."

"I'd give it back soon as we're finished."

Atkins looked up. "Goddamn. I said I'm fine, Hayes."

"Sure, no need to get hot about it. One more thing, though. Don't call me Hayes. I don't want anybody knowing my name around here. The law and I aren't too friendly with each other."

Atkins snorted and spat on the ground.

"Somehow, that don't surprise me much."

Hayes opened the jailhouse door and gestured for Atkins to go through first. Atkins touched his hat brim in mock thanks and went into the brick building. He found himself in a large room that smelled like cigar smoke and coffee and had three cells at the back. To his left was a table where two men sat playing crib, to his right a large oak executive desk behind which a portly, gray bearded man sat smoking and reading a paper. All three looked up as they entered, studying them. "Morning," Atkins said, removing his hat and stepping toward the gray bearded man. "Are you the sheriff?"

"Far as I know," he said, smiling as he laid down his paper and offered his hand. "Jeremiah Taylor."

Atkins shook his hand.

"Milo Atkins, sir, and that fella there is Mr. Elwood Smith."

"Pleasure to meet you," Sheriff Taylor said, nodding to Hayes. "What can I do for you, gentlemen?"

Atkins took a breath and pressed his hat against his chest, wondering how best to explain it.

"We're just in from Red Earth. Actually, I'm the camp's sheriff."

"That so?" Taylor leaned back in his chair, resting his hands on his round gut. "How's that mine coming? Still yielding high grade, I hope. Y'all only been on it for what, two years?"

"That's why we're here, actually. They had a problem in

the mine."

Taylor frowned and twiddled his thumbs.

"Collapse?"

"Worse than that. They found something in the mine that started killing the men and they couldn't stop it."

Taylor looked from Atkins to Hayes to the deputies across the room.

"You mean like poison gas? Like a coal damp?"

"More like a demon, or a devil, like. He tore through the miners then came up to the surface. We tried collapsing the mine, but he just tunneled out. Every man he killed seemed to make him stronger. I called a town meeting, but he showed up there, too, and killed about anything that moved, including women and children. By the morning, he'd killed near everybody in town."

Atkins paused, giving the news time to sink in. The sheriff's face had frozen at the word "devil" and remained that way.

"Elwood and I are the last folks still breathing air. We came to Rawlins to warn you he might be coming here, or already is here. He looks like any man, really, though he walks stiff, like there's a rod run through his back."

"A rod run through his back?"

"That's correct, sir."

Taylor licked his lips and a twinkle came into his eyes. His face broke into a broad smile as he sat forward again in his chair, setting his plump hands onto the table.

"Doc Osborne put you up to this, didn't he?"

Taylor started wheezing until the wheezing changed to laughter.

"That old son-of-a-bitch. First he turns Big Nose George into a pair of shoes, now he's trying to fool me."

The deputies guffawed at their table. "He's trying to get your goat," one of them said, fanning himself with his cards. "Thinks you're plumb simple, J. T."

Taylor crossed his arms across his chest, his laughter turned to chuckling.

"If that don't beat all, fellas. A demon killing a whole camp."

Hayes pushed his hat up his forehead and looked around the room, letting his glance linger on each man. His eyes had gone flat and hard, like a hawk's, and he didn't speak till the others had gone silent again.

"I don't know who Doc Osborne is, but this is no jest. Sheriff Atkins is telling the God's honest. My brother was one of the killed. So was Atkins' wife and son."

Sheriff Taylor's grin faded, though his eyes still had that twinkle.

"I'm sorry to hear that, Mr. Smith."

"Sorry's got nothing to do with it. We came to warn you. How you take it is your concern."

"That's right," Sheriff Taylor said, nodding. "So, saying this all happened there in Red Earth, what would you like me to do about it? Send a crew of gravediggers into the mountains to bury the whole town?"

"You needn't do that," Atkins said, his hands curling back into fists. "The miners are sealed below ground and we burned the townsfolk in a pile."

"That must have been a sight."

"It was," Hayes said. "Won't be nothing compared to all the folks in Rawlins heaped together, if he decides to set loose here. You tell your deputies to keep their eyes open for strangers acting peculiar."

"Like the two of you, you mean," the other deputy said. "I'd have to say you two boys sound about as peculiar as it gets."

Atkins forced his fingers to uncurl and set his hat back on his head. "We'll be staying in town for a few days if you need us. He favors a straight razor, though he's strong enough to rip a body apart if he's inclined."

Hayes and Atkins headed for the door, but Atkins paused before crossing through the doorway.

"I don't know how many deputies you got, but you'll want to see to adding as many more as can shoot a gun."

Taylor smiled and sat back in his chair.

"Thank you, Sheriff Atkins. I'll take your idea into consideration."

Atkins nodded and stepped out. As the door swung shut behind him, he heard the deputies inside bust into laughter, braying like a couple of asses.

"I thought as much," Atkins said to Hayes, who'd hooked his thumbs through his belt and was standing in the middle of the street, looking both ways. "They figured us for a pair of loons."

Hayes shrugged, studying the folks passing by. "They've been warned, Milo. We can't do more."

A man rode by on horseback, chased by a yipping terrier with a tatted left ear. Two women, out window shopping in their fancy lace dresses, pointed at the yipping dog and giggled.

"He'll sweep through this town like a brushfire, Elwood."

The older man nodded.

"If he wants."

Hayes wanted to wander the town some more to properly scout it, but Atkins was too worn out from riding through the night and begged off. Atkins dragged himself back to the hotel and dropped onto his bed, removing only his gun belt and boots. He could hear the traffic passing by in the street—the clopping of hooves, the shouts of children, the guttural laughter of men—but the noise came to him as from a great and clouded distance. He drifted asleep but woke several times in the late morning and early afternoon, his room growing ever warmer, his pillow hot beneath his head.

Finally, at dusk, Milo Atkins broke free of sleep's groggy tendrils and rose kicking to the surface. His blankets lay tangled around him, damp with his sweat. When he turned onto his side, yawning away the sleep, he expected to see his wife there, smiling back at him.

But she was not.

This was not Red Earth.

This was Rawlins, Wyoming, and no one he loved was here.

Atkins turned onto his back and gazed up at the stamped tin ceiling. More traffic passed below—early evening traffic. Folks taking the air, couples heading to dinner. When he and Violet had been courting, they'd loved watching the sun go down—they'd felt as if each setting was for them and them alone, as if Nature sensed the fierceness of their new love and wished to reflect it back upon them ten-fold. He could still recall her cool hand in his. The soft blue light after.

Atkins rolled off the lumpy hotel bed and onto his feet. He put on his boots and his gun belt and splashed water on his face from the wash basin. He could hear voices murmuring through the walls of his room—the hotel had filled up while he'd been sleeping. They'd come into town on the daily train, he supposed. The depot was only a few blocks away, along Front Street. The newcomers would have proper, stiff-sided luggage, traveling clothes, and purpose. You didn't come to this part of the country without a good reason.

Atkins exited his room, went down the hotel stairs, and stepped out onto the street. The evening sky had turned the dark purple of a bruised plum. Atkins entered a saloon beside their hotel and found it packed with folks eating and drinking at small tables, with more men sitting elbow-to-elbow up at the long counter. Elwood Hayes was sitting at the far end of the counter and staring into his beer. He looked like he'd had a bath and the cut on his face was freshly bandaged. Atkins felt an urge to go over and join him, but then he remembered they weren't exactly drinking buddies. Barely associates, really, with the only thing shared between them the horror of the last few days, the Charred Man and the wickedness he had wrought. What would they talk about except death? What else was there to talk about anymore?

Hayes lifted his beer, finished it in one swallow, and signaled the bartender for another. Atkins left the saloon and returned to the street, walking without any particular aim. Couples strolled by, arm in arm, while their unruly children ran ahead, laughing and arguing with each other. Men stood in doorways, smoking, while old women sat rocking on their front porches, mending piled high in their laps.

Atkins found himself turned north, where he could see hills rising and the streets ended. To his right, atop a gradually sloping hillside, was the Rawlins cemetery. He strolled up the hillside, watching the grass for snakes and gopher holes, and approached the first line of graves. The cemetery was set in a grove of trees, as if the dead required shade even six feet beneath the earth, and the wind was strong enough to set their branches rustling.

"Evening," Atkins said aloud, speaking to gravestones. "Y'all don't know me, but I thought you might appreciate the company."

He walked down their line, reading the names and dates. None of them were older than 1868, some as fresh as '89. Yet, unlike Red Earth, this looked like a town that would take. The railroad was here and more folks would come. The town's heart would beat on and on, as long as there were people who didn't mind the wind and the hard winters and the loneliness of so much wide country. Rawlins might never be a Chicago or a New York, but it would survive in its own dry, stubborn way.

A squirrel jumped to a higher branch, riled by his presence. Atkins reached the end of gravestones and sat down beside the last. He made to remove his hat but then recalled he'd left it in his hotel room. "A man without a hat is no man at all," Milo Atkins said aloud, echoing his father, the true Sheriff Atkins. He unbuttoned his revolver from its holster and held it in his hands, examining it. He looked up at the bruised plum sky and felt a dull coldness flow through him.

"Truly, I am sorry," he said, his words rising into the sky. He placed the gun's barrel in his mouth and bit down, the metal tangy and sharp on his tongue. He let his mind empty. He listened to the branches rustling and the wind feathering through the grass. He thumbed back the revolver's hammer, took one last sweet-smelling breath, and pulled the trigger.

32

They buried young Milo Atkins the next afternoon, right where he'd died. Elwood Hayes paid for the coffin, the plot, and the service with the Dennison money he'd lifted from Revis Cooke's house (he figured the miners would have appreciated their monthly salaries going to such an affair, seeing that none of them had been given such honors themselves). The burial was sparsely attended by Elwood, Sherriff Taylor, and a handful of curious old folks dressed in their faded Sunday best. The preacher was an overstuffed old codger with a walrus mustache and a fancy navy blue suit. He went on about how men were not but dust, life was brief, and the world was nothing more than a veil of tears, his deep voice booming across the bone orchard and disturbing the squirrels as they frolicked. Elwood bore the preaching patiently, listening to the trees rustle with the occasional breeze and the mosquitoes whine past his ears.

The preacher halted his yammering and asked Elwood if he'd like to say a few words about his friend. "Yes, I would," Elwood said, stepping up behind the grave beside the wheezing preacher. He looked at Sheriff Taylor and the old folks grouped behind him and squinted in thought, noticing the patches of sunlight that poked through the trees and lay bright on the grass.

"Been a hard week," he started, deciding to lay it all out. "Milo and I come recent from a town called Red Earth about fifty miles south. I was just passing through, but Milo was sheriff there. When the town was attacked by a devil last Saturday evening, he did his best to stand tall."

Elwood paused, putting his thoughts in order. The old folks exchanged looks with each other like they didn't know if they'd heard right.

"Sorry to say, it wasn't enough. Most of the townsfolk were slaughtered, including Milo's wife and boy. I don't know what you think about a man killing himself, but Sheriff Atkins had his heart broken back in Red Earth and couldn't see past it. You may think what he did here is a sin, but I do not blame him for it. I was in Red Earth last Saturday night and the wickedness I saw done there puts most anything else to shame."

Elwood looked down at the coffin exposed in its open grave. He kicked a clump of dirt on top of it and started down the hillside, not wanting to hear another word out of the fat preacher's throat or answer thick questions from the old folks. Nobody would believe him, anyhow—as soon as that bullet had blown out Milo Atkins' brains, Elwood had been made the last person alive who knew what truly had happened in Red Earth, and one man alone with a wild story was nothing but a lunatic to other folks, no matter how well he told that story.

Elwood walked back through town. Folks stared as he passed and he was glad he wore his gun hidden, though there wasn't anything he could do about the swath of bandage on his face. And the cut was itching, too, itching so bad he had to restrain himself ten times a minute from ripping the bandage off and clawing at the wound with his fingernails. He'd gone to a sawbones on Cedar Street the day before, an old man who'd whistled when he'd seen the cut and started telling stories about the Civil War. He'd smiled while he'd sewed Elwood's cheek together, tugging at the thread like he was mending a shirt.

The hotel appeared suddenly as if Elwood had dreamt himself there. He went past the entrance and went into the saloon next door, which was half-empty because it was ten in the morning on a Wednesday. He walked along the bar, which ran from wall to wall, and bellied up to the far end. He asked for a bottle of whiskey and a glass and paid in full.

"Looks like you're bent on doing some damage."

Elwood glanced sideways at the man who'd come in behind him. He pulled at the whiskey bottle's cork till it popped out, sounding like champagne.

"Howdy, Sheriff."

"Mind if I join you?"

"Go ahead."

Elwood poured the whiskey into his glass. Sheriff Taylor sat down on the stool beside him and set his elbows on the bar, letting out a long sigh.

"I have been to this place too many times, after too many funerals."

"Whiskey?"

"Can't," Taylor said, glancing at the bartender. "I'm on duty."

The bartender nodded and poured the sheriff a cup of coffee.

"Always helps to have coffee and food in a saloon. Helps keep folks from acting the fool."

Elwood threw back the glass of whiskey and poured himself another.

"That what you think of me, Sheriff? That I'm acting the fool?"

Taylor blew on his coffee and pushed the steam around. He sipped gently at it, hissing softly from the corner of his mouth.

"At first I was inclined to that idea. Now, I'm starting to wonder."

"Yeah? It only took Milo chewing on his revolver to start you round?"

Taylor licked his lips and took a longer sip.

"I was rounding before that, actually. Mr. Dennison's people have been inquiring about a payroll stagecoach that was supposed to have returned to Rawlins on Monday. Say it's two days late and their man's never late."

Elwood smirked and threw back his second glass.

"He's late because he's dead. They're all dead."

The sheriff nodded and turned toward Elwood on his stool. "I told them about you and Milo Atkins, also. What you'd said happened."

"That so?"

"Yeah. They said Red Earth did have a lawman named Milo Atkins, but they never heard of anybody named Elwood Smith."

Elwood refilled his glass, the itching in his wound starting to lessen.

"They'd heard of an Elwood Hayes, though. Said he was a small time crook who'd been buzzing around Colorado for the past couple of years."

The room, not loud to begin with, had quieted. Elwood noticed the bartender had gone down to the opposite end of the bar, where he pretended to read the paper while he eavesdropped. A barking dog ran past the bar's doorway.

"Never heard of any Hayes," Elwood said, speaking as though he was tasting the name on his tongue. "Though I reckon any man named Elwood can't be all bad."

The sheriff laughed and raised his coffee cup.

"Here, here."

Elwood lifted his whiskey glass and threw back his third, starting to feel the earth's roll. The sheriff finished his coffee and slid off his stool, setting a couple of pennies on the counter.

"Anyhow. When I got the news from San Francisco, I sent two men out to Red Earth. They should be back in three or four days. If you and Atkins were speaking the truth about the camp, you'll be vindicated soon enough."

Elwood nodded, though he no longer cared one way or another about vindication. He just wanted to drink from his bottle of whiskey until it was late enough to eat dinner and go to bed.

Taylor set his hand on Elwood's shoulder, making him wince.

"I'm sorry about your friend, Mr. Smith."

"Thank you," Elwood said, exhaling whiskey fumes. "Milo would appreciate that, coming from a fellow star."

The sheriff laughed, though Elwood didn't think what he'd said was that funny. He watched Taylor amble out of the bar and was glad to see him go. He still bore no fondness for the law.

As Elwood drank the rest of the morning away, he recalled things he did not particularly wish to recall. Mainly, he thought about those last crowded moments in the Runoff Saloon, picking them over to see if there'd been anything he could have done different to bring his gang out of it alive.

That heavy pounding on the Runoff's front door.

The way that lit bottle had sailed past the Charred Man and burst into flame.

How the other men had opened fire, their aim wild and shots unmeasured while the Charred Man crossed the room, seeming like he was still walking but going too fast for that, too fast for any bullet to hit.

How the Charred Man circled round the bar and closed

in from the side, holding a straight razor high above his head like he was proud of it, like it was a kingly sword, and Clem Stubbs screaming from his first strike, a slash right across Stubb's eyes. The other men so worked up they shot Stubbs instead of the demon, plugging the big man four or five times before they realized what they'd done and adjusted their aim.

And from there, nothing but men dying as the Charred Man set upon them like a whirlwind made flesh. The demon fought low to the ground, dropping the four unarmed prospectors by severing their hamstrings and slicing their throats while they writhed on the ground. The bartender, Caleb, ran at the demon with his empty scattergun raised like a club, getting in one good hard swing before the Charred Man stepped aside and cut at his ankles, sending him sprawling into a pile.

Hayes, his own revolver still in its holster, had just enough time to light a second bottle of moonshine while Roach Clayton and Owen stumbled backward, fumbling bullets while they tried to reload. The Charred Man running at them, then breaking to his right and coming for Hayes instead. He'd hurled the second bottle, aiming for the demon's chest, but missed with that one, too, and felt a streak of fire raking across his face in consequence, followed by a rising as the Charred Man lifted Hayes into the air with one arm, squeezing his windpipe shut while he looked him over.

Hayes tried to cuss him out, but his words were nothing but choked sputtering, gargles of sound, and then he was already flying across the room. His last sight was the saloon going up in flames and the widowed ladies raising their heads above the bar like three pale, blinking ghosts, uncertain of the ugly sight before them.

And where was Ingrid? Why hadn't she come to the stairs?

"You all right, sir?"

Elwood raised his head. The bartender had come over

and was drying a beer mug with his apron.

"Want some water to go with that whiskey?"

Elwood frowned at the bottle at his elbow—he'd gone through a third of it already.

"What time is it?"

"Just past noon."

"Noon," Elwood said, rubbing his face and sliding off his stool. "Well, might as well get some grub." He headed for the saloon door and the bartender called after him, reminding him to take his bottle along. Elwood waved off the suggestion and pushed his way through the saloon's swinging doors, the sun blinding him with its noonday glare as he stepped into the street. "Goddamn," he shouted, addressing no one in particular.

He started walking along the storefronts, peering into each window, but after a few minutes Elwood made his way to a short order down the street, a place he hadn't been to yet, where he bought himself a plate piled high with stringy, peppered chicken and watery potatoes. He ate with relish, elbows on the table, and drank cup after cup of coffee as he bolted the mess down. The food revived him. When he finished eating, he pushed his chair back and let out a loud belch of appreciation.

A portly, thick-necked man sitting at the table beside his looked up and whistled. He was wearing a shabby tweed coat with the elbows patched up, like a farmer wore when he was visiting town and thinking he looked pretty fancy. He smelled like manure and wet dog.

"My Lord," the farmer said. "Haven't seen food put away like that since I fed the hogs this morning."

"I was hungry," Elwood said, patting his stomach. "I buried my friend today and that can put a man to feeding."

"Did he feed like that, too? That so, he must have choked to death."

The farmer chortled at his own joke, his fat cheeks bunching up beneath his eyes. Elwood sprung forward, crossing the distance between their tables and tackling the farmer off his chair. They rolled around on the floor, the farmer screaming murder, and Elwood started working him over, increasing the jolt behind his punches the more the farmer hollered.

"You fat sack of cow shit," Elwood shouted, his mind filled with an angry buzzing. "Lay still and take your goddamn beating."

Something cracked in the farmer's face, probably his nose, and Elwood felt himself pulled off by several strong hands. He thrashed wildly as they manhandled him, not finished, but he stilled as he felt a knife's blade at his throat. The farmer sat up, clutching his face.

"Wash only joshing," the farmer said, his words muddled through his hands. "Wash the hell wrong with you?"

"I wouldn't know where to start with that," Elwood said, raising his hands to show he was through and extracting himself from his handlers. "You just remember to watch your words, you old hog."

Elwood pushed his way through the crowd of gawkers and left the restaurant. He went back to his hotel and climbed the stairs, his legs quivering and knuckles swelling. He went into his room, gathered his few belongings, and threw his saddle bags over his shoulder. Always, it turned like this. Always, always, always.

Elwood went back downstairs and exited the hotel. Clouds had blown in, making the sunlight tolerable. He went down to the livery stables and sold the four horses they'd brought from Red Earth to the livery's owner, who gave him a fair enough price. From there he walked down to the train depot on Front Street and spoke with the stationmaster, who told him the afternoon train was due in twenty minutes, headed for Cheyenne. He bought a one-way ticket and sat down on one of the platform's benches. He rubbed his swollen knuckles, enjoying the pain. He pictured the farmer's surprised face and smiled, feeling the warmth of his morning's whiskey returning.

As the train's arrival time neared, more folks stepped onto the platform. They waited with their heads turned to the west, like turkeys hoping to be fed. Elwood wondered—

What was that smell?

Elwood sat forward on the bench, sniffing the air. He smelled something peculiar. Something like…

Char.

The last drop of alcohol fled from Elwood Hayes' blood, flushed by a sudden and joint-locking certainty that every person on the platform was about to die. He sat back against the bench slowly, trying not to call attention to himself, and scanned the crowd as they waited for the train.

He picked out two families, holding no luggage, and figured they were waiting for somebody to arrive. He counted eight women and ten men, standing either in pairs or alone, with luggage piled at their feet. Everyone wore some kind of hat, the women in hats and gloves. Turned west slightly, he could make out each face in profile, but even as Elwood studied the men, he realized he had no solid idea of what the Charred Man looked like. The first time he'd seen him, he'd still been half-covered in char, and the second time he'd been more worried about aiming his throw. Now, pressed to it, he could only recall a man's pallid, smooth face, glistening like it was wet.

Shiny, Father Lynch had said.

Shiny like a new penny.

Elwood sighed and reach slowly behind him, unbuttoning his gun from its holster and preparing the way for a clear draw. The burnt char smell had faded and been replaced by perfume, too much perfume. Elwood scowled at the old woman sitting beside him and rose to his feet, moving as natural as he could as he watched the men standing in the crowd, trying to keep an eye on each one at the same time.

He was tall.

He remembered that. The Charred Man fought low to the ground, but he was—

"Sir?"

Elwood sniffed the air. He'd caught the burnt scent again. He was here, in the crowd. He was near.

"Sir?"

An old woman's voice, rising shrill. Elwood turned, hoping she was talking to somebody else. She wasn't.

"Sir, you forgot your luggage," the old woman he'd been sitting beside called out, waving at him and pointing at his saddle bags with her foot. Elwood felt the crowd eyeing him curiously and kept his back turned so nobody could see his face.

"Thank you, ma'am," he said in a low voice, gritting his teeth. "I was only getting up to peer down the tracks a moment."

"Oh," the old woman said, deflated. "I thought—"

"I appreciate your concern, though. It was mighty kind of you to call me back like that. Mighty kind."

The old woman brightened, twisting her gloved hands in her lap.

"No bother. No bother at all, sir."

Elwood smiled through clenched teeth and counted to five, letting the crowd lose interest and return to their westward gazing before he pivoted round again, hands clasped behind his back. He expected to find the Charred Man already upon him, straight razor lifted, but nobody was at his back—the crowd was milling about ten feet away as the train, now a smoking speck on the horizon, blew its horn to alert Rawlins of its arrival.

Elwood drew his pistol and stepped up to the rear of the grouped men, nostrils flaring like a hound's. He noticed one of the taller men, a gentleman in a fine suit and black bowler hat, had lost interest in the approaching train and was studying one of the women on the platform. His arms were thin, like stovepipes, and hung limply at his sides, as if separate from the rest of his body and waiting to be told what to do next. Elwood closed in on the man, careful to keep at his blind. He thumbed back the gun's hammer, a small noise lost in the train's second whistle. The smell of char grew stronger as he neared the man, so pungent he wondered how the others on the platform could tolerate it. He raised his pistol and aimed it just under the brim of the man's bowler, his eyes watering.

He'd made mistakes. He could be killed.

"Red Earth," Hayes whispered. The man's shoulders flinched and Elwood shot him in the back of the skull, his gun a dry pop as the train rolled into the station, brakes screaming as steel pressed steel. The man wavered on his feet a moment, absorbing the shock, before his knees buckled and he pitched forward onto the platform.

Elwood thumbed a second round into his gun's chamber and rolled the man over with his foot. The bullet hadn't passed through—the man's pale, glistening face was still intact, his dark eyes open and showing their surprise. The man opened his mouth, tried to say something, and shut it again. Elwood fired two more shots into the fallen man's chest and delivered a hard kick to his side.

"You know what that's for, you bastard."

The Charred Man flopped about on the platform and red-black ooze dribbled from the corners of his mouth. The train blew its whistle a third time. The other passengers had collected their luggage and were boarding as if they hadn't noticed the shooting at all. For a short, dreamy moment

Elwood considered grabbing his saddlebags and joining them, going to Cheyenne as if nothing had happened and moving on from there, living like a king on the Dennison money.

Instead, Elwood holstered his gun and dragged the demon across the platform, aiming for the little wooden shack the stationmaster sold his tickets from. He couldn't tell if the char smell had lessened from the train smoke, but he knew this needed to be a certain thing. He knocked on the stationmaster's door and the gaunt young man came out straight off, trembling hands raised. He shouted something but Elwood couldn't make it out. He waved the boy off, allowing him to tuck tail and run, and dragged the demon into the shack—the Charred Man's tall frame filled the small building so greatly Elwood had to raise him by the shoulders and prop him up until he resembled a man reading in bed.

An oil lamp and matches sat on a shelf beside the shack's window. Hayes unscrewed the lamp, dumped its contents both onto the demon and the walls surrounding, and stepped back out through the doorway.

"You ready?"

The demon had stopped its sputtering and flopping. It regarded him in a cool, hard manner, its dark and bottomless eyes fixed upon his face. Hayes, who could feel his flesh crawl and threaten to run off, struck a match on the doorframe and tossed it inside. The match's flame dimmed for a moment then bloomed in a fine way.

Soon enough, the shack was burning like it had been made for it. Hayes heard no screams, no curses uttered with a final vehemence. The train had pulled out of the station and was rolling east once more, picking up speed as it belched along. Hayes left the station to find the nearest stack of timber he could lay his hands on—one or two wagonloads would see this last bit through.

Epilogue

Elwood Hayes was scheduled to hang in mid-September. The time before the hanging passed both quick and slow, with summer taking its gradual leave of southern Wyoming as Elwood paced his narrow cell daily, wishing he was back in Colorado, or even on the old farmstead. He'd written to his parents about his brother's death and his own impending but no reply had come, which did not surprise him much.

Then, on the morning of the big day, Elwood was visited by a ghost.

The ghost was let into the jailhouse by a Rawlins deputy. Dressed in a stiff brown suit of rough linen, the ghost wore his brown hair slicked back, like a lawyer or politician. He came up to Elwood's cell and gripped a bar with each hand.

"Hey there, El."

Elwood stoop up from his cot, his astonishment genuine.

"Johnny? Johnny Miller?"

The ghost smiled and Elwood stepped closer, getting a proper look.

"Christ, son. I thought you were dead."

"No, sir," Miller replied, shaking his head. "The sheriff let me loose and sent me packing. I figure he already had enough on his hands, what with the Indians about to attack and all."

Elwood rubbed his eyes with his palms.

"There weren't no goddamn Indians, Johnny. That's a lie the papers made up, like how they call it the 'Bone House Massacre' to sell more papers."

"There weren't no Indians? What hit town, then?"

Elwood leaned toward the bars and lowered his voice. "It was the goddamn miners. They blasted too deep and woke a demon."

Miller smoothed his hair, which was already lying flat. Elwood watched him absorb what he'd said like he'd been told how to sight a rifle, or saddle a horse. Miller had never been the swiftest thinker, but he did give things his full consideration.

"That man I shot here in Rawlins? That was him, Johnny. No matter what they say, that was the demon as sure as I'm standing here. I was lucky and got the drop on him."

"Lucky? They're going to hang you for it, El. I saw them setting up the gallows in front of the courthouse."

Elwood shrugged. "Could have been worse—he could've torn through this whole damn town if he'd had a mind to. Besides, they're really hanging me for that payroll in my bags. Mr. Dennison's making sure I get strung before the whole world to set a proper example."

Miller scratched his cheek, still digesting the idea. He looked strange with his face clean shaven.

"That demon killed Roach and Clem, then?"

"Yes. My brother also. And he gave me this pretty scar on my cheek and threw me through the goddamn saloon wall."

Miller whistled softly.

"Well, I guess I owe you thanks for handing me over. You hadn't done that I'd be a goner myself."

Elwood snorted and paced around his cell, of which he knew every quarter inch by heart. Miller cleared his throat.

"I came to apologize, El. I shouldn't have killed that National man like I did. You took me in and showed me how things were done and I went off and did something small like that. I deserved to get knocked down and handed over. I deserved a hanging."

Somebody shouted outside Elwood's cell window. People liked to shout into the jailhouse, knowing Elwood was there to be shouted at. They came and hollered at all hours, night or day, sober or drunk.

"From here on out, I plan to live a clean life and not let my temper best me," Miller said, pushing his face between the cell bars. "I'm going to get a job with the railroad and thieve no more."

Elwood stopped his pacing and looked the young man in the eye.

"That's good, son. You stay clear of trouble."

Miller grinned in earnest, showing the boy he'd once been, but his grin faded as the jailhouse door creaked open behind him.

"I'm sorry they're going to hang you, Elwood. You're a good man. I'll be there to see you off and pray for your soul."

"Thank you, Johnny."

They shook hands through the bars of the cell and Miller, satisfied, showed himself out. Two hours later Elwood Hayes was standing on the trapdoor of a temporary gallows, listening to the same blowhard preacher that buried Milo Atkins hollering about mortal sin and the Lord's justice and the eternal flames of Hell. They'd been right to choose a Saturday for the hanging—a full crowd was in attendance, filling the square and spilling into the streets beyond, men and women and children who all looked, from up here, like people Elwood had seen somewhere before. He let his thoughts drift to Ingrid

Blomvik as the preacher thundered on, recalling the warmth of her body against his, her soft blond hair and sad blue eyes. He wondered if he could have settled down and loved a woman like that for fifty years, if they could have grown old and happy together in some calm place, perhaps a house tucked near the ocean.

When the preacher asked him if he had any last words, interrupting his pleasant reverie, Elwood Hayes said no, he did not. He figured some things you just didn't come back from.

Acknowledgments

The author would like to thank Mark Rapacz, Jason Stuart, Karen L. Williamson, and the entire Burnt Bridge crew for bringing this strange beast of a novel to the world so beautifully. He would also like to thank his agent Jonathan Lyons of Curtis Brown, LTD. for all his tremendous insight, effort, and often baffling doggedness. Finally, as always, the author would like to thank his friends and family for their love and unflagging support. You are the light out of the dark.

About the Author

David Oppegaard is the author of the Bram Stoker-nominated *The Suicide Collectors* (St. Martin's Press), *Wormwood, Nevada* (St. Martin's Press) and *The Ragged Mountains* (eBook). David's work is a blend of science fiction, literary fiction, horror, and dark fantasy. He holds an M.F.A. in Writing from Hamline University and a B.A. in English from St. Olaf College. He teaches at Hamline University and the Loft Literary Center and works at the University of Minnesota. He lives in St. Paul, MN.

You can visit his website at davidoppegaard.com.

CPSIA information can be obtained at www.ICGtesting.com
Printed in the USA
LVOW12s1743070414

380670LV00008B/1188/P